The Hit

Code name: "the Big Event"

« The one thing we do know is none of the [assassination] teams knew the existence of the others... When they heard the shots, they would flinch because they weren't sure that they'd been spotted and somebody was trying to take them out... You can put a smile on the shooter's face because then he realizes that it's a super-pro job and there are backup and decoy teams and that's where those shots are coming from. Silencers were used extensively... »

- Gerry Patrick Hemming

Note to reader

This is a novel, a fictional work... fiction! The Hit is the <u>English version</u> of the French novel *"Le Contrat"* produced by the same author... Enjoy!

Hoover memo: On November 22nd, 1963, the afternoon of the assassination of John Fitzgerald Kennedy, even before the investigation began, FBI Director J. Edgar Hoover sent a memo to his executive saying that he had spoken on the phone with Attorney General Robert F. Kennedy and that he had informed him in these terms: *"We have the man who killed the President!"* For many it was irrefutable proof that Lee Oswald had acted alone.

"The thing I am concerned about is having something issued so that we can convince the public that Oswald is the real assassin..."

J. Edgar Hoover, Director FBI

From the same author:

Lève-toi et marche… ou crève!
Les aventures d'un Pied-Noir en Algérie
www.fouillez-tout.com/edition, 2007
ISBN : 978-2-9809849-0-7

Bienvenue sur Galaxya 7.0
En route pour Alpha Centauri
www.fouillez-tout.com/edition, 2008
ISBN : 978-2-9809849-1-4

Confessions d'un collabo
Vous irez cracher sur ma tombe!
www.fouillez-tout.com/edition, 2009
ISBN : 978-2-9809849-2-1

59,35 ARPENTS
La Romance d'un vin
www.fouillez-tout.com/edition, 2010
ISBN : 978-2-9809849-3-8

La Croix du Sud
La Cruz del Sur
www.fouillez-tout.com/edition, 2013
ISBN : 978-2-9809849-4-5

La route d'Espagne
La ruta del vino Somontano
www.fouillez-tout.com/edition, 2016
ISBN: 978-2-9809849-6-9

Le contrat
Code name: the « Big Event »
www.fouillez-tout.com/edition, 2017
ISBN: 978-2-9809849-7-6

To Giuseppe
& to my wife Rosy...

The Hit

Code name: "the Big Event"
Based on the original title: «Le Contrat»

Alain Bellemare

NOVEL

FIRST EDITION

Dépôt légal: 2e trimestre 2018
Bibliothèque nationale du Québec

Bellemare, Alain
The Hit
Code name: the "Big Event"
ISBN: 978-2-9809849-9-0

Published with the help of my Credit card in 2018

"J'aime mieux raconter des histoires. J'en raconterai de telles qu'ils reviendront, exprès, pour me tuer, des quatre coins du monde. Alors ce sera fini et je serai bien content.

(I like telling stories better. I will tell of such that they will return, on purpose, to kill me, from the four corners of the world. So it will be over and I will be happy.)"

Louis-Ferdinand Céline,
Mort à crédit I

The Hit

Code name: "the Big Event"

When the alarm went off, the morning of the "Big Event", I had not yet managed to really close my eyes during the night. I always had trouble sleeping on the eve of a mission, my brain stubbornly refusing to sink into this restorative coma called "a good night's sleep", and instead of resting as did most people, I was thinking rather of the job I had to execute on the next day. I had wandered between two worlds, alternating dreams and nightmares, half asleep, half awake, and when I finally got back to my own self... I couldn't remember where I was! And during that split second, a moment that seemed like an eternity, I thought I was still in Bône, Algeria... in the middle of a fuckin' civil war! And I panicked; I had lost my points of lair... I was completely lost!

I tried to pull myself together and take stock of my situation... exasperating! And then it came back to me... In an instant... I knew where I was... And above all, why I was there.

It was one of those sad skies of November; it was the morning of the 22nd day of the year of grace 1963; I was going to execute the contract in Dallas, Texas; and the name of my client was John Fitzgerald Kennedy... The elected president of the United States of America!

And from that moment on, I started breathing... normally.

When Jack Ruby came to the house with his disguises at seven o'clock in the morning, the Dallas sky was still overcast: it was raining a little. Lucien Sarti, who was not an early riser but a night owl of the worst kind, was all smiles: he was finally going to wear a uniform of the US Air Force and play little soldier boy. He had made a fool of himself to get one and absolutely wanted a police officer outfit or one the US Army. Now, he was going to be happy like the little motherfucker he was and stop pooping all over us most of the time.

Beau Serge had opted for a loose but short windbreaker, navy blue, with a decorative silver badge on the heart and a cap of the Dallas Cowboys on the head. For my part, I had preferred a long-sleeved white shirt and a trench-style beige raincoat, a classic, with a felt hat and a pair of glasses with horn mount. To complete the picture, I had stuck a little mustache and had darkened my face with make-up, war paint that would allow me to pass for a South American "*de vacaciones*". But soon after I wondered who would be foolish enough to go on vacation to Dallas in November?

Sarti was going to carry his 7.65 mm Mauser wrapped in a blanket to keep it out of sight; Beau Serge was going to hide his Fireball XP-100 - a mini-rifle or some kind of big handgun - under his short coat, and me, as the metal stock of my Savage 7 mm was foldable, I had recycled a long strap of leather which, wrapped around my neck, would allow me to keep the rifle on the side of my body, under the cloak. My only problem was the silencer, which added a good 25 centimeters in length: I was going to keep it in an inner pocket of the raincoat and screw it on to the rifle at the very last moment. I had made a slit inside the right pocket of the raincoat, opening that would allow me to hold the barrel of the weapon glued to the thigh by passing a hand through the pocket and thus prevent the weapon from wabbling, when I would walk around Dealey Plaza... Nobody would know that I was carrying a long gun under the coat!

In addition to all of that, I kept a little Walter .380 stuck in my belt... For close encounters of the third kind!

Since we had received the formal order not to harm the First Lady, Sarti and I had prepared three dum-dum bullets each, fragmentation projectiles that would allow us to do the greatest possible damage but without the missile going through the target and continue its course and wound another person - In the Foreign Legion, in special circumstances, I had taken the habit of notching the point of my ammunition and make a cross at the tip so that the small bullet would split upon impact -. However, we knew damn well that we wouldn't have time to fire more than one shot, maybe two, at most...

Beau Serge, as the bullets of his gun did not weigh heavily - they weighed only 60 grains while ours were more massive at 165 grains -, would shoot with a full metal jacket projectile, an armored missile which, in theory, was not going to break up upon impact and continue its course through and through. He was ordered to fire only if he was certain of his shot. We had been told that these instructions came from the highest echelon of all... the big boss, himself.

Jack Ruby picked us up at around 10:45 a.m. in an old pick-up truck, and since there was only room for two more people in the cabin and that we were three triggers, Sarti had to take place in the cargo box of the small truck. Fortunately for us, the sky was clearing, and despite gusts of wind of 15 to 20 miles per hour that blew from Love Field Airport, it was going to be nice for the rest of the day: sunny skies with a maximum of 67 degrees. We were told that Indian summer had made an appearance in Dallas, even though Texans had wiped out most of them by the end of the 19th Century... along with the buffaloes. However, in addition to a mild weather working day in Texas, it meant that Secret Service would be taking off the car roof of the presidential limousine and that we would have no trouble finding our target: they would surely give us the green light for the hit.

Despite this benevolent climate news, promise of a beautiful sunny afternoon in Dallas, Ruby was making a face behind the wheel.

- You look a little tense, Mister Ruby. Is everything OK? I had launched as I was taking place at the front, with Beau Serge.

- Yeah! You better believe it, Jo... It looks like a fuckin' hitman convention in Dallas!

He was over-excited behind the wheel and even had trouble shifting gears. Was it a clutch problem? ... Or maybe just alot of miles on the clock? ... I don't know? Because the Ford looked like and old Betsy that had been around the block more than a couple of times.

- Why do you say that, Mister Ruby? ... I don't understand?

- I've seen at least a dozen hitman walking around Dealey Plaza when I drove downtown... It's a fuckin' zoo out there! I saw Roselli, Eugene Bradin, Larry Flower, Johnny D's, Nicoletti, even Eduardo and Bush, those CIA cocksuckers, Mac Wallace, LBJ's personal fuckin' assassin, Harrelson, Frank Sturgis, Morales... And some Cubans from Operation Mongoose that I forgot the names of... Like I told you, Jo, it's a fuckin' hitman convention in Dallas!

- And? ... Why should I give a shit about that, Mister Ruby? Are they gonna be a problem for us? Do we have to abort the mission? Are they here to kill us? What? ... You tell me, for fuck's sake... What?

- No! ... No! Don't worry, Jo... I think alot of these guys are just here to see the fireworks!

- Fuck me man! ... To see the fireworks, you say? Well! Fuck them and fuck you too! ... We came here to do a job... And they better not get in our way, I tell ya, because we're gonna hit your beloved American President, and then, we're gonna pop a couple of your hitman friends just for the fun of shootin' clay pigeons in Dallas... Is that fuckin' understood, Mister Ruby?

- Don't you get mad, Jo! I just wanted to let you know that...

- ... Well, consider it done!

Ruby drove a little and I had time to calm down a bit and get into my "let's kill every-fuckin'-body who gets in the way" mood.

Jack's face was ruby red... He was pumping oil like his old truck engine.

Attention à l'angine de poitrine, M Ruby! (Watch out for an angina attack, Mr Ruby!) I taught.

Coming near Dealey Plaza, when Jack Ruby told me he would drop us off in front of the Grassy Knoll - the idiot! -, I told him "no"... And I got out of the pickup truck with Beau Serge on Houston Street, at the corner of Elm. We were going to walk to our location, because I didn't want people to see all three of us descend at the same spot as during the Normandy landings and draw attention on us.

- After the hit, one of the Joes with Roselli or Frank, I don't know who, exactly, will be driving you out of Dealey Plaza in a station wagon parked on Houston, across the dirt parking lot...

- The car? ... What color?

- It's a light-colored Rambler piece of shit wagon. You can't miss it... It's the ugliest car ever made in the States!

Ruby drove around a bit, and then he stopped in front of the Texas School Book Depository to let us out...

- Okay! Here we are... I'll see you guys at the safe house after the hit. Good luck to you, Jo!

- Yeah! Better believe it! ... We'll need all the luck we can on this one, Mister Ruby...

We got off the pickup truck at the corner of Houston and Elm. I motioned to Lucien Sarti to stay in the cargo box, just as he was about to get off, and said: "*Tu descendras en face de l'escalier* (You'll get out in front of the staircase)".

Then Ruby went on his merry fuckin' way down Elm Street. He left Sarti out in front of the stairs leading to the pergola and the Grassy Knoll dirt car park, stopping only a moment in the avenue because there was a lot of traffic, and, slowly, I saw the old Ford Pickup disappear on the other side of the Stemmons Freeway overpass.

When we ultimately arrived at the Grassy Knoll, Lucien was already at his post, at the foot of the viaduct, and was walking along the end of the fence, impatiently; he was going back and forth while smoking a cigarette. Fiorini, Roselli with his two Joes, and another guy, a Cuban whose name we didn't know, took out their fake secret service badges, half jokingly: they were going to play the role of "special agent" so that we could work in peace on the little hill; they would chase intruders out of the perimeter and control the crowd so that we could leave without any problem once we've finished our work.

Frank introduced me to another guy, a man dressed in a railway worker's shirt; he looked like a Cuban, too, a lowly smiling guy who was going to take care of Sarti's weapon after the hit. Fuckin' Lucien! The guy was a lot of management; we always had to do something special to make him happy...

I went to see Frank Fiorini, and asked him:

"How will we know if we can execute the contract? Will you be the one to give us the signal?"

- Jo, we'll be patrolling behind of the fence and give you the green light with a thumbs-up as soon as we get the OK from our radio coordinator.

- And if I cannot see your signal... What then?

- There will be two of our guys at the bottom of the knoll, right in front of you. One is a radioman; the other one will have an umbrella and will open it to greet our dear President's departure for the other world, just as the car starts going down on Elm Street. That's your green light! ... You cannot miss that.

- OK... Got it, Frank. Thanks for everything!

- Good luck to you, Jo! Fiorini wished me, when we left each other... Good hunting to you and to your guys!

- It's not luck that I need, Frank... I just need to know where-he-is!

I had answered, sweeping off Elm Street with my index finger, as if pointing an invisible gun and firing with my digit.

After talking to them both and retransmitting the instructions to make sure they had understood, I left my fellow French colleague behind the Grassy Knoll's fence and went to my site.

I grilled cigarette on cigarette while surveying the place until five minutes to noon. Then, concentrating on the task at hand, I went to settle in the cement pergola. Folks had already started gathering at the corner of Houston and Elm Street, it swarmed with people down the Texas School Book Depository, but around the Grassy Knoll there was no crowd; there were only a few onlookers on the sidewalks and a meagre herd of admirers of the presidential couple who were waiting for the procession to come to them in an immense manicured lawn... Several bystanders were directly in my line of fire.

From my spot, in addition to having tree branches and the Stemmons Highway traffic sign to block my view, a couple came to plant themselves right in front of me on a cement promontory that bordered the staircase leading to one of the ends of the pergola. A woman escorted a man who had a cine-camera and was preparing to shoot the presidential procession, just like me, and I was going to have to aim just next to their heads - or even between their two skulls! -, as the supersonic sound of the bullet would produce a loud noise as it passed close to them. My only hope was that they wouldn't turn around after my shot, panicked, and that the amateur filmmaker would continue to fire at the presidential car while I would finish dealing with the leader of the greatest economy on the planet. I wanted to stay hidden for as long as possible... at least until the gunshot festival ended in Dealey Plaza.

I looked in the direction of Fiorini, still busy chasing people who wanted to stand in front of, or behind, the picket fence so they could watch the procession, and when he finally looked in my direction to make sure that everything was fine for me, too, I pointed a desperate finger to the guy who was getting ready to film, hoping Frank would chase him and his girlfriend out of the promontory.

But Frank just thumbed up to let me know that everything was OK: Frank Fiorini did not realize that these people were in my line of fire.

Fuck me man! ... Talk about an impossible shot to make! I would have to aim between two heads to hit the target... *Deux têtes valent mieux qu'une!* (Two heads are better than one!) Used to say Aunt Titine.

The presidential car finally turned the corner of Houston and Elm Street at around 12:30 p.m. The limo had almost made a complete stop as the driver probably misjudged the bend and made a slow wide turn to correct his course... Fiorini had surely received the green light from the radio operator, because, all smile, he raised a thumbs-up in my direction, articulating slowly: *"We've got a go..."*

It was pretty much all I could decipher by reading on his lips.

The umbrella man pumped his little black parasol several times, but I had already deduced that the procession was on us when I saw the crowd shouting madly at the corner of Houston and Elm Street.

As the presidential car barely moved away from the Texas Book School Depository to go down towards the Grassy Knoll, we heard a loud firecracker bang coming from the general direction of the Texas School Book Depository... Followed by another one less than a second after the first one!

Two shoooters, I tought!

From inside the cement vestibule, I had to change position at the last moment to better follow the leading car with the scope. I needed to post myself against one of the walls of the small concrete porch to increase my angle of fire and to better circumvent obstacles that obstructed my view: the limousine would be cruising from left to right...

In theory, I must wait and shoot only when the target will be almost in front of me. So, I will try to make myself as discreet as possible, and, since the crowd is looking at the president's car and onto the street... I should remain almost invisible with my light coloured raincoat against the cement wall.

I follow the lead car in my scope, the view partially obscured by tree limbs, but I know that the presidential limousine will be in my window of opportunity very shortly. I'm nervous like a maid in a castle 'cause it's my first honeymoon in Texas. I can hear my heartbeat pulsing in my ears; my eardrums vibrate at a brisk pace; the frenzy also wins the anxious crowd; my brain is nothing but a pious delirium; the green hill of the Grassy Knoll leads to another existence; I am the actor of my own rebirth; to the west of Nirvana, my legendary Hollywood; it's the death of a president who will finally unite us forever; with one bullet, I will bring down the democracy of an entire nation; the most beautiful country in the world, assassinated; *the Land of the free* with its gigantic amusement parks, annihilated; the dazzling rockets of *the Star Spangled Banner,* eradicated; with one shot I will rebuild everything; I am a shaper of worlds; it is a rather strange fate which leads a Bônois to the Texans; but a destiny which passes through Marseilles and Dallas is another one; I am the Mediterranean Sea creeping at the foot of Dealey Plaza; I am the cry of the cormorant which flies painfully from a cemetery of the Blue Bayou; watch over my own little private Idaho, O! Angel of stone; it's the miracle of chance that creates a new era; from ashes to ashes, dust to dust, it's a world from which everything will be reborn again; I am made of star dust and my ashes will collapse on Hyannis Port like those of a Gas Giant; I am the Supernova who has had everything aborted, and then gave birth to everything; I swapped the Kennedy's Dynasty for the Bush's; push push in the bush... I am death blooming in a desert of Paris, Texas; I am the sum of all that has ever been drunk from Pomme de terre river, in Missouri; two million years ago I came out of my cave, crawling; I am a Pied-Noir virus that has the power to kill everything in site; it was General de Gaulle who gave me birth in the late fifties; where I was sent, I have killed them all; I am the man who saw the man who saw the bear; from North Africa, I landed in North America; the America that chews and divides men into pieces; the land of the free; the America who gives death by gun in the inner city... And, precisely, I came to Dallas to grant it to some unlucky fellow citizen!

The presidential car is coming... It's here! No more time for delirium, now... I'm just a trigger... The extension of Texas Oilman's hatred for their President... The end point in the unfinished personal diary of John Fitzgerald Kennedy's presidency!

The president and his wife are within sight... The first lady wears a beautiful fuchsia set... She is radiant and she smiles... What a flirtatious woman, the First Lady! ... The President looks to his right and sends a hand to admirers... Then, for a moment, I lose track of the limousine behind the Stemmons Highway sign... *Wanted for treason* is stuck on one of the posts... After two beats we meet again on the other side of the road sign... Then, to improve my angle, I slip to the far right of the small concrete hall and must shoulder from the left, 'cause I have to negotiate with the heads of the amateur filmmaker and that of his partner who, partially, obstruct my line of fire.

Finally, the radio operator raises one arm in the air, clenching his fist, and steps into the avenue so that the driver of the limo cannot miss it... *"We've got a go... We've got a go... We've got a go..."* Is he is transmitting on a monotonous tone to all, thanks to a microphone hidden in his sleeve...

The driver of the presidential limousine has understood the instructions, a closed fist being the signal that the military uses between militaries to signal a "complete stop" during a patrol, and the federal agent immobilizes the vehicle in the central lane like a good little soldier boy, just in front of our team...

I take the time to aim good... Tac! A muffled shot echoes from the fence of the Grassy Knoll... Bang! Pigeons fly off the roof of the TSBD... The president then raises both elbows at shoulder height... He cannot breathe anymore! ... He has been hit in the throat... He chokes! ... The bullet has passed through the front window of the limousine... But the windshield is not bullet proof... No more than the bumpers of the Lincoln are a shield for American democracy... And just at the top of the presidential tie, a small hole of 6.5 mm in diameter appeared just below the Adam's apple!

The driver takes time to look behind... He too heard firing sounds... The president is perhaps already dead? ... The secret agent keeps his foot on the brakes... The car stays motionless for a few seconds in the middle of the avenue... Time has stopped in Dealey Plaza: a kind of invitation to complete Beau Serge's work... The First Lady approaches her husband... She inspects the damage caused by the armoured projectile... She sees blood spurting from the trachea... *"My God, he's been shot!"* Exclaims the First Lady... But she's still in my line of fire... And if she does not move her head from there, I will never be able to fire and justify the wages of death.

Then, while everything seemed to be lost for me, it's the miracle that occurs... O! Sweet Jesus of Nazareth, why did you grant thy wishes?

(Tout vient à point à qui peult attendre...) Everything comes to those who can wait...

The First Lady changes position on her seat... She barely moves her head for an ultimate face to face with her husband...

There is my chance!

And I point my cannon through the cameraman and his female colleague, who are always at the top of the stairs, just in front of me...

Tac! ... Zooooom!

The supersonic bullet nibbles away at their ears as it makes its way into Dealey Plaza, chewing the air like a parasitic worm chasing a head of lettuce... But the guy with camera still goes on shooting the procession, even if he has wobbled a bit on his legs... I aimed behind the right ear of the President of the United States of America so I would not risk hitting the First Lady... Who will not be for much longer after my shot... And then, as I was leaning on the trigger to strike, a simultaneous shot from the viaduct reached the president in the head.

A scarlet droplet now adorns the top of the president's forehead, just below the forelock, as well as behind his right ear... Like the crown of the king of Nazareth because of the long spines that had pierced his flesh!

The head of the president of the Americas is projected towards the back and on the left side... Two goads of metal ploughed trough his head... It is the big financiers of this world with the corrupt politicians, the mafia, the American military-industrialist complex, fallen government agents and Texan oil magnates who crucified you, O! King of the Americans... It's Jewish Easter and Passover all wrapped into one, but in the month of November... I wash my hands like Pontius Pilate in the Passion... Forgive me for having driven this last nail in thy cross, oh! Sweet Jesus of the Americans!

And the back of the head of the President of the United States of America bursts open like a melon that would have fallen from the window of the second floor of the White House: dum-dum bullets, it appears, do not forgive at all... With a single shot from a long rifle, I helped bring down American democracy!

A police biker thought he'd seen a sniper on the Grassy Knoll... He also detected small puffs of smoke floating on top of the fence of the small hill... He then passed between the stopped cars of the procession and tried to climb the mound with his motorcycle... Who ends up down the hill... He then abandons his Harley Davidson and tries to rush to the fence... To hell with the bike!

At the same moment, five secret agents throw themselves on the presidential limousine and surround it... One of the agents picks up a fragment of bone that a child had recovered on the lawn... Another climbs into the car to check the state of health of the president... He then turns and throws a thumb down to his boss in the following car...

The president is dead on the spot!

And the agents are recalled in order to protect the car behind; where the Vice President has already been hiding behind the seats for a while, as if he had known in advance what would happen in Dealey Plaza today! ... O! Dear Vice President of the Americans, why be one with the carpets of your limousine?

The king of the Americans is dead. Long lives the king! ... A Texan! And the bullets continue to ricochet in the avenue to celebrate his long-awaited advent...

They still shoot from the TSBD and from behind... More than a dozen shots were fired in Dealey Plaza, a green square that has been turned into a mousetrap:

"Welcome to Texas, Mr. President!"

It's Lyndon Baines Johnson who must be laughing in his beard. He ransacked his rival for murder in Texas where he and his friends control all the tricks of the state: judges, politicians and police... Even the FBI is in his back pocket!

On the sidelines, just behind the presidential limousine, a police biker was sprayed with bone, brains and blood. He pats his upper body and looks for the invisible wound that would have made him bleed... Despite the sound of his Harley Davidson's engine, he thought he heard shots coming from the Grassy Knoll... Even saw a small purple cumulus floating up the grassy hillock under the trees and thought bullets had rammed him. He palpates his chest, but he's not hit... It's the presidential car and its occupants who were struck down!

The First Lady, too, has pieces of flesh, bone fragments and blood all over her face. Her beautiful Chanel set is also stained with gray matter and bits of bloody brain... What remains of the head of the president rests for a moment on her fragile knees... She cradles him gently as to comfort a child who would have had a headache... Mechanically, she smooth's his hair to hide the gaping opening in the back of the skull... He was so beautiful, her president! ... She talks to him, whispering in his ear an ultimate word of affection... As one accompanies a loved one during his brief passage to the afterlife... The beautiful blue eyes of the President are open wide... Frozen in the nil, they look at the infinite Texan sky...

"Why did we come here?" Sighs the First Lady... "We had been warned of the danger!"

Seeing his petrified gaze through the lens of my high-precision rifle, I know that the President is dead... Dead on the spot... Even if the presidential heart may still beat in his chest and has not yet realized that everything was over: I have killed my first president... The President of the United States of America!

The work completed, as in a military parade set to quarter turn, the presidential car leaves, but without too much of a hurry... The First Lady then gets up from her seat, leaves the president for a moment in the back, and climbs on the trunk of the car to retrieve a big piece of skull... And, at the same time, a secret service agent manages to jump at the back of the limousine to protect the presidential family... To make with his body a bulwark against dictatorship! ... And big capital! ... And the hatred of Texas oilman! But alas! ... It's already too late for American democracy in the United States of America.

The *coup d'état* executed masterfully, the presidential car, gone, I stopped to scan through the lens of my Savage 7 mm. Crouched on the cement floor, I hid for a moment in the little concrete hallway as I picked up the ejected shell of my high-precision rifle, well away from the inquisitive gaze of the crowd who cries and mourns the loss of this dear beloved president...

Most of the people had thrown themselves to the ground... Panicked! ... They were lying on the Grassy Knoll mound... On the lawn on the other side of Elm... On the wide cement sidewalk... All were afraid of being shot by a new salvo, because someone was still firing from the Dal-Tex building and the Texas School Book Depository... The diversion promised by the Secret Services!

And it's this moment of confusion, orchestrated masterfully by the *friends* of the president, who gave me time to unscrew the silencer... Which I put back in the inner pocket of my raincoat... The smell of the powder greyed me for a moment... Next, I let my gun hang down on my thigh... Put on the trench coat and the hat... And, without hurry, I walked away from the pergola and took the direction of the car park.

One of two coloured folks sitting on a park bench in front of the fence, just alongside the cement stairs, had dropped his lunch bag and a bottle of soda, which made a loud pop when it exploded on the concrete, while the amateur cineaste, paralysed by what had happened or by the bullets that still ricocheted into the street, flinched a little as if the noise had awaken a wino filmmaker from the drunken stupor he was in.

As he awoke, he screamed: "They killed him! ... They killed him!" Afterwards, he quickly inspected his camera to make sure his Bell & Howell had captured the carnage, and when he finally decided to look around and survey the bottom of the hill, shell-shocked, almost everybody was laying down on the ground... Except him!

Beau Serge was already moving away from the Grassy Knoll to the Texas School Book Depository, when I went around the pergola to join him. I saw Sarti take a few steps towards the railway, and then, immediately after, he threw his Mauser to the guy wearing a railway employee's shirt, which caught the rifle as when seizing a child in full flight. Sarti then straightened his officer's uniform, took the time to adjust his cap, and he headed for the TSBD car park to join us at a good pace.

Lucien had not made two strides that the railwayman was already kneeling, hidden behind a junction box of the railway, and with dexterity, as if he had done this during his whole life, the dude with the striped shirt took the time to disassemble the rifle into several pieces. After unscrewing the gun suppressor, the Cuban stowed the gun in spare parts in a bumpy toolbox of beige color; he then walked towards the railroad as if nothing had happened... As if he belonged to the rail! Afterwards, he skirted the railway before disappearing at the end of the endless parallel lines...

As panicked people rushed to the Grassy Knoll by the dozen, the Dallas police biker, who had climbed the little hill with the gun in his hand, was leading the charge of his fellow countrymen. At the top of the mound, the officer immediately rushed at one of the Cubans who acted as a secret agent during the shooting, and the man immediately raised his hands in the air when he saw the gun pointed at him. Afterwards, after having talked a little with the cop, the Cuban took out his Secret Service agent badge from his jacket and quickly waved it in front of the policeman's face like a magic wand, and the piggy immediately left him alone when he saw that the dude was *"family"*.

Afterwards, the Cuban pointed a finger at abandoned cars on the other side of the railway line, probably to distract the policeman as the crowd began to mass more and more at the top of the mound... All were trying to catch the murderers of the president! Nearly a hundred people were shouting everywhere, all of whom were convinced that the shots that had hit the president's head came from the Grassy Knoll.

While the very "special agent" was directing the attention of the biker cop to the rail yard, we were leaving the car park on the side of Houston Street, on the opposite end of the Grassy Knoll, just behind the Texas School Book Depository, and were walking without saying a word through the cars parked like sardines in a tin box.

As we emerged on Houston Street, a light-coloured family car was waiting... Frank Fiorini saw us coming out of the dirt car park and immediately made us a sign to reapply, rapidly. The engine of the station wagon seemed to purr with joy when we arrived, with horses under the hood that seemed to paw with impatience when Fiorini opened the door...

2

We quickly got into the car; I sat at the front, next to one of the Joe's who accompanied Fiorini. Sarti and Beau Serge climbed behind and hid on the floor of the car to go unnoticed. As soon as the doors were closed, Frank managed to sneak through the pedestrians of Houston Street, where panic was already beginning to set in, and afterwards, as if nothing exceptional had happened in Dealy Plaza, he turned right on Elm Street and took the path of the presidential motorcade...

The fuckin' nerve with this Fiorini!

I was really amazed by the balls on that guy... But there wasn't a single cop to block off the road or to prevent us from crossing. It was organized confusion at its finest; no one knew what the fuck was going on; and on top of that, the police radio channel had been jammed... Courtesy of a policeman of the Dallas Police Force who, coincidentally, had left is mike open!

A few seconds later, at the same place where the presidential limo had been struck by bullets, Fiorini slowed down and stopped for a brief second in the middle of the street! ... Then, out of nowhere, one of the Cubans who had taken the role of *secret agent* behind the picket fence ran down the slope with great strides to join us, and, as soon as the dude had sit inside - he had to go around the car and to the left side of the station wagon as Sarti and Beau Serge were lying behind the right passenger seat -, Frank Fiorini floored the gas pedal of the Rambler... Pedal to the metal... Ramble on!

Once on the other side of the Stemmons Triple Overpass, Sarti and Beau Serge took their seats... And we all started breathing again, normally.

As soon as we crossed the viaduct, Frank asked me, a little worried: "Now you tell me, Jo... How did it go?"

He didn't know we two-timed the president in the head...
Fucked him really good.

- Fine, Frank. A real no-brainer! ... One in the throat; one in the forehead, just above the right eye; and one behind and above his right ear! After the last two shots, the back of his head shattered into a million little pieces in the air: the mark was dead before the limo went under the Stemmons...

- ... Are you sure, Jo? Are you absolutely sure of this? It's important... I heard on the radio that he was just injured and...

- ... Don't believe everything you ear on the radio, Frank! ... He's dead! As dead as the sun sets in the West... As sure as Jesus Christ died on the cross to save humanity!

Even though we all were baptized and confirmed Christians in the car, I immediately regretted saying this because I was not even sure that our Lord Jesus had only existed...

And since he had supposedly resurrected on the third day, according to the *Hollywood Bible,* it may not have been a very good comparison to make here.

- Good Lord! Very good, guys... Excellent shooting! This calls for a little celebration. And I think that...

- ... Yeah! Let us... please... going to... the...

- ... But not right now, Lucien. Had cut Fiorini, dryly.

- *Putain, Jo! On se fait une petite virée au Carousel Club! Faut absolument fêter ça avec les filles du pédé! Non?* (Damn it, Jo! We have to go to the Carousel Club! We must absolutely celebrate with the bitches of that fag Ruby! ... No?)

When Fiorini heard the words *"Carousel Club"* coming out of Sarti's mouth, he surely deduced that Lucien wanted to party there, even if Frank didn't understand a fuckin' word of French.

- No! No Carousel Club for you, guys. You fellas have to keep a low profile and stay out of site for a while... Especially you, Lucien! We all know what you're capable of... And on top of that, I have a little stop to make before we take you back to the safe house. So...

- ... A stop, you say? But? ... What the fuck for, Frank? All the cops are gonna be gunning for us in the city! You crazy?

- Not all of them, Jo... Don't you worry about the cops. I just need to talk to someone and pick up a package... It's important: part of the plan, if you want to know. But I won't be long. Promise. We're cool, guys... Don't you worry about anything: we'll take good care of you.

- *Ouais! Une balle dans le dos et addio amici!* (Yeah! A bullet in the back and goodbye my friends!) Said Sarti out loud.

- What's that he's saying about his friends?

- Bah! Nothing important, Frank; you know Lucien is... He's always complaining about something.

- Well! He'd better shut the fuck up and walk the line with his ass real tight, I tell ya! Otherwise...

But Sarti was absolutely right: we couldn't trust any of these guys. None of them... Not even Frank Fiorini who was our friend, supposedly.

After getting rid of our gear and weapons in the parking lot of a gas station in Oak Cliff, I had kept my white shirt with long sleeves and put the rifle, the hat and the rest of my clothes in the trunk, Frank coasted for a good five minutes in the neighbourhood where our hideout was located, but he had no intention of dropping us off...

Fiorini looked everywhere as we were passing the cross streets: he was moving very slowly... What the fuck? Every available body with a badge in Dallas was now looking for us, and this motherfucker was taking a promenade in the city!

- Fuck me, Frank! ... What's you looking for, man? I asked.

- I'm looking for a police officer of ours...

- ... A police? What the hell for, Frank! ... You crazy, man?

- Don't you worry, Jo... Officer Tippit is working for us. Christ! Half of the Dallas Police force is on the payroll! ... That cop is supposed to deliver a package for us. But? ... Where the fuck is that cocksucker hiding?

We drove another ten minutes more in Oak Cliff. Fiorini was still inspecting the crossings and looking for his famous police car. A ghost! Then, parked near a sidewalk in the shade of a tree, we finally saw a patrol car... Inside, there was only one pig, and the cop seemed to be waiting for something or someone... I thought it must have been for Frank. But nobody knew at the time that Fiorini wanted to make blood sausage with the piggy... my preference being Canadian bacon and not black pudding.

On the door of the police car, sandwiched between the words Police and Dallas, was painted the number "10": car number 10 of the Dallas police force, Texas.

Fiorini parked the Rambler a little way back at about thirty meters, just passed the corner of a side street that intersected with East 10th street, and then he ordered:

- Joe, take the wheel.

He had spoken to the other Joe, I understood it well, but when he repeated "Jo" for the second time, he was speaking to me:

- Jo, I want you to come with me... You'll be my backup man on this one.

Sarti had more or less understood the words of Fiorini, because he immediately launched, very animated:

- *Je veux y aller moi aussi, Jo. Je veux vous accompagner...* I am... wanting to...to go, too... with you... me...

But Fiorini cut him dry, pointing a threatening finger at him as if he had deciphered what Sarti had to say, and he told Lucien, in Italian:

- *È... Tranquilla! Non si muovono da qui.* (Hey! ... Quiet! You're not moving out of here.)

Lucien had to stay in the car and was really pissed off about it: he had the look of a guy who could kill everyone in a hundred mile radius.

But Fiorini didn't want him for the job... He didn't need a fuckin' unstable Sour Puss drinker with him!

- What do you want me to do, Frank? ... I don't understand?

- Just fuckin' come with me, will ya!

- Why? ... I don't understand what I have to do...

- ... Don't question everything for once in your life and just fuckin' do what I tell you to do... And be ready for anything. You've got a gun on you?

- Yes, Frank... I'm packing. Got my Walter on me. But...

- ... Good! Now follow my lead and don't say another fuckin' word until I say otherwise! ... You can do that, can you?

I nodded... 'Cause I wasn't aloud to speak! But Fiorini was stepping all over my First Amendment: the freedom of speach.

I followed Fiorini, like a docile dog would his puppet master, but I still didn't understand what he was expecting of me, exactly. I still had the fear of being shot by one of his goons, by the CIA, the FBI, or indeed by a cop in service! And it rattled me a bit: I didn't trust him completely, this Frank, although he looked like an OK guy to me.

But they were all motherfuckers until proven otherwise...

We crossed the intersection in a hurry, and, on the passenger's side, Frank approached the police officer and started knocking against the window.

I was a little behind... The backup man!

Then, spinning a finger that operated an invisible reel, he motioned to the officer to lower the window...

They both seemed to know each other very well, and officer Tippit never seemed frightened to see him appear on the sidewalk: he had to be waiting for him.

The cop turned the crank of the door and lowered the glass, halfway. He took a look at me as to size me, surely wondering what the fuck I was doing there... Covering Fiorini's back? ... He made a face... Maybe he felt that something was wrong? ... I donno? Then Frank leaned in and it was he who shouted first, irritated:

- I don't see Oswald! ... Where the fuck is Oswald? He should be handcuffed in the back of your car... Or did you put him in the trunk? ... Where's my package, Tippit? ... Where the fuck is he?

- I don't know, Frank? I don't know? ... Don't you get mad at me. I've been looking all over for Lee, but I just couldn't locate him. So, you probably won't be able to drive him to Red Bird airport before dinner, as planned.

Yeah! Red Bird! ... Before dinner... Ha! Sure! Frank probably wanted to chopsuey Oswald real good and then dump his body in Garland's Chinatown so they could make chicken soo guy with him... Erase all traces of the plot with cherry sauce!

I was a little scared for my skin, too.

- And Ruby? ... Where the fuck is Jack Ruby? Have you spoken with him? ... He was supposed to wait for your call and meet us here. Christ! I tell ya! ... Where are the fuckin' fags when you just need one?

- I don't know, Frank. I couldn't get him either. I tried calling. He could have gone to the hospital... Possibly to check on the President condition! I don't know what to tell you, Frank...

I knew very well in what state was the Constitution of the United States of America, or for that matter the health status of the President... They both were D.O.A! But I didn't interfere with their pleasant conversation and didn't say anything.

- Tippit? You fool! ... What have you done with Oswald? Tell me the truth... **Now,** would be a good time! We don't have time to play 20 questions. This is important... Hurry! What have you done with him? ... Jesus Christ! Don't fuck with me, Tippit. Otherwise, I'm gonna squeeze you by the balls and make you squeal like the little skinny piggy you are until you tell me where the fuck he is...

- ... Oswald is not my fuckin' problem. I'm police. I don't have to answer to you, Frank. So, fuck you... Find yourself another fuckin' killer. I don't want to do your dirty work no more. You get my drift? ... Now, fuck off, Frank, and leave me the hell out of your shit bath!

And with that being said, Tippit operated the crank and went up the window, while Frank thundered, banging one fist on the roof of the patrol car:

- Fuck off, you say? ... You want to fuck with me, officer Tippit? Really? Come on out of the cruiser, you little piece of shit... I'm the fucker who's gonna fuck you over twice on Sunday!

And it was after this tempestuous verbal exchange that Tippit got out of his car, gun in hand, looking for his pound of fresh meat. He was furious and was about to discharge his weapon at Fiorini... Or was it Fiorini who was going to do the shooting first? ... I donno?

Fuck me! ... I wasn't gonna to do a cop on top of everything else?

I searched my back and grabbed my Walter .380, but Fiorini had been faster than both of us and already had the jump on the cop, and like a bobcat from Montana, he leaped to the front of the car before Tippit was even ready to discharge his weapon.

As officer Tippit finally aimed in an attempt to fire at us and save himself, Fiorini lodged a good five or six bullets at close range in his chest; emptied his revolver on the cop...

I'll plead the Fifth on that one, your Honour! And Tippit collapsed to the ground, straightaway...

A fuckin' sac of potatoes!

I got frightened for an instant. Fearful that Fiorini would turn to me, next, and gun me down... Just like Tippit!

Then, I told myself: Relax motherfucker! Relax! ... He's empty... He emptied his revolver on the cop, not you. He's not gonna shoot you. At least, not now... And if you still can ear the shots ringing in your ear that means it wasn't meant for your sorry ass. So, chill the fuck down, dude!

And a little shaken with the whole affair, I finally turned my attention to the situation at hand...

Tippit was lying on the ground. The cop was probably dead before tasting asphalt; his plumbing was leaking from every-fuckin'-where: there even was a puddle of blood already stretching towards a nearby sewer... The scarlet stream was pushing one of Tippit's uniform buttons torned and scarred by the shelling!

However, as Tippit shuddered a little - but in my opinion, for having bumped off several dozens Muslim terrorist scumbags in Algeria, it was more like involuntary muscle spasms than muscular-voluntary activity -, Fiorini ordered me to complete his masterwork...

- Now, finish him off, Jo!

He was smiling...

As he laughed a little, he started to eject the cartridges from the barrel of his revolver, one by one, dropping them onto the pavement... Near the *dead* body of officer Tippit!?!

Jesus Christ! ... What the fuck was he doing, that cunt?

- What's that you're saying, Frank? ... You're fuckin' with me, or what? ... I'm not sure that I got it.

- I said: finish him off... Just fuckin' do him, for Christ's sake! ... For you it will be just like doing JFK for the second time!

- You fuckin' crazy, Frank? ... Have you gone completely insane? That cop is dead... Fuckin' dead! And so is JFK... I should know this since I'm the one who popped him in the head and watch his brain explode in my scope!

- Jo, my little Jo... I said: fi-nish-him-off, for Christ's sake! Are you fuckin' deaf or what? ... You know damn well that we can't leave any witnesses behind. So, come on, Jo... Just get on with it already!

- But Frank? ... He's already dead. Deceased! As dead as a fuckin' doornail! ... What do you want of me? ... Make him just a little more dead than he already is?

I didn't understand the "why" and it fuckin' scared the bejesus out of me! My only hope was to understand what was going on in order to survive this journey... To understand the "why"... The "why" that divides the wolf from the sheep... Because the "why" is the only real power of life, when you are an elite soldier, and without it you're defenseless and can't survive the crossing...

And this is how Fiorini was coming to me: without the "why"? ... Without any fuckin' knowledge?

I was just another link in a long chain of actors in the plot, and since I wasn't very good at following orders blindly, I almost wanted to tell Fiorini to go fuck himself with his little piggy friend, and run back to the car!

- What? ... Have you suddenly lost your tongue, my little Jo? ... Just do him, for fuck's sake, and stop arguing with me all the time like a little girl with her panties in a bunch!

And on top of everything, Frank Fiorini was making fun of me, the bastard!

I was wavering between being mad at him or just being scared of what would happen to me afterwards if I refused to do what he said...

- *Putain!* (Damn!) Do him, you're saying? ... But? ... Do what, Frank? ... What? ... That cop is a deadbeat! Dead! ... What's there to finish?

- Are you some kind of fuckin' doctor, Jo?

I shook my head...

"No? ... So, how the fuck can you tell if that cocksucker is really dead or not?"

- Um! Maybe by just looking at the corpse, Frank... By observing at the **huge** bullet holes you've made in his chest? The blood is oozing from his hart, for Christ's sake! ... I could try to bring back the poor bastard to life by giving him mouth-to-mouth resuscitation... And then kill him again! At least, that would be killing him for real...

- Then, if he's already dead, what's your fuckin' problem, Jo? ... Just finish the motherfucker for a second time, for crying out loud! ... Just do it!

- But...

- ... No buts! ... Just fuckin' do him, will ya? And stop arguing all the time like a little brat from southern France!

I watched him without understanding what was going on in here, exactly... Without the motherfuckin' "why"...

Then, I responded:

- Okay, Frank. Okay. If you insist, I'll put a pill in his head and do him... Juuust to make you happy! Will that work for you?

- Fine! ... Good boy! ... Now, just fuckin' do him and stop debating like a fuckin' French motherfuckin' politician bitch!

I ignored Frank's Frenchy flavoured comments, and asked:

- Open casket or casket closed?

- Um! Very good question, Jo! ... Better open, I think... We may need the motherfuker later on... Who the fuck knows?

Need him later? ... What the fuck was Fiorini talking about?

After these words, I bent over Tippit's body to put a pill in his head... I put my pistol on the back of his neck and looked up at Frank to see if it was what he wanted... Location! Location! Location! ... The three L's of the killing business!

Fiorini shook his head...

Fuck me! This was not the right spot, according to him...

I pointed the gun a little higher, on top of Tippit's skull, and then looked up at Frank before pulling the trigger... But he shook his head once more and motioned a little lower and more to the right with his index finger in what I understood as being: popping the cop in the right temple...

- The coupe de gras, Jo! ... The coupe de gras!

Fuckin' Americans! ... They could'nt promounce *coup de gras* even if their life fuckin' depended on it!

Damn! ... Fuck me, man! What a fuckin' nightmare, this hitman profession! I may just need a fuckin' vacation afterwards just to keep me from going completely insane!

I finally did dropped the hammer on the motherfucker...

The bullet made its way into the moribund temple: Tippit's cranium did not even quiver a millimeter. He was indeed dead... Really fuckin' dead! As dead as JFK was... A goner!

But, I already new that...

However, what I didn't know at the time was that Fiorini's friends were going to tamper with the photos of the autopsy of the president and use Tippit's body for some *official* shots of the head, Tippit being some sort of JFK look-alike... A double with the back of the head *in one piece!*

When I picked up my Walter's still smoking casing on the asphalt, trying not to put my foot in the pool of blood that was still growing, I exclaimed:

- You happy now, Frank? Is he fuckin' dead enough for you or do I have to do him for the third time?

- Good fuckin' job! ... Super, Jo! I think JFK is really dead, now.

The bastard! ... He just wanted me to take part in the murder of Tippit: a Dallas police officer.

- He's got at least half a dozen bullet holes in him, Frank... We've killed the poor son of a bitch a good four times. At least! ... Fuckin' waste of ammo, man, if you don't mind me saying so!

I had been taught in the Foreign Legion the importance of not wasting ammunition. When you have no more cartridges and that you are in an ambush, you cannot fire to save your life... And I had once or twice had to kill enemies with a bayonet, just before they invaded our perimeter, to later recover their weapon and keep on firing on Fellaghas (Algerian freedom fighters) with their own AK's, in Algeria.

But Frank didn't care about ammunitions... or even for my opinion. And he smiled as if he was really proud of himself...

He later claimed that JFK had been killed twice. But I didn't know at the time that, because of his striking resemblance to the President of the United States, officer Tippit's nickname was "JFK" amongst the Dallas police force. A pejorative diminutive, it goes without saying, because very few policemen liked John Fitzgerald Kennedy in Texas... The tendency was rather on the side of the KKK, in Dallas.

Several politicians and police officers were active members of the Ku Klux Klan in the sixties; some even claimed that Lyndon B Johnson was a member, too; many cops had an emblem on their uniforms used by many right-wing groups... including the triple K!

Then, from a distance, we saw a big black magic woman coming down the street...

When Frank saw her tumbling towards us like a wine barrel of Châteauneuf-du-Pape rolling down a hillside of the Côte du Rhône, he immediately ordered me, while he finished reloading his revolver:

- Go back to the car, Jo. Go back... Now!

- OK, Frank. But? ... What about you?

- Just go, for fuck sakes! Faster the fuck up...

I stuck my Walter in the belt and ran for the Station wagon. I just had crossed the street when Frank started yelling at me, waving furiously:

- I'm gonna go the other way... You guys can pick me up further down the street.

I nodded...

I sped up towards the car, while Frank was trotting in the opposite direction, with the gun in his hand.

When the huge women arrived at the scene to notice the death of Officer Tippit, I was already far away. And I said to Joe, as I entered the car:

- Frank wants you to pick him up down the street... Hurry!

- Got it... I'll go around the block and fetch him on the other side. But Jo? ... Do you know what the fuck just happened over there?

- Yeah! ... Frank went postal!

- But? ... Why?

- I have no idea what that was all about? I'm just like you, Joe... I just fuckin' work here, man!

- But? ... We can't leave one of our cops like this in the middle of the...

- ... We'll light a candle for him later! ... Okay?

- Shit! ... Everybody is gonna be looking for us, now.

- Ho yeah? ... Well, you deal with Frank on that one, Joe. Because, killing cops... that ain't my fuckin' specialty!

We quickly went around the block, and then Joe picked up Fiorini a little further down the street.

- Frank? You tell me... Why the fuck did you leave your spent casings at the scene? Have you gone completely mad, or what?

- Spur-of-the-moment kind of thing, Jo... So it looks like Oswald just killed a cop. He's got a .38 on him. So, you do the math...

Sarti looked at me with envy... He who dreamed of doing an American cop!

- And what happens now, Frank?

- Nothing will happen, Jo... Nothing. You guys are going back to the safe house so you can rest and celebrate. I've got to tie up some loose ends... So, I can't stay with you guys and party. Tomorrow, when the cops have their man at the morgue, we'll get you Frenchies out of town in a flash. Transport has already been arranged for you and your team. And from now on, do not worry about anything; all the Dallas police force is gonna be looking for a cop killer... **Officer down** will be dispatched on all radio frequencies, and anyone with a gun in Dallas will be looking for the cop killer whose name happens to be: Lee Oswald!

- OK! ... Got it, Frank. Sounds like a plan.

- And Jo... Please keep an eye on your two Frenchy friends for me. I'm counting on you... And I don't want any waves like the last time! Make sure you tell your bozos so they understand.

- Don't worry, Frank... I'll but fuck them with my Walter to keep them quiet if I must, too... And take one for the team!

- Fine, Jo... Fine! You do what you have to... But make sure that you do what you have to in order to keep a handle on things. Whatever it takes... We don't need any more fuckin' problems! ... Is that clear?

- Yeah! Yeah! Got it, Frank!

- I said: is that clear?

- Cristal! ... Don't you worry about a fuckin' thing.

When Fiorini left us with a smirk tattooed on his face, Sarti had already taken out the bottles of Whiskey. Beau Serge came back from his room with some dope; he had shut up some shit in his veins... And we all got drunk like Popeye the sailor man.

Finally, in the wee hours of the morning, I finally managed to escape the hold that the two Corsicans had on me and crawled all the way back to my room... I was fuckin' dead drunk!

3

When I woke up, it was still dark. I was tired. As if I had just laid down a few minutes ago on the bed. And I freaked for a moment... 'Cause I did not remember where I was! Then, in the darkness that crushes everything, dominating this moment of fear with the help of moonlight that filtered through a slat of wood shutters, I quickly realized that I was no longer with my troop, holed up in a manhole, but in my bed. And I immediately searched under the pillow... My gun.

I tried to go back to sleep, with the sensation of not having closed my eyes during the night, turned several times on my bed, adjusted, a thousand times, my pillows to find the perfect position that would allow me to lose consciousness... even for a single minute! Then, glimmers appeared... Later, it was birds chirping. And, in the relative heat of my bed, I had only time to yawn a big blow before the muezzin singer pushed his long never-fuckin'-ending lamentation... Damn! I was just waiting for that... With his fuckin' call to prayer, the bastard Muslim wakes us up every morning from the first lights of dawn! ... But for the Pieds-Noirs of Bône, they rather looked like the hell fires of shame.

The window continued to blush while I tried to steal a few more seconds, rolling on the mattress, then machine gun fire made me jump out of bed... Through the double shutters, an old Jeep... The 4X4 was still sprinkling the buildings when I looked between the slats.

Fuckin' Fellaghas (Algerian nationalists), they never get tire, the motherfuckers! I live on Caroubiers street. Previously, it was one of the peaceful neighbourhoods of Bône. Nowadays, they're shooting all over the fuckin' city... From top to bottom... No favoritism... Randomly fired bullets... Everyone gets what he deserves... Surved on a siver platter... There's no twenty-one ways to eat your fuckin' Algerian couscous, dude! ... And yo-ho-ho! And onnnnnnne bullet coming straith back down at us!

Takers? ... Anyone?

I must admit, I don't know what day it is... Maybe it's Tuesday? ... Or is it Wednesday? I don't fuckin' know! And since it's all over for us in Algeria, it doesn't really matter anymore. Every day it's the same routine; the civil war still lurks at the corner of avenues; at every turn of a crossing, there is a terrorist waiting for me... With my compatriots who collapsed under bullets or fell under Arab blades in the public markets of the city! The lucky ones have already set sail towards the motherland... Before dying! One after the other, I see them leave, and soon, I will not have any.

But if I stubbornly stay in the country the Muslims now call their own, it's to pay them back in their own coin... To wash the honour flouted of my friends who have bitten dust at the hands of the Fellaghas... Those who fell for this France outside of France... This France that no longer exists for us! ... And it's with lead bullets that I want to pay them back.

Many times they missed their attempt to kill me. And I had luck on my side... Lots of luck! But I'll be the one to kill them all, these shit heads! Because danger doesn't scare me; I play with it daily; I have the recklessness of an experienced blaster: I must have blowned everything at least once in my life... Everything! ... Except myself.

A hoarse voice comes out of my throat: "*Dio cane! ... Mais qu'est-ce qu'ils foutent encore ces putains de Melons?* (God is a dog! ... What are they still doing, these fuckin' Johnny Jihad?)"

My voice, I barely recognized it! It's surely because of the two packs of Gitanes... Yesterday, I smoked like a chimney; my lungs are going to hell and the rest of the body is not too far behind.

I took out my gun, checked that it was fully loaded, that the safety catch was on... The kind of good habits that can save your life! Because, in a city where the hunt for Europeans is open all year round, a guy better have a firearm on him at all times.

The sun is barely up that it's already hot. It's only June, but it's gonna go up to 45 (one hundred ten) degrees, today. I rinse my face with fresh water, take the opportunity to look at myself in the mirror: I have hollow and sunken eyes. A Fellagha must have grafted tea bags under my eyes during the night. But how the fuck did he do it? ... Because, I almost didn't sleep at all!

"*C'est une sorte de maladie chronique professionnelle, soldat* (It's kind of a chronic occupational disease, soldier)", had said the Legion's doctor. It was during a routine medical checkup; I was still on duty and "*mon mal s'était développé au fil des ans* (my pain had developed over the years)", he had said, "*sans que personne ne s'en aperçoive (*without anyone noticing)"... Me, included! I had spent more than three years patrolling Algeria up and down; East to West; right to left; right or wrong: the generals had made me eat Fellagha kebabs non-stop. I had survived during all these years without sleeping for more than a couple hours in a row. In the long run, it makes your face look older, insomnia, as if I were born old and would die young! ... Or was it the other way around? And when I returned home after a three-year tour of Algeria, my father said that I looked like a twenty-one-year-old senior fuckin' citizen!

I have known several legionary friends who have fallen... Fallen into a catatonic state! ... Those who slept too well at night! They usually ended up with a bullet in the head in the wee hours of the morning, the hours of the morning when morning wood is at its peak in the brothels of the city, or was it with the throat cut in the military whorehouse of a madam? The mouth was wide open... It looked like a call for help... A request for reinforcement... A fuckin' supplication! ... But our generals would never hear it. And today, my companions are dead: their eyelids are now indifferent to human misery. They fell for Algeria... The Algeria of the Pieds-Noirs... The Algeria that general de Gaulle has sold for all the black gold of the Sahara! "*Je vous ai compris!* (I understood you!)" He had told us all. But after his speeches, no one understood anything, anymore... And de Gaulle's Algeria is now the Algeria of shame.

Towards the end of the afternoon, some friends came to get me to go for a tour of the city. *Bône la coquette* (Bône the handsome) as portrayed in Odé, the collection of French tour guides. She's really elegant... A small friendly port city of a hundred thousand inhabitants, perhaps more, with the clear majority of Italian origin! The weather is good all year around, except when it rains in the winter. It's a kind of paradise that the Romans founded, then abandoned, in Antiquity: Hippone... With Roman ruins and all that goes with it. A paradise, yes! But that's not counting with those Muslims. And especially... The Fellaghas! Muslims, too, but rebellious Muslims. And it's there that I was born... In the Arab district with the non-nationals and the underprivileged of North Africa. I attended the same schools as they did; I learned Arabic in the same back alleys... In the same classes! A long time ago... A very long time ago... The French had locked up my father at the very beginning of the Second World War because he was of Sicilian origin, and Peppé was still behind bars the day I was born, even though he had been living in Algeria for at least ten years. But as he had never taken the trouble to regularize his situation, for the French, Giuseppe would always be an Italian. And since France was at war with Germany and Italy, politicians had him incarcerated... By pure prevention... Because Peppé would never have hurt a fly!

I never had the head for politics; neigther did my friends. And we, moreover, never listened to anybody... Neither the prophets of misfortune nor the politicians of the right... Even less those of the left... The Commies! All would pronounce elegant speeches, make their marvellous promises, but they never did anything for us, those idiots! ... Only promises. And I, tired of their inaction, went to serious things with ours. And with my friends from the OAS (*Organisation armée secrète*) we took care of the terrorists of our zone; us too we began to terrorize... To clean up the city!

Like most *Bônois* of my generation, I'm satisfied with fugitive moments of happiness gleaned here and there... Of picnics at Saint-Cloud beach, dinners with friends at the Simoun, our weekly *belote* card games washed down with anise with Salvatore, the dominoes with Tic-Tac, the chess games with Uncle Nino, when he gets out of his farm to come sell his cheese and makes his tour of the city... Nothing much! But I know each of the customers of the neighbourhood's bistro. Many are good friends. Childhood friends... And even of Arab origin! Hey! Yes, I have several... Many that I saved from trouble when I could. But they, too, did the same for me when it was possible, because I lived for a long time with them... Among them... Like them! We were like brothers before this fuckin' civil war broke out. I even sucked on some nice Arab tity early in life, because, when I came into the world, my mother was seriously ill, and as a neighbour next door, too, had given birth, I was able to enjoy *Sarrazin* (Sarasen) milk at a very young age. I, like many of my friends, enjoyed the simple pleasures of life; I had little money in my pockets, but a lot of joy in my heart.

Our small town stretches on the Mediterranean coast. Near the sea, its avenues are transformed into a landing stage on the harbour, just before diving into the briny waters. I like swimming in the ocean, too, and I often went fishing for oysters, in season, and not only to eat them, but also to find pearls... Little wonders that I sold to the Jewish jeweler or that I traded for American watches in the Arab market of Place d'Armes. And I've stayed almost three full minutes under the water... For real! It was my girlfriend Ariane who timed me, and more than once. I remember it very well; because, during my diving record, she was very scared when she looked at the needle of the chrono go around several times... My friend Salvatore told me that she kept saying things like: "*Mais y remonte plus! Y remonte plus! Mais qu'est-ce qu'il fait, celui-là?... Y remonte plus!* (But he's not coming back up! He's not coming up! But what is he doing, that one? ... He's not coming up!)"

It's nothing to write home about, but it's home. And our simple pleasures, young Pieds-Noirs of Bône, it's to hear the shout of the vendors of lamb kebabs or merguez sausages of the

Place d'Armes... "*Des merguez aussi petites que la quéquette d'un chat!* (Merguez as small as catdick shit!)" Always said Salvatore, laughing, but who smelled so good; it's the pleasure of walking the avenues of the Saint-Cloud district with friends; it's to take a stroll through the crowded alleys of Cours Bertagna with a beautiful girl hanging on the arm, on Sundays... These are all the ingredients of our happiness on a land that is now hostile to us.

I lingered for a moment on the bridge of la Tranchée. Leaning against the guardrail, I eagerly admired the fishing boats at berth. They seamed to be dreaming, lazily, in the little seaport... If only I could sleep a little, I, too, would be able to dream... As much as I want! Finally, I took the path to the Place d'Armes with a good step; I wanted to eat kebabs in the shade of arcades with my friends.

The heat is always suffocating, and the closer you get to the market, the more there is in the air a whole mix of exhilarating smells that make your mouth water: lamb kebabs from Constantine with potato bricks spiced with garlic and parsley. All Bônois know the place for its animation and its businesses, but past the cafés and the bistrots, it's now a true cutthroat district... It's the Arab zone that shelters the houses of tolerance and of debauchery for soldiers... A total fuckup in a sector that never sleeps at night... A monumental tangle of streets that ends in a cul-de-sac: Algeria is going down to hell and I'm running straight for it, too.

I go up the walkway to find other friends near Le Simoun. They are waiting for me in the shade of a palm tree and are grilling cigarettes. Le Simoun is a small building with whitewashed walls to kill insects carrying malaria. The Seybouse River carries them and they often agonize against the walls of buildings by sticking on to them instead of trying to sting us with malaria! My dad got it and became very sick. He almost died... Of fever! And since that day, his liver has been annihilated. Not far from the café, there is a nice little cinema: the Olympia. The Fellaghas threatened to blow it up several times. They claim that the owner is showing films considered immodest by Allah. But what the fuck does he know about cinema, the motherfucker? Men are sometimes seen kissing women and we sometimes see half-portions of naked breasts. Teenager, I used to add them together and it made me one complete!

The owner of Le Simoun is a former captain of the Foreign Legion, a tough guy; an especially "hard to kill son of a bitch!" He survived French Indochina war, the unhealthy Algerian countryside of 1954, and French army's food... Quite a feat! The name of its bistro comes from *samoûn,* the Arabic word for the dry and hot winds of Arabia and the Sahara.

When the keeper of the café sees our little troop coming from afar, he gives us hand signs of warning of some kind...

I approximately deciphered his gestures; I understood: "*Ne pointez pas vos tronches du côté du café!* (Don't point your asses on this side of the café!)" And I must admit that, at first, I didn't react. So, not to look too stupid in the eyes of my friends, I beat the torrid air heavy of humidity with the hand...

Then, a young Arab in his early twenties crossed the Place crowling with passers-by to come my way. I recognized him at first glance; it was Abdel: Abdel Kassem. We had shared the same poverty and had grown up in the same backyards of the Arab quarter, and he told me, continuing his way without stopping or even giving me his hand: "*Déscends dé la rue! Rétourne-toi vite et déscends! Rétourne vite chez toi! Ils sont fous... Ils veulent vous tuer à tous!* (Get off the street! Go back quickly and get out! Quickly go home! They are crazy... They want to kill you all!)" The whole thing happened like in Hitchcock's spy movies, except that I was not as elegant and slender as Cary Grant. My alley buddy seemed to be afraid of being butchered by Fellagha's bullets... Even if he was a Muslim, too! And at the same moment, there was a click that occured in my head... And I put my hand in my back... Dug under my sweaty shirt... Grabbed the butt of my 9 mil automatic pistol stuck under the belt... Took it out... Removed the safety...

Then, I let the weapon hang on the side of my thigh: it is now the prolongation of my hand! ... A hand that could kill anyone who wished it... And I immediately felt relieved because I was ready... Ready for what? ... That, I didn't know it, at the time, but I was ready for something... Ready for anything just like the last fuckin' Boy Scout of Bône!

Passers-by looked at me funny, when they saw my caliber: a handgun dangling at the end of my arm like a pestilential outgrowth. I looked like a guy who got scabies... A contagious sicko, but without the motherfuckin' mental problems!

"*Mais y a pas de quoi se flinguer, Signora Pasquale!* (But there's no point in shelling me, Signora Pasquale!)", I said to a neighbor, still searching the crowd, the senses on alert. And, despite my experience of urban guerrilla warfare, I didn't see the threat. Not yet. But I felt the danger... It was here... Waiting for us... I even had fuckin' goosebumps! ... A sixth sense that I developed at the Foreign Legion... A capacity for anticipation that allowed me to survive all that the Fellaghas sent my way... And it started to trouble me! ... Because, I couldn't see the threat... Put the finger on the problem... What the fuck man?

"*Moi, je monte pas là!* (I'm not going up there!)" I voiced to my friends.

- *Hoon! Mais on va manger des brochettes, Jo!... Voyons les gars!* (Hoon! Let's go eat kebabs, Jo! ... Come on, you guys!)

Nico was rubbing his belly because he was very hungry... That guy seems to want to eat all the fuckin' time just like the ogre of the fable!

- *Non! Je ne monte pas, moi! T'as vu l'Arabe qui vient de nous croiser... Hé! Bien, il m'a dit de retourner à la maison parce que... Parce que... Y a quelqu'un qui veut notre peau, ici... Y a quelque chose qui ne tourne pas rond... Je le sens!* (No! I'm not going up there! Have you've seen the Arab who just crossed us? ... Well, he told me to go back home because... Because... There's someone here who's looking to kill us... There's something wrong, here... I feel it in my gut!)

I shouted at his face, tiptoeing on the sidewalk, because Nico is a hulk that's almost two meters high... A fuckin' giant!

- *Tu as peur! Ho! Ho!* (You are scared! Ho! Ho!)

Nico began popping pecs: a real motherfuckin' gorilla! But brute force of ignorance doesn't stop bullets. Being smart, does!

- *Ouais! Certain que j'ai peur... J'suis pas fou comme toi!* (Yeah! ... Sure, I'm scared. I'm not fuckin' crazy like you!)

My hazel eyes plunge diagonally into those of the colossus, because I barely reach him from the top of my meter seventy-five, and I had not only finished swallowing my saliva that it began to explode... Everywhere In Saint-Augustin street, the bullets whistled in gusts and pierced the flesh of bystanders to the sound of Fellagha's rallying shouts: "*N'katlan n'sara!* (Kill the Christians!)" The projectiles ricocheted on the pavement and finished their trajectory against the walls or windows of shops. No need to know how to shoot, because at this busy hour the pedestrian avenue is crowded with people. Folks are fleeing in all directions... The less fortunate whine on the ground, often hit by deadly shootings of 7.62 mm AK-47 automatic rifles.

With my friends, I raced across the small Arab place, bent in two to present the least favorable target to the Fellaghas who, in addition to shooting at us, still bark to raise their passive brothers: "*Ouktelhou, eddeblhou!* (Kill them, kill them!)"

Many Arabs look at the scene with dread, while I stagger... I apologize... Almost... When I bump into friends or acquaintances of the neighboorhood: "*Salut! Ça va, la santé?* (Hi! How's your health?)" That I swing to Omar, a good friend who was in primary school with me. He's terrorized, too. But many Pieds-Noirs are already lying on the ground. They are wounded or just terrified by bursts of AK-47 and do not know what to do to get out of there, alive... So they hide on the ground and try to become one with the stones of the pavement and they wait for the slaughter to end... A real bunch of fuckin' ostriches in a desert of stones!

We finally arrive at Le Simoun at full speed... It's organized confusion in the streets, and at no time was I able to fire even a single shot... Too many folks in the way! The old legionnaire is waiting for us at the door of Le Simoun. He seemed to want to taunt the Fellaghas by braving enemy bullets with his chest, and, with big reels, he urges us to hurry in. It was like in rowing competitions when the skipper mooves his arms for the rowers to move faster, but with him I'm sure he's not gonna lead us astray. Captain! Old captain please lower the iron curtain...

And as soon as we throw ourselves inside, rolled-up, a few bursts intone on the metal door the first measures of a concert piece: "Tac, tac, tac, taaaac... Toc, toc, toc, toooc... ". It looks like fuckin' Beethoven music! ... Or is it the Ride of the Walkyries on hash? ... Good fuckin' shit, man! ... With deadly virgins shooting at us and all the rest... *Speaking in a secret alphabet... No time for another cigarette... Learn to forget...* There you go, Jo! It's the fuckin' music of terror directly from Le Simoun's soul kitchen! ... Why didn't I think of that one before?

Then, a patrol of the French Army arrives in the Place at full speed... The shots of the rebels alerted them, or it is the colonel of the garrison who's been disturbed during his dinner? But in French *"trouille"* rimes with *"patrouille"* - to be *scared* (trouille) rimes with *patrol* (patrouille) -, and young recruits are fearful. Expatriated from France because of the unfortunate circumstances affecting the Algerian colony, they all were forced to serve in Algeria, and, as soon as they'd gone down the trucks, they started shooting everywhere. The captain had said to them: "*Faut nettoyer la Place... Exécution!* (You must clean-up the Place... Execution!)" And they did it... Execute the orders and shoot everything that moved in the arcade. And by cleansing the Place d'Armes, they'll have a lesser chance of being crippled for life by the Fellaghas' bullets or of falling for France.

But the French berets do more harm than good with their indiscriminate shooting: it's as if the officer had given machine guns to blind soloists with permission to fire at whatever they wanted. And the *barbouzes* (anti AOS soldiers) scare the civilians and injure others, for whom everything will now end with a song... I immediately recognized this great Algerian concert music, because for more than three long years, I had often played it, too!

Only thirty seconds elapsed before the Fellaghas evaporate into nature, and then it is silence... Total. The French instruments had stopped making harmonies with the Muslim terrorists. Later, everything will be noted and recorded by the troop's concert leader with music paper with staves and key...

Once the Place died down, an Army doctor came to the rescue of the wounded. He examined them, took their pulse, palpated them everywhere... A real doctor! Or rather a god who has the right of life or death on his patients, because he's the one who will designate those who will be sent to the hospital in priority: "*Lui, là-bas... Oui! Lui aussi. L'autre? Le barbu? Non! Laissez-le... C'est déjà trop tard pour lui!* (Him, there... Yes! He too. The other? ... The bearded one? ... No! Leave him... It's already too late for him!)"

The Legion doc called this procedure "*triage*", triage being like deciding who lives and who dies on a battlefield. But they kept calling it murder when I did the same in the streets of Bône!

The prelude had been well orchestrated. In the Place, we only heard a succession of quaver rest... The final rest... That of the dying spread-eagled on the cobblestones with their most precious possession... gone! When I was still serving in the Foreign Legion, the unlucky ones, we finished them on the spot... We couldn't take prisonners... A bullet in the back of the head and their case was quickly settled... "*C'est pour mettre fin à leurs souffrances inutiles* (It's to put an end to their unnecessary suffering)", said our captain of the 1st REP (*Régiment Etranger de Parachutistes:* Paratroopers) who justified our *humanitarian* action with a smirk.

Suffering is always useless... Except maybe in Tlemcen, when I took part in the interrogations of the *Deuxième Bureau* (Military intelligence Bureau). During my service, when I wasn't patrolling with my band, I often served as their interpreter, because at the battalion, I was one of the few who spoke fluent Arabic. But it was also because the commander had discovered in me some natural abilities to make people talk. He said that I had a certain talent for communication: "*Un don inné...* (An innate gift...)" My job was to set tongues wagging using a military campaign phone. The waterboarding technique, simulated drowning, didn't really work in Algeria... First, it's because in the *djebel* (mountain) we didn't really have any water to waste, there wasn't even enough water to take a shower; also, it's because a drowning man cannot really communicate with you, and your client just wants to come up to the surface to breathe. So...

What fascinated me the most in my work with the Bureau was to make a good connection with my Muslim clients... Turning the magneto! And it's amazing the words you can put in anyone's mouth by establishing a direct circuit from the testicles or the anus of your client... Whether he has something to say or not! Thanks to the magic of the military telephone, a strange communication was established between us, while my Fellagha, laid bare to humiliate him just enough, pissed on himself and trembled while unpacking his shit. However, several Fellagha *(road cutter terrorists)* didn't make it up to the end of our communication sessions, but as it was to save Pieds-Noirs lives, our superiors often told us to keep the conversation going... Until the last word had been said! The guys of the *Bureau* alleged that it was to make sure our Fellagha didn't change his tune... And thirty minutes later, effectively, the client couldn't change it anymore even if he wanted to.

At the very beginning, during my first work sessions with intelligence services, I found it a bit difficult. Subsequently, with hundreds of hours of practice behind you, and because you believe in a cause, you discover that you feel nothing for your clients: that you've shielded yourself from their pain. And your captain claims that you are now a true communication expert... A machine that makes people talk! And it's amazing what you can do to your peers in the name of... whatever the fuckin' cause may be! But I always felt helpless when I saw one of my own suffering and agonizing in the streets of Bône.

4

After the carnage, I got out of Le Simoun with my friends. We all had gone hungry because no one likes to see their own brothers' and sisters cut into pieces... Muslim terrorist's massacres kind of make you lose your appetite that way.

In the almost deserted Place, two soldiers were busy picking up corpses. They stacked them up in a transport truck and grumbled things like: "*C'est pas juste!* (It's not fair!) Or "*c'est toujours moi qui suis de corvée.* (I always get the chores of no real utility.)" The usual recriminations... That's what happens when you're not a fuckin' general, you fuckin' assholes! And it was while crossing the square that I recognized one of my cousins... A distant cousin. He was on my mother's side and had become further distant after her death. Mom died because of a heart murmur, a valve problem that my turbulent coming into the world had only worsened: from birth, I had already started to kill! ... Kill your mother, and they'll call you a murderer... A matricide! Kill thousands and they'll say that you're a conqueror! I must have had the stuff rulers were made of! And after my mother's funeral, I didn't see much of her family's... and my cousin, too. Especially after my father remarried.

Barely twenty-six years old, my cousin was laying on the cobblestones of the Place. Frozen dead in spite of the heat! He already had a strange scent, when I leaned over him to notice his death, with hints of shit and urine that attacked my nostrils. I knew this perfume well: it was the aroma of abandonment... The smell of death!

And I made a face because of the foul fragrance, but my cousin's face still gave a vague smile anyway... It looked like an expression of relief, like when you're at the cinema and that you want to go to the lavatories during the entire duration of the projection and you can finally go, when the projectionist is running the credits and everybody gets out, rapidly.

My cousin had only one bullet in him, but it was *the* one... The one you've been waiting for part of your life and that finally comes for you! The bullet had torn off the upper chest of my cuz and a good part of the heart, the rest having been slashed away eight years ago, when Arab terrorists raped and slaughtered his fiancee in front of him. Since that day, my cousin had been angry enough with himself to die... For a man, a true man must protect his beloved fiancée at the peril of his own life and that he had been powerless to save her from the claws of the Fellaghas.

Once everything had been piled up neatly, the truck quickly went away; the avenue was now peaceful; but a hint of death and burnt powder still intoxicated my nostrils. And it had made me furious to see the inert carcass of my cousin laying on the ground... I should avenge him, and quickly!

Later in the evening, I'll pay a last visit to my cousin and family. I spoke with Ariane, my fiancée, and explained that I would not be able to go out with her tonight: no dancing at La Colonne dancehall, as promised...

She didn't look terribly happy and even made a face, when I added, to try to justify myself:

"*C'est pas ma faute à moi si mon cousin s'est fait gommer par des putains de Fells... Bordel de merde!* (It's not my fault if my cousin was slayed by fuckin' Fellaghas! ... Fuck that shit!)"

But when I saw her reaction to my words, I thought that, maybe, I shouldn't have told her that. Or at least, not that way... And she didn't say another word after her little fit. Then, she closed her door for the evening. Maybe for even longer. It will depend on her. And it will be for me some kind of passage to purgatory forced by uncontrollable circumstances that affect the French colony...

In a torrid country like Algeria, one does not waste time in vain procedures, when it comes to burying one's dead. Here, in a few hours, one can go from life to death... And sometimes without even noticing it! One roams aimlessly the streets of Bône with his dog, and then, the next morning, one finds himself between the four planks of a coffin at the bottom of a grave. No

matter how hard one tries to remember, nothing comes to mind...
And everyone is wondering what the fuck happened!

Everyone? ... Well! Except for the wife who's crying at the cemetery, already hanging on the arm of another guy... And even one's faithful dog already pisses on the grave! So...

Peppé says it's because of the scorching heat.

***

My cousin is resting in Aunt Anna's living room. This is the largest space in the apartment. At the entrance, there is a hanging chain: it usually gards the entrance to the room which has been transformed into a small mortuary for the occasion. The whitish walls reflect a pale light provided by two small decrepit chandeliers, with two large antique-style couches that are covered with plastic to protect them from guests' affronts. My aunt has stuck them to the opposite walls: they seem to be waiting for the callers with impatience.

Usually, my cousin does'nt have the right to enter the living room because it was designed only for distinguished visitors, but I think Aunt Anna made a small exception for him tonight.

Several chairs are arranged in a semi-circle, with in the center two easels on which seems to rest the body. The coffin is open and my cousin has put on his best Sunday clothing... He almost seemed relieved to see so much affluence! But I knew better... The real reason for his little death smile.

Near the casket sits the closely related family members of my cousin, and I almost need a good ten minutes to do the circuit and finish with the accolades, the kisses on the cheeks, the "*ça fait longtemps que j't'ai pas vu!* (it's been awhile since I have seen you!) And the "*mon Dieu que tu ressembles à ta mère!* (my God, you look soo much like your mother!)"

Mom died when I was six, and it must have been a good ten years since my aunt has seen me show up at her home. But as she has never invited me even once to come for coffee and hear from me, I don't have to feel guilty about anything.

50

After the usual condolences, I sat apart from the rest, caught up in the fatigue of the day, and I left the immediate family of my cousin tear each other over who was to be blamed for this useless death. The death of a Pied-Noir by shooting is useless already... And I didn't dare interfere. But I could have explained that my cousin had already been deadened for the last eight years; that it happened the day the Fellaghas abused her fiancée and killed her in front of him; that he had been unable to protect her and felt guilty as sin; and that he already was dead since that fateful day. However, I didn't have the balls to tell my aunt... because the dear girl had never even noticed it!

I yawned a good part of the vigil, not daring to push rudeness and grill cigarettes in my aunt's living room, but that was not for a lack of desire. In addition, it was very hot... I was choking! So, I loosened my tie to breathe a little, though we shouldn't usually do it at a wake.

At around eleven o'clock, I took advantage of the human tide that was coming out to try to leave my cousin's *funeral* home on tippy toes... But I got caught just before the exit. And I only took my leave after promising my auntie to come back more often... On the Bible! But as I had my fingers crossed in the back, when I swore that I would soon go back to visit her, it didn't count for real! And I don't think that I will have the opportunity to get back there anytime soon unless I lose another cousin... Which is not at all impossible given the circumstances that affect the French colony.

And it took me another good ten minutes before I could set sail...

To finish the evening, I smoked cigarettes and had a few drinks with my uncles at a local café. They had insisted that I go join them: they had a lot to say about my cousin, and about French Algeria.

5

The day after the massacre, we attended the funeral mass of my cousin. I had smoked some kif (a mix of hash, opium and black tobacco) with friends before entering the church, just to pass the doldrums that we all felt since the slaughter of our Pieds-Noirs compatriots, and I was really fucked... as high as a kite!

Aunt Titine, Dad's sister, was hanging on the trembling arm of Aunt Anna, the mother of the deceased. One was crying and had a long face; the other was praying our sweet Jesus for the both of them. We were sitting in a small section reserved for relatives of the departed, but my father had preferred to stay outside with distant relatives, because the practice of Catholicism "*c'est dur pour les genoux!* (Is hard for the knees!)" He preached.

The coffins were parked in the central aisle in double file because of the high number of caskets. Aunt Anna, who had lost her son to the hands of Muslim terrorists, was crying like a madwoman in front of a huge Jesus nailed to his cross: he almost looked delighted to be part of the ceremony.

"*Pourquoi m'avez-vous pris mon fils bien-aimé?* (Why did you take my beloved son?) Had shouted Aunt Anna between two sobs.

Jesus seemed embarrassed by the question. And so was I, I must admit, because, now, we had the entire church watching us!

I then tried to calm my auntie and stop her tears with Titine and a handkerchief.

"*On croyait en Vous et Vous nous abandonnez!* (We believed in You and You have abandoned us up!)" Had dared complain Aunt Anna, morally weakened by the death of her son.

The statue of Jesus had seemed to move the head a little...

"*Qui va s'occuper de nous... Hein? Maintenant qu'il est mort?... Pourquoi l'avez-vous laissé crever comme un chien?* (Who will take care of us... Huh? Now that he's dead? ... Why did you let him die like a dog?)"

She had pointed a threatening finger at Jesus as she sniffled.

And that is when I heard the words, "*Mais qu'est-ce que je fous ici, mon Dieu Seigneur?* (What am I doing here? O! My Lord and God!)"

Dio cane! (God is a dog!) I exclaimed in Sicilian, totally stunned... Was I hallucinating, or what? ... It seemed to really come from the statue of Jesus!

Fuck me man! ... Un-fuckin'-believable!

Aunt Titine, however, wondered why they didn't let the Son of God rest in peace on his cross. And besides all that, she hit me smack in the face because I had dared call her motherfuckin' God: "dog".

I, who had been a pagan since my first and last communion - as a choirboy I had not really appreciated that, into the sacristy, the priest had grabbed me by the cruets after Mass, the cruets being usually parked next to the altar -, I wondered which actor they had taken for the role of Jesus, because that one... Good fuckin' Lord! ... I couldn't even start to describe how real the motherfucker was on the cross!

And it was very realistic, the staging of the priest. Finely chiseled! They had to keep him, this mothefuckin' Jesus on a stick... Absolutely! With him on the pole, they would fill the church every single fuckin' day... Certain! And it wasn't long before I started to applaud like the world's fastest clapper, but since it was the funeral of my cousin, I had to restrain myself after a few claps... and I especially did not want to disturb my aunts and spoil their liturgical show.

Finally, the ecclesiastic began to flatter the divine assembly with small blows of the thurible, and, arrived before the alter ego, he finally took the floor: "*Dominus vomiscum...*"

- *Es com spiritoutounne!*

The faithful spectators of the first rows had answered in chorus, and then they began to make the sign of the cross in successive waves, breakers that ended up contaminating the other faithfuls sitting behind... And let it be so, amen!

The incense burners went full volley and let escape small clouds of submission and sparks, choirboys dragging the hat on the chains, violently. I had deduced that it was surely to make them spit the smoke faster... And after the nails, the thorns, the whip and the cross, poor Jesus was the victim of flattery.

"*Mes très chers frères... Ce qui intéresse votre Seigneur, notre doux Jésus et moi-même, ce n'est pas le bonheur de tous les hommes... Mais bien celui de chacun d'entre vous...* (My dear brothers, had professed the representative of God on earth... What interests your Lord, our sweet Jesus and myself, is not the happiness of all men... But that of everyone and each of you...)"

- *Amen!* Had answered the audience made up of captives of religion and holy Joes.

The clergyman had really lost me, and I think that the only Son of God was a little bewildered, too, because he had only started to pay attention to the priest when he heard his name spoken out loud: "Jesus!"

It was perhaps his turn to play his character in the mass, but he understood nothing of all the litanies of the priest... Neither did I! But I wasn't Christian religious royalty, for fuck's sake! I was just a fuckin' regular guy... An ordinary sinner!

Meanwhile, the poor officiant was desperately searching for his breviary. I thought that he couldn't remember his text... The magic formulas... Fuck if I know!

And where was the bloody fuckin' prompter?

Tired of resisting, while his liver was gnawing his voluble abdominal, he decided to improvise: he played so well the comedy when he wanted it, too, relying especially on the ignorance and the credulity of the good people... and also on the Latin language!

Except that in Bône, unfortunately for him, we also spoke Italian. It increased the difficulty of his play...

Since he was hungry like the wolf, he went directly from the *Agnus Dei* to the *Confit de porc*, it immediately eliminated any Arab or Jew from the religious ceremony, and then, he obliqued by the *Asparagus* and the *fromage Kyrie eleison.* When at the sound of the bells the devotees lowered their heads to adore him, he took the opportunity to swallow large chalices of wine in secret. After, Hostia! He threw himself at the sacramantal bread. Then, he went on to do the clown with St. Matthew: "*... Et c'est à ce moment-là que les disciples s'approchèrent de Jésus, après avoir mangé des fayots judéens toute la soirée, et Simon-Pierre demanda: Rabbi?... Qui donc est l'homme dont le pet porte le plus loin au royaume des cieux?... Ô! Doux Jésus, ô! Rabbi Jacob... Qui d'entre nous est le plus grand des péteurs?* (... And it was at this time that the disciples approached Jesus, having eaten Judean beans all evening long, and Simon-Peter asked: Rabbi? ... Who is the man whose fart carries the farthest to the kingdom of heaven? ... O! Sweet Jesus, O! Rabbi Jacob... Who among us is the greatest of the farters?)"

I had thought, for a moment, that I had seen move the actor who played the role of Jesus on the cross... He had raised his head and seemed to try to better understand the holy text... Because it was implied that he was the origin of the script! ... He who thought he had explained that he was the source of eternal life and stuff like: "Let the little children come to me..."

But that's about all the Catholic priests seemed to have retained from his doctrine!

Once the long funeral mass had ended, the cathedral emptied quickly, and the faithful gathered at the bottom of the stairs in large numbers. The funeral procession then shook towards the cemetery, with the families of the departed dragging behind the officiants and the caskets, but, on my side, it was the aunties that I had to drag... They wanted surely to make me earn my way to heaven even if I didn't want to go!

An infernal sun was burning the streets. It must have been forty degrees in the shade, and I could have fried an egg on the hood of a car, so it was hot!

That day, going to the cemetery would be a real descent to hell for all those people who were mourning.

Throughout the procession, onlookers discovered themselves with respect, and after having made the first hundred meters in the suffocating heat, like in a mirage in the Algerian desert, there were only the coffins and the immediate families of the disappeared in the procession, so hot it was. Some of the people in the march, feeling themselves on the verge of fainting, would sneak into the cafés and disappear to cool off and regain their strength with an anisette while playing belote and dominoes to pass time with friends.

Many Bônois were fearful because there had been shots fired by Fellaghas on funeral processions in the previous weeks, and relatives in mourning had been killed: they had been shot down from the roofs by young Muslim recruits who tried to make a name for themselfves.

Sometimes, a Muslim douchebags would throw grenades at the funeral procession and mortally wound passers-by, the Arab terrorists even pushing the audacity to plunge long steel spears through the coffins... The dead, thus pinned to the pine for eternity, had only one last little jolt... Almost imperceptible... And end of their sad journey on Algerian soil with a shake!

Finally, the caravan arrived at the cemetery. I was dying of thirst... Everyone would have killed for a good glass of water! And from a distance, seeing the crypts and gravestones of our fallen comrades, I immediately started to think about my mother...

Mom was buried here, dead from a heart weakness after I came into this world, and it was my aunt Titine who had served as a replacement mother before dad remarried, a few years later.

And it was only then that my heart of stone began to pound into my chest, as if it had started beating again only when I thought of my mother again.

The priest finished the ceremony with a very quick occasional lecture. Because of the heat! He then gave blessing and sprinkled the assembly with stagnant blessed water... Forbidden for consumption, but not for benediction!

However, we still wanted to drink a sip anyway, so we were thirsty!

Afterwards, the priest blessed the caskets... And the crowd dispersed, very quickly. Some were crying as they went...

I left Auntie Anna with Titine and took advantage of the funeral to go and take a moment's rest at my mother's grave, and five minutes later, because of the suffocating heat and a thirst that would have overwhelmed even the Spirit of the Holy Ghost, we went back to the cafés in the Arab quarter to refresh ourselves with something cold.

Anything that wasn't hot pissy Arabic tea would do... Even a clairet from Château What-the-fuck-for in Bordeaux! They've had so many châteaux over there that it was hard to keep the fuckin' count.

Revenge-thirsty friends were waiting for me with a frosty drink in the hand, but for one of the first times in my life... I was just thirsty for something cold and nothing more!

6

I remember that, when I finished my stay with the Foreign Legion, at the end of my third year of military service for the Nation, my captain of the 1st REP (First Foreign Parachutists Regiment) had the tear in his eye just to see me leave, his "*traducteur favori* (favorite translator)" he had said... "*Le seul du Régiment qui n'ait pas froid aux yeux!* (The only one of the Regiment who isn't scared shitless!) And then, he added that "*dans la vie, il n'y a que deux sortes d'hommes: ceux qui savent pas tuer et ceux qui savent...* (in life there are only two kinds of men: those who cannot kill and those who know how to...)" And that I was an integral part of the second category.

Afterwards, he had recited his official blah blah blah to get me to reenlist. In his eyes, I was a monster and a heartless yougmen for wanting to leave this great family that was the Foreign Legion, he who treated me like a son and who now feared for me... His child of legalized terror! He saw my return to civilian life with an evil eye and said that the Foreign Legion would suffer a lot from letting me go...

If he thought he could convince me to reenlist with such arguments, he had bet on the wrong horse!

And I said, "*Capitaine! Ô Capitaine! ... Non! Merci, mon Capitaine!* (O Captain! My Captain! ... No! Thank you, my Captain!)"

And then I left the Foreign Legion. Forever!

I departed from my Airborne Division for good because it was time for me to return to civilian life. As my family was eager to see me again, Mémé and Peppé were holding on to me as if I were the apple of their eyes, I brought myself back home as soon as possible. I was about to be twenty-one, and besides all of that... Ariane was waiting for me, impatiently!

But I barely had time to embrace family life and the numerous feasts I had had with my friends, uncles and cousins that I already had to been sent on *"vacances forcées* (forced holidays)"... A stay of several months at my paternal grandfather's farm: a grower settled near Palermo, Sicily.

Since my return to bourgeois life in Bône, I kept fighting and beating up some of the citizens of the city. It was enough to look at me sideways in a café for a war to break out. In addition, I had had many altercations and serious problems with the conscripts of the continent, the *barbouzes* (General de Gaulle special force: the "bearded ones" or "fake-beards" were a group of armed counter-insurgents established for the purposes of suppressing the OAS in Algeria), and the local police...

The chief commissary, who had friendship and esteem for my father, had suggested to Peppé to send me on *judicial vacations* before he would be obliged to lock me up in one of the cells of the police station of Bône... A reform school for big boys!

In Sicily, on the outskirts of Palermo, I digged acres of vines, milked the ewes, fed animals, picked fruits and vegetables that grew in abundance on the farm, and especially olives that we marinated in large barrels or the oil that was drawn by pressing them. The weeks of difficult manual work followed, one after another, and I was able to decompress, gradually: I had finally returned to better sentiments *vis-à-vis* humanity. And it was only from that moment that I was able to stop wanting to kill all the people I met on my way...

Uncle Vito, who had come to visit family in Palermo - he had emigrated to the United States a long time ago and had taken advantage of a business trip to visit relatives and spend his holidays in Sicily -, told me that, the day that I would decide to leave Algeria for good, he would be there to help me settle in the USA. He said he was working in *Bro-ké-lin* for an import-export company that specialized in importing olive oil to the States, among other things, in a neighbourhood in New York where many Italian families lived, and told me that "*A giovane come te che non aveva i piedi freddi (*A young man like you who is not

afraid of any challenges [literally: who didn't have cold feet])"
would easily find himself a good job... and make a good living.

He was going to give me all the help I needed and facilitate
my integration into America, and invited me to think about it,
seriously, seeing that we, the Pieds-Noirs of Algeria, couldn't
stay in North Africa for a much longer time: "*Pensateci!* (Think
about it!) He had recommended.

I thanked *Tio* (Uncle) Vito for his tempting offer and added
that, for now, I had no intention of giving up my native Algeria,
and as I did not have a perfect command of English at the time,
the United States of America may not be my first choice the day
that I would want to leave my native country...

I spoke and could write in French, Italian and Arabic... And
could still manage a bit of English, language that I had learned
while in contact with the G.I's stationed in Bône, after the
Second World War. At the time, I was just a little shrimp and,
under the supervision of *tio* Vito, I was stealing food under the
kaki tents of the Americans to help my family survive.

Since there was nothing to eat at home after the end of the
Second World War, almost all the heads of family (of Italian
origin) still being in prison, I was plundering left and right to
help provide for the necessities of life... Like eating! And one
day, I was five or six at the time, my uncle Vito, who was about
sixteen, took me on his bike frame to go for a "*travail de
dernière minute!* (last minute job!)" in *les Santons.*

Les Santons was a district of Bône where the American
army had installed a camp for a whole battalion of soldiers. On
the vacant lot of the city was a store of ammunition... And food
in abundance well hidden from view in large kaki tents of the
American army. An immense barbed wire, two and a half meters
high, ran tirelessly around the American compound, with some
sentinels guarding the entrance of the camp. Other G.I.'s were
patroling around the fortified area, by Jeep or on foot, and
provided security for the small US base.

Uncle Vito knew in what tent the food was piled up, for he
had already done minor work for the American administration.

"*On va là-bas!* (We're going over there!) He had ordered me... his most valiant and the youngest of his nephews!

He had pointed out the place from which stood a huge tent from the lot: that one was twice as big as all the others.

Uncle Vito and I had turned like vultures around the barbed wire fence. Then, when the sentries had finally gone out of sight, I went pilfering on behalf of the *familia.*

Vito had gently lifted the barbwire with a long club, and as I was very small, I was the one who volunteered to loot. I was able to sneak up without being skinned alive by the sharp blades and crawled to the big tent without anyone seeing me. During my incursion into enemy territory, Uncle Vito made the *djaya,* the watchman, in Arabic, and was to alert me if anyone ever approached the marquee.

Under the great circus tent, there was a multitude of boxes: canned food to supply the entire population of Bône's Arab district. It was heaven on earth: I was going to feed my family for an eternity!

My uncle had told me to look for big boxes of yellow metal, containers of salted margarine, and I quickly located them in a corner of the Ali Baba's barrack: there was a whole mountain of canned food!

I grabbed a crate of margarine by the handle... But as it was very heavy, I had to drag it and fight with the ground that made the maneuver difficult. Then, while I was still battleling with the vegetable fat, a huge G.I. came in like a gust of wind, spitting and swearing in American... He was furious!

But I didn't understand a fuckin' word of his verbiage. And, as he was cutting off all retreat, I realized that I was caught like a rat in a trap...

I waited to see what would happen to me before I'd start crying... And I didn't even have time to be afraid that the G.I. had sent me slaps and bangs in titanic proportions. The next moment, I was promoted to the rank of little rocket man; and next, I took a swan dive under the big top... In the seconds that followed, I went from first flying drummer boy to the rank of scout Squadron Airborne; made a free fall without a fuckin' parachute; tasted the fear, the blood and the leather of an American boot up the ass: "*This is not America, no... This is not, sha la la la la!*"

That day, I climbed to unreachable peaks before another soldier broke into the tent. It was a beefy chocolate milk skinned man, that one... I thought it was the end or my career as a thief!

Welcome to fuckin' America, my little Jo!

"What the fuck, man?" The cocoa-skinned soldier said.

Fortunately for me, he seemed to be a human, that one, and I was happy for humanity in its whole when my savior fired a powerful right hand to the jaw of the child molester.

The American soldier ended up on the ground, dizzy Deaned by high stinky cheddar flying at the head...

"Are you-O-K-boy?" Had articulated the chocolate man, showing teeth that looked even whiter than life.

I didn't understand anything of what this guy was saying to me, and I could have tried to save myself from the *tin shelter* during the moment of confusion that followed the punch, but I rather kept an attitude of gratitude towards this variety of military policemen, true protector of the citizen, and I waited to see what would happen next... without flinching.

The American trooper, who knew the conditions of precarious existence of the inhabitants of the city, had taken two large containers of margarine from the pile and deposited them near the exit. He then filled a large canvas bag with the provisions that were stored there, three or four cans of every kind: corned beef, tuna, sardines, râgout, and canned vegetables of all kinds... Afterwards, he took me by the hand and led me to his Jeep: "Come on! Don't-be-scared-boy! I'll-take-you-home."

He raised the little sac of shit that I was and gently put it on the front seat of the military vehicle. "What-is-your-name-boy? ... My-na-me-is-Geor-ges. Geooorr... ges", had made the American, pointing to his chest... "Geoooooooorrges!"

- *Oh! Tu veux savoir mon nom?... Moi, c'est Joseph!... Non! Non! Pas comme ça... Écoute bien, Geooorrrrges! Jooo... Seph!*

Jo-seph... (Oh! You want to know my name? ... I'm Joseph! ... No! No! Not like that... Listen well, Geooorrges! Jooo... Seph! Jo-seph ...)

- ... Jooo-sef!

- *C'est bien! Tu vois que c'est facile, Geooorrges.* (Good! You see how easy it is, Geooorrges.)

- Show-me-where-yo-live? ... Jooo-sef... *Maisooooon?* He risked.

- *Ah! Tu veux savoir où j'habite... C'est ça?* (Ah! You want to know where I live... Is that it?)

We drove during some time in his Jeep, while I showed him how to get to my house, showing him where he should turn in *les Santons.* We tooked the path of Chaud'Eau street, then I pulled the sleeve of the military man and pointed right, on Victor Hugo, and then again to the right, on Sainte-Monique. Big Georges then took Narbonne Boulevard, turned right on Algiers, after which he stopped on Maulinais street...

During the whole trip, Uncle Vito followed on his bicycle and made himself as small as possible, in case of a problem...

Finally arrived at my house, the *Samarican* soldier stopped his Jeep. He took me down, and, immediately after, he carried the victuals to the door: two big loads, in all.

- Now-you-be-a-good-boy! Joo-sef? ... Promess? He had said, looking severe.

I didn't understand what the hell he was saying, but I liked the music that made his voice, and, finally, I nodded...

I had a fifty-fifty chance that this was the right answer!

I shook the soldier's hand and then watched him leave. And that's when my uncle Vito arrived on his bicycle...

A small tear of joy had dug a groove on my filthy cheeks. Mom, who was very sick at that time, was going to be forced to wash my face with her big bar of lime soap... And it's by keeping contact with this Geooorrges, this American G.I. coated with milk chocolate, a good guy that I saw several times a week during his interminable quartering in Bône, that I learned some American English on the spot...

* * *

After a forced stay of several months in the Sicilian countryside, I finally took the boat for Algeria. As the olive harvest and the bulk of the work in the orchards were over, my grandfather had judged that I had calmed down to a lesser degree and that I wasn't any longer a walking threat to anyone.

Upon my return to Algeria, as I was an experienced soldier and that things had been getting worse in Bône, I was immediately assigned to the *Unitée Territoriale* (Territorial Units) of the city: a formation of reservists of the French Army coming from all departments of Algeria. My job at the UT was to patrol the streets and keep citizens safe during the night. It started at sun down, three or four times a week, and since I was used to this kind of work, almost of routine and of second nature to me, I didn't find myself at all displeased with the work.

A legionary friend of the OAS (*Organisation Armé Secrète;* Secret Armed Organization: a clandestine French political-military organization created to defend the French presence in Algeria by all means) had found me a paying job at Salem to thank me for my involvement for the cause. But blowing up Arab shops with plastic explosives and gunning down Fellagha terrorists, I would have done it for sport.

Salem was a lighterage contractor for whom I transshipped sea freight on the port, because the city was teeming with activity despite the troubles... As if everything was fuckin' normal! I was on call with the UT for the protection of the Pieds-Noirs of the city, while working for the OAS (under the cover of the UT). I was a medic who could urgently be summoned to save a member of the Pieds-Noirs family; I had become a sort of doctor without Borders working on the night shift: Bône was now my vast operating room. I was a surgeon who had swapped the scalpel for the bayonet, the microscope for the scope of a high precision rifle... And with my friends from the OAS, and all those who wanted to keep their country and

64

their French heritage, we were going to cleanup the city and save *our* Algeria... The Algeria of the Pieds-Noirs!

I worked for Salem, and a little for my own benefit, for a little over six months. Then, I quickly left the stevedore, who had complained of large installments perceived on suspicious lighterages that I had made for my own benefit. Subsequently, I was hired on a construction site that belonged to an Italian-born contractor named Butta Cavoli; my father had been working for him for several years and had helped me to enter in the construction company: Peppé was the foreman of one of the many projects the big boss was erecting.

Butta Cavoli was a structure heavyweight specializing in bridges, roads and low-cost housing. He was a powerhouse of contruction that employed thousands of workers, Arabs usually being low-level laborers, underpaid lick-ass slaves or modern-day cheap labor. The employer pressed them like lemons to extract their juice. Then, when they were emptied, he would throw them and hired new ones... My Muslim friends used to say that: "*mathal Yahud motherfuckin, yumkin lilrujul aldaght ealaa eurq albueud!* (like the motherfuckin' Jews, the guy could squeeze the sweat of a mosquito!)"

Europeans occupied the jobs of specialized workers and contractors. Peppé and I earned a very good salary while unskilled laborers only collected crumbs. It allowed the capitalist-Christian boss to earn gold with the sweat of the subjugated Muslim laborers with the support of the local republican authorities and the blessing of the clergy, who allowed exploitation of the Arab population to the maximum. Since they were not even Christians... They had no soul!

But all these projects of society had been built on unstable political foundations... And on the backs of the Muslim brothers with whom I had grown up. They revolted more and more: civil war was raging throughout the country and no one felt safe... Neither did my Arab friends and the moderate Muslims population!

7

One evening, after *a hard day's night, I been working like a dog* on the Elysa construction site, I went down Garibaldi Avenue to join my friends in Cours Bertagna. This great boulevard was like the Champs Elysees, but even more beautiful... and more intimate! It had been named after a former mayor who had left his mark on the city: Jérome Bertagna.

The Cours was a large esplanade divided into three parts by rows of majestic trees: on the right, it was the alley of the young; the central aisle was the widest and descended to a bandstand and a huge garden; on the left was the quiet alley of the elderly... They were following the movement between old friends, hobbling behind with their walking stick.

The pedestrian walkways were protected by century-old palm trees standing guard; the Cathedral of Bône valiantly barred the passage to the infidels at one end of the Place, the port did the same office at the other end. Large arcades were home to the city's chic shops, cafés, pubs and restaurants. There was the municipal theater, a mecca of Bônoise culture, the Transatlantique Hotel-restaurant, a meeting place for high society that I was not part of, banks and other shops for the rich and famous...

During the day, the sun was beating hard and sweeping the Place with sparkling luminosity; at night, it was the softened light of lamppost that gave youths renewed ardor. My eyes crossed the defensive line of the chaperones and I could glance at the girl I was in love with... And that's where my eye caressed my sweet Ariane for the first time.

To show her my affection, I had offered her an ice cream and an *oublie*. An *oublie* was a kind of lace crepe; it was as fragile as true love, and, if one was to squeeze it too hard, it disintegrated in the hand... disappearing between the fingers like tentative love! It was above all traveling salesmen who offered them to the passers-by and shouted: "*Oublies à la vanille... Qui veut des oublies!* (Vanilla *oublies...* Who wants an *oublie!*)"

As the sun was still falling, inhaling the air laden with the scent of flowers, I looked for my friends. But I was especially eager to connect with Ariane: I was feeling like cupid just by thinking of seeing her again!

On either side of the promenade, there were intimate hotels, restaurants renowned for their seafood, and friendly cafés with tables and chairs running along the aisles. The sun was already flirting with the sea, when I finally spotted my friends: Salvatore, my best friend, who was a carpenter for another contractor; Tic-Tac, who worked as an industrial draftsman; Lucky, who was with the CRS (police); and Ariane, who worked as a shorthand typist for CFAR (Crédit Foncier of Algeria and Tunisia).

Ariane immediately hung on my neck... She nibbled at me indefatigably and chewed at my eager ear with love bites as we wandered together on the wide sidewalk that bordered the shops. There was still a crowd at this late hour, surely because of the heat, and we were strolling without hurry, taking advantage of the last orange-rays, which were still writhing with the waves.

A few young women followed us at a respectful distance and seemed to be praying who knows what pagan god of love, while my bachelor pals turned from time to time to give them a little wink or make eyes at them. The girls then burst out laughing, fluttering their eyelashes, hiding their mouths with a trembling hand while cooing I don't know what in the ear of a friend.

And that's when I saw a young Arab shoe-shiner take off on the other side of the pedestrian mall...

It had intrigued me to see him go that way, but I thought at the time that he may not have given the change to his client and that he was running away with all the dough. The young Muslim seemed to have about no more then twelve years of age, at the most, with the traditional box with brushes and waxes in his hand. During his desperate flight, the towel-head youth had overturned a table and passers-by. The next moment, I thought I saw a dark pellet the size of an apple flowing towards us; the spheroid rolled awkwardly under the tables of a nearby cafe, and, despite the rumor that rose from hundreds of strollers in the Cours, I still could perceive the distinct metallic sound that the object made while twirling on the pavements... Tac! Toc! ... Tac! Toc! ... The round stumbled towards us with the uncertain slowness of a petanque ball landing on the jack!

After a brief hesitation, I finally recognized the danger... and I leaped over Ariane, shouting with all of my strength:

"Grenaaaaaaaaaaade!"

I had screamed those few syllables of death, lying on top of Ariane to screen her with my body, while the explosive wrapped in metal still pirouetted on the smooth stones of the alley as in a film played in slow motion. The little bomb was still barreling on itself when it stopped on the border of the sidewalk, nearby. My childhood friend, Salvatore, still busy detailing the girls, I suppose, or surprise shot, perhaps, had not reacted quickly enough... And he had only time to utter a single word... More an exclamation of suprise... An ultimate interjection: "*Hein?* (Huh?)"

That would be the last word coming out of his mouth...

And as he vocalized this one and only outcry, a loud detonation shook the Pied-Noir's Cours. The next moment, there was whining everywhere... The wounded were on all sides!

Ariane had been spared. Me too. But my friend Salvatore had been hit... He had taken on the forehead a tiny flush of nothing at all... Hardly as big as the nail of my little finger. But the little mouth of metal had torn everything in Salvatore's skull, making its way out of the back of the head...

A tiny scarlet droplet was dyeing his short chestnut hair, when I went to help him... Salvatore's eyes had only time to pass on a languid exclamation of surprise for already a last breath seemed to abandon him forever. His chest was tense with the pain of an unjust death while I held him with a hand under his neck to support his softened head, like when holding a newborn baby in his arms to keep the head upright.

I hugged him to repel the inevitable... I felt his heart... It still throbbed in his chest... Salvatore might not have died yet?

I shook him softly, whispering:

"*Reste éveillé, Salvatore. Ferme pas les yeux!... Faut surtout pas fermer les yeux!... On va t'emmener tout de suite à l'hôpital... Reste avec moi, je t'en supplie... Salvatore!* (Stay awake, Salvatore. Don't shut your eyes! ... You mustn't close your eyes! ... We'll take you to the hospital right away... Stay with me, I beg you... Salvatore!)"

But my hand had already started to blush... Warm blood!

Afterwards, it was the cobblestones... They had taken a scarlet color where Salvatore had laid. And it was then that I fully realized the finality of his predicament...

I had tears in my eyes as I rocked him in my arms to keep him awake, and then I implored:

"*Pars pas, Salvatore. Pars pas!... Accroche-toi!* (Don't let go, Salvatore. Don't let go! ... Hang on!)

But the blood was now oozing from his nose. A second after, it would be with from one ear... With the mouth still open twisted by a last and almost unpronounceable syllable that seemed to come from beyond: "Ooooooooh!"

It was death that had come to rob him from us...

An ironic bite had already taken possession of his half-opened lips, when I let him go on the bloody pavement: Salvatore had just died in my arms. And, with his gaze fixed on the hereafter, his only answer to this unjust death, when you barely are twenty-two years old, had been to kiss death on the lips and to sketch a sarcastic smile.

And death, I knew the fuckin' bitch very well. I had seen her in action several times, the tramp! But this time was very different... She had just mowed my best friend... A childhood friend... A brother! ... A young Pied-Noir of Bône, like me.

There were screams and howlings under the archway; a clamor of indignation and hate then took possession of the Place, but as I was busy with Salvatore... I had not even realized it. And when I raised my head to look around, a good dozen Pieds-Noirs were writhing on the wide, bloody sidewalk. Within a radius of ten meters, the deadly machine of hate had pierced bodies and upset the course of lives forever. The edge of the sidewalk had surely spared some Pieds-Noirs... But Salvatore, no!

Subsequently, by agreement, without a single rallying cry, the majority of the Pieds-Noirs in the Cours began to chase the Arabs wandering around: and a *ratonnade* (raccoon hunt) followed. In an instant of pure human madness, the collective IQ of the Bônois population had regressed to zero... And a hunt for *Ratagaz* (Muslim rats) was engaged in Bône, even though the word *Ratagaz* was not yet valid in scrabble.

I left Ariane, the dead and the wounded: "*Reste-là!* (Stay there!)" I had ordered. Then I started looking for my pound of Arab flesh with my friends Tic-Tac and Lucky...

The men beat up Muslims with their feet, chairs, table legs and knives. Adam, a colossus of nearly two meters high who had been spared by the detonation, had had the fright of his life! He had seized a frail Arab of only five feet tall, lifted him from the ground in a single block, and had burst the *djounoud's* (Algerian Moudjahidin) head against an oak tree knot after a gyration. A poor guy on his bicycle, who was hanging around and was coming back from his underpaid work, did not get very far. The women, by the dozen, had laid him on the ground and had begun to crush him with the slender needles of their shoes. They put the *innocent* terrorist in lint in less than two minutes...

After a brief lull caused by fatigue, disgust or the lack of Muslim martyrs, we finally organized ourselves with other friends... And despite the fall of the night and the curfew, we went down in droves in the Arab district. Initially, we were only a dozen; a few minutes later, due to a ripple effect or pure xenophobic patriotism, we were a few hundred who ransacked everything in our path. There, all the unlucky Arabs we met were beaten and sacrificed on the altar of collective vengeance.

It was like in a big mass, except that *I* was the priest of it all... And it wasn't crucifixes that we forced them to kiss!

Many favored the delicate touch of the knife: I kept my pistol and the few bullets contained in my single charger for emergencies. Almost all men had a knife, in Algeria... Especially the Arabs! And it gave me a real pleasure to feel my victim agonize in my hands and hear them flinch as I turned the blade inside the ribcage of my *Ratagaz...*

I had learned the dead-on martial technique at the Legion in hand-to-hand combat classes. One mustn't go into the ribcage and simply plant and remove his bayonet. One had to stab and turn... Stab and turn... To avoid only hurting the opponent to death... an adversary who could still kill you before dying. In this way, the Muslim cocksuker was obliged to die, for a piece of liver was torn from him or was it the heart and a piece of lung that went off to rat shit?

For each *djounoud* that I stabbed, I avenged Salvatore death, and while I stabbed and turned, knifed and twisted, tirelessly, my shirt was gorged with the blood of my victims. And once again I avenged my friend Salvatore knifing and weaving... With a cry to the sky so that he could maybe hear me: "*Celui-là c'est pour toi, Salvatore!* (This one is for you, Salvatore!)"

The *ratonnades* (hunt for Muslim rats) was for several Pieds-Noirs the definitive moment to settle personal accounts with the towel heads. For me, I didn't make any fuss at all, and it didn't really matter to me who the Muslim was... My dagger trusting the hazards of chance! I was using a Schlash retractable knife: a six inches switchblade.

Sometimes, the victims were pursued into their homes, some pushing the odious to smash the locked doors from the inside. The police forces of Bône were completely helpless and unprepared to deal with this oldest form of social justice on the planet and preferred to hide behind bars and wait it out, safely, in the confort of their own jail cells.

I don't remember how many *djounoud* I eviscerated that night, and when I returned home, the shirt soaked with the blood of my victims, I felt as if I had accomplished my duty: I had avenged the death of my best friend, Salvatore... Sal who had gone on to the afterlife in my arms! Later, a couple blocks from my house, I stopped near a public fountain to wash and quench my thirst. Killing Arabs with a blade can make you quite thirsty... And I drew the pure water with my soiled hands, moistened my face with the purifying substance, and then I gave myself absolution. When I arrived home, Mémé and Peppé almost fainted so the sight of my bloodied shirt had affected them. I had only received light knife strokes that had slipped on the floating ribs... some Arab brothers that had not been easily convinced.

Earlier in the evening, a benevolent friend came to tell my father that I had been killed near a small café on Cours Bertagna; that shrapnel had ravaged my head... A little Arab shoe shiner who had thrown a grenade into the Cours. And since we didn't have a phone, yet, the neighbourhood wasn't even connected, the communications were done in this way; and it was often by friends or neighbours who reported, from another source, what they had been told... The whole thing being as reliable as *le téléphone arabe* (hearing it through the grapevine) (Arab phone, in French: *téléphone arabe*)!

My fiancée, too, had received such sad news; her mother had consoled her for a long part of the night. She had been told that I had been stabbed in the Arab quarter... It was probably because of my shirt soaked with blood that she had received the false information of my death. Ariane had cried until morning and already saw herself a widow before only being married... She had spent the night, and a good part of the next day, thinking that I was dead! And when we saw each other again, the next night, she almost fainted when she opened the door. Subsequently, she tried to tear me a new one! ... But it wasn't my fault, because I didn't know someone had announced my passing to her!

My brother, my friends, my uncles, my cousins and all the family I had in Bône had been put to work... All of them had been looking for me that evening, trying to find my body... The body of the deceased!

And I came back whistling as if nothing had happened.

I must say that they had already told my father, during my service at the Foreign Legion, and at least on three occasions, that I had died for my country. Once, the Army sent a courier to my house and a corporal had read the usual formula of military condolences, telegram and medal in hand... Cross my heart and hope to die! Peppé had been mourning for three long weeks before I got back home, officially declared *"Tombé pour la France!* (Fallen in the service of France!)" I had survived an ambush and had been the only survivor of my patrol, but since I had been found three days after the massacre, the Legion had already declared me dead in the service of the country... By mistake! And had sent the bad news to my family. I had not been aware of it and only found out when I got a ten days leave and dropped by the house... So Peppé, thanks to his previous experiences with the Foreign Legion, had waited to see the body before starting to prepare for my burial.

The whole family was crying, when I arrived; the prodigal son was coming back from a mortal fight with Arab devils... Safe and sound!

But for all the torments I had caused my parents, I had ended up depicted as a heartless man... Which is what I had become, really, by dint of killing so many people!

However, despite all that I had done to others, I had a clear conscience: I had killed because I had to do it. I wasn't ashamed of any of it. And my motto was derived from my training with the Foreign Legion and from my experience in urban guerrilla warfare in the streets of Bône, as well as the little religion that the priests had managed to inculcate into me by force, in primary school...

And my rallying cry was: *"Lève-toi et marche... ou crève!* (Get up and march... or die!)"

8

In the following weeks, life would gradually resume its course, and since I wasn't on duty at the UT every night, I often had to return to work on the construction site to justify my salary in the eyes of the entrepreneur.

That morning, Peppé had taken his usual place at the back of my bike, when I throttled up to the yards of the Élysa, propelled by tiny cumulus of oil and gasoline.

The Élysa was a vast complex of three thousand homes that the French Government was building for the homeless Arabs... *HLM's* (low-cost housing) intended for people who preferred to live with their flock of sheep in caves or tents, rather than owe anything to the French. The leader of the whole kit and caboodle was called Rassmussen...

Rass was a good guy, slightly carefree guy who was about sixty years old. He was simply happy not mingling with anyone and did his best to be fair to all the workers; the only thing that really interested him was a job well done: "*Le béton est-il bon? ... Le fer est-il à la bonne place?* (Is the concrete good? ... Is the iron set at the right place?) He asked, before pouring the cement of another retaining pillar.

He was meticulous, only passionate about his work, and noted his appreciations on everything in lead pencil in a small pocket book he kept preciously in the right-side slot of his pants.

"*Non! T'as pas fait ça? ... T'as pas fait ça?* (No! You didn't do that? ... Tell me you didn't do that!) He reproached me, when he met me on the site.

My face immediately took a culpable color... Even though I didn't know why, yet!

"*Qu'est-ce que j'ai encore fait de mal, Rass?* (What have I done wrong this time, Rass?) And Rassmussen took up his notebook again and noted that there wasn't enough iron in a pylon, that there had not been enough support for a floor, or any other kind of stuff related with rebar!

"*Remettez encore du métal... Remettez-en, messieurs! Encore du métal!... Encore et toujours plus de métal!* (Put some more metal... Put on more, gentlemen! More metal! ... More and always more metal!)"

And the men would put more metal under the protection of some UT members who, like me, always came to work with their pistols or their machine gun. Once, a worker dropped his firearm in a work form where we were pouring cement, and Peppé said to the guy: "*tant pis! On ne va pas arrêter la coulée pour un idiot qui ne sait pas prendre soin de son arme!* (Too bad! We're not gonna stop the pour of cement for of an idiot who can't take care of his gun!)" ... And he had called this type of cement: "*du béton armé!* (Armed [reinforced] concrete!)"

As I got closer to the yard, having parked my motorcycle in the corner reserved for European motorized workers, I was surprised to see a crowd of workers bunched up: a few hundred Muslim workers had gathered at the bottom of one fo the towers... There wasn't a single European in the lot! Maybe we were late? ... But? ... Late for what, exactly? ... And what were those idiots doing? ... Why weren't they working?

These labourers, I almost knew them all by name, or at least from sight, because on top of estimating of the volume of cement to be prepared for each day, I also helped to calculate the pay of the workers. I was not only skilled at killing Fellaghas... I was also very good with Arabic numbers.

In the middle of the nearly perfect circle that formed the Muslim workers, there was a body... The round had partially opened to let us pass trough, when we came closer to see what the fuck was going on in there. The face of the guy was resting on his side, cheek on the ground, with the prisoner's cigarette in his half-open mouth, the paper still stuck against the lower lip: the inert carcass seemed to be smoking, even though the heart wasn't in it, anymore.

On the sleeveless work shirt, in the back, there were seven large reddish stains embedded in the fabric, with seven holes inside, resulting from the seven stab wounds that had been given to him... It was indeed Rassmussen who was lying there.

We went to him. Peppé had a tear in his eye; to see his friend stretched on the ground had troubled him. So, it was I who leaned over the inert body and looked for the carotid artery... Rass's neck was still hot, but even when I tried very hard to feel something... There wasn't anything pulsating in there!

These fuckin' sand niggers had killed him!

Despite my growing anger at the free bee assassination of a man who had remained neutral in this conflict, I still had the impression of hearing old Rass repeating to me: "*Faut mettre du métal, Jo! Encore plus de métal!* (We must put more metal, Jo! ... Much more metal!)"

Except that, this time, it was Rass who had taken everything in the back!

I removed the cigarette end stuck in his lips, closed his wide-open eyes, and, mechanically, took the butt to my mouth. Next, without even thinking about it, like a nicotine withdrawal automaton, I pulled one or two puffs, looking pensive.

The Arabs watched me with astonishment and had a general recoil impulse, when I walked out of the circle of workers making smoke rings with Rass's coffin nail. Daddy too... As if I had committed sacrilege by stealing the butt of a cripple, or desecrated a gravestone in the middle of a graveyard!

Hey! For fuck's sake! ... Rassmussen was dead! ... Dead!

I took a last puff, staring at them, all, and then I put out the cigarette... To the great relief of Peppé, who had only begun to breathe when I extinguished the roll-your-own. Rass still held his black booklet in one hand; the pages seemed to be fighting with a light breeze blowing from the coast...

One of the Arabs in the circle formed by the Muslims was named Hussein. We had been to school together, high school,

and he said to me: "*Va-t-en vite!... Va-t-en!* (Go away quickly!
... Go away!)"

- *Non! Je ne m'en irai pas!* (No! I'm not going away!) I
snapped back.

And I leaned over the dead body of good Rasmussen so I
could take his notebook... And then, immediately after, I
extended a hand to my father, in tears.

- *Allez-vous-en vite, qué jé vous dis! On peut plus lé
arrêter... Y sont fous! Y sont dé l'autre côté du bâtiment... Y
cherchent des Européens pour lé tuer, tous! Allez! Vite! On pé
pas vous garder ici plus longtemps, sinon, ils vont nous tuer à
nous aussi...* (Go away quickly, I tell you... Go! We cannot stop
them... They' crazy! They' on the other side of the building...
They' looking for Europeans to kill them, all! Come on!
Quickly! ... We can' keep you here any longer, otherwise, they'd
kill us too...)

A few terrorists armed with semi-automatic rifles and
antique single shot firearm had come out of a building under
construction at the other end of the building site... They were
slowly coming towards us.

"*Mé ti piges rien à rien, toi?!?* (Hey! ... You don't
understand anyting, you?)" Hussein had told me, screaming.

That's when I really understood the danger and ran to my
bike. I made it start at the first stroke of the heel and went back
to pick up my father. Peppé was still frozen in front of the
remains of his old buddy, with the precious notebook in his
hand... A Rassmussen who had killed himself at work all the
years of his adult life... for nothing!

I grabbed Peppé by the arm and almost snatched my father
from the Arab workers, when I picked him up, pulling him
sharply towards me so that he could climb from behind in a
jiffy... Dad caught on, but he wanted to put the notebook in his
pocket... "*Laisse tomber, papa!* (Forget about it, Dad!)" I
ordered... "*Tiens-toi bien!* (Hang on!)"

It was raining bullets, when I drove away from the
construction site like a maniac...

I jumped a sidewalk with my Push, an agile 250 cc bike made in Austria, spanned a ditch of at least two meters wide, while my bike seemed to fly over it at full speed... I waltzed in the street zigzagging to the sound of the well-timed music that the Fellagha's guns were playing... Bing! Bang! Boom! ...

Didn't like their fuckin' music at all!

Bullets ricocheted all around us like river pebbles when you throw them to make them jump, echoing: Ziiiing! Zooooung! ...

But without hitting us!

Didn't know who they were fuckin' with, these motherfuckers! ... And they sure couldn't shoot for shit! Otherwise... We'd both be dead!

I drove like a nut and had only stopped at the edge of our neighbourhood, drowned in the Pied-Noir mass that was already crowding the street around us to find out what had happened at the Élysa construction site.

Peppé and I patted each other's bodies, trying to make sure we had escaped the terrorist's bullets: two St. Thomas who were examining the wounds of 2 Jesus of Nazareth, in Bône! But Aunt Titine, who was twice as religious as a nun from the Vatican, would have alleged that there were one Jesus too many.

Fortunately for Peppé, I had not managed to put my finger in any new orifice whatsoever... But our family doctor, to make sure that everything was in good working order, would have surely put a finger up our ass, ordering:

"*Dites trente-trois!* (Say thirty-three!)"

On that specific morning, no one could have beaten me in a motocross race, and Peppé gave me a friendly pat on the back, adding: "*Bon boulot, mon fils!* (Good job, my son!)"

This paternal recognition, alone, was worth more than all the shitty fuckin' medals I had earned at the Foreign Legion...

A few minutes later, we saw a huge column of smoke emanating from the construction site; the Fellaghas had put fire to the wooden formwork for concrete, the scaffolding and all that could burn on the site: they were going to lay off thousands of Arab workers... What a fuckin' revolution, I tell ya!

***

Later in the evening, I went to see my lieutenant of the Territorial Units (UT). I reported to him at least once a week: he supervised the work of the UT from Bône to Constantine, and also worked on the side, like me, for the OAS, in an attempt to accomplish specific damage to the Muslims. He was a small sized man, the hair cut in brush with ears like barn door that seemed to want to take off on their own at the first gust of wind. I had told him one day, jokingly, that with such ears he'd better pay attention to the Fellaghas hunting for trophies, the Fells (short for Fellaghas) having the habit of making collars with the auricles of their European victims. He was a true Pied-Noir, like me, and in addition to reporting to him to engineer the atrocities against the Muslim terrorists, I had come to ask him for personal advice...

There was a young Arab in the city that was seriously beginning to fuck with my head. Mohamed Salahim, was his name... Killing innocent people, was the game... He was a young activist of the FLN (National Liberation Front, the political wing of the ALN who fought against the French colonial power: us, Pieds-Noirs) who had tried, and more than once, to kill me in the city... To make me "un-fuckin'-alive!"

The Fell claimed that I had killed his brother on the College's playground - we had attended the same institution, his brother and I -, a duel *mano a mano* in which I had sent the Muslim motherfucker for a forced stay at the hospital.

But, I hadn't killed him! So? ... What the fuck was he talking about, that cunt?

But a year after our fight, *le frère* (the brother) died of a heart attack. And a few years later, his family claimed that he had died of complications resulting of our fight... From a punch he would have received to the heart, according to them. So, it was my fault: I was therefore the culprit of his untimely death.

Anyway, the Fell's family took advantage of the turmoil in Algeria to try to send me to hell, attempting to avenge the *honor* of their son at the same time... And I had been unable to find this dear Mohamed and settle the account once and for all with his family... I couldn't find the cocksucker and set the record strait... Punch his fuckin' number!

It was very likely that it was this Fellagha who had killed people around me, missing me while undertaking my premature disappearance. I was now afraid for my family, and especially for Ariane... And the murder of dear Rassussen, like the assassination of my best friend Salvatore, was perhaps related to his promise to suppress me and avenge his brother.

"Tu sais ce qu'il te faut faire?... (You know what you have to do? ...)" My lieutenant friend told me, *"Va falloir aller au... Hum! ... Tu sais où il est?... Le centre présumé du FLN, à Bône?* (You'll have to go to... Umm! ... Do you know where it is? ... The alleged center of the FLN, in Bône?)"

- *Ouais! Je sais c'est où* (Yeah! I know where it is), I had answered, quietly.

- *Eh bien!... Va falloir que tu ailles là-bas et que tu montes les voir pour parlementer avec eux.* (Well! ... You'll have to go over there and parlé with them.)

- *Ho! Mais t'es fou ou quoi?... Ils vont me faire la peau, ces cons... Illico!* (Ho! But you' crazy, or what? ... They'll fuck me up good, these assholes... Illico!)

- *Mais non! Mais non! Je ne suis pas fou, Jo. Va là-bas, que j'te dis! Et si jamais quelque chose t'arrivait... Mais ils savent très bien qu'on va tout raser les Melons du coin si jamais ils osaient te faire quoi que ce soit. Alors, y feront rien contre toi là-bas... Garanti!* (But, no! No! I'm not crazy, Jo. Go there, I tell you! And if something ever happened to you... But they know damn well that we'll just slaughter all the Muslims in the area if they ever dared do anything to you. So, they'll do nothing against you in there... Guaranteed!)

I took some time to think a little... And then I said to my Lieutenant:

- *Bon! Puisque je n'ai pas tellement le choix... J'irai.* (OK! Since I haven't got much choice... I'll go.)

But if I went, I was going backwards!

The headquarters of the FLN in Bône was located in a huge Arab shop at the top of the Place d'Armes, just next to *la Tranchée Bridge.* I knew the area very well because it was in that district that I was born. They sold rugs, carved furniture and other typical Muslim craft concoctions for the well off of the city. Everyone suspected that this trade center was a meeting place of the FLN, but nobody had ever dared do anything about it since the sand niggers had *gained* their independence. The French Army had only doubts as to what was really going on in there, but as the colonel of the garrison had been expressly ordered to remain neutral in the conflict between the FLN and the Pieds-Noirs, one way or the other, I was going to somehow confirm it for everyone...

I knew the owner very well, because he had taught me mathematics at l'École Polytechnique de Bône (Bône's polytechnic school). He was a Muslim intellectual educated in France: an academic named Abdel Tahar. I had only retained from his higher academic teaching the rules of trigonometry and the striking of his rod on my phalanges... The price to pay to amuse the class with my fallacious answers during his class.

The mathematician had once broken a yardstick on my fingers, and as a macho I was, I burst out laughing!

The next day, it was the teacher who giggled, when he found out that I couldn't write anymore with my right hand. But I still had my left to sent him a "fuck you" with the middle finger...

I introduced myself to my former teacher, still lost in my memories of class, and a big hoarse voice leaned onto my young face:

"*Qu'est-ce que tu fous ici, toi?* (You? ... What are you doing here?)"

- *Vous le savez bien ce que je fais ici, Monsieur Tahar.* (You know damn well what I'm doing here, Mr Tahar.)

I had replied most politely as I took the humble tone of the apprentice in the presence of his old Kung Fu master.

But his mastery was of mathematics...

- *Viens ici!... Et suis-moi!* (Come here! ... And follow me!) He had ordered.

The math genius then dragged me into a maze of carpets hung on high iron wires; they served as divisions in the vast open-plan commercial space: partitions generated by large wool carpets. I still had my automatic stuck in the belt, and, left to die, I was going to bring as much as possible to the other side with me. I was fearful and disoriented, after all the bifurcations we had taken: on the right, and on the right again, and then on the left, and another time on the right, and...

I, who had the sense of orientation and could find my way in any *djebel* (mountain) of Algeria, I was completely lost!

And... Fuck that shit!

I had two extra clips in my pockets... 24 shots, in all! In case of a glitch, I just had to shoot everything that moved and make beautiful nine millimeters holes in their fuckin' new Arabic carpets... *Yalla! Shoot.*

My former teacher had probably read the concern on my face as easily as an axiom from which he drew the logical consequence, because he had told me, rather dryly:

"*On ne te fera aucun mal, ici! N'aie pas peur!* (We will not hurt you in here! Do not be afraid!)"

- *Non! Non... Je n'ai pas peur, parce que le premier qui va morfler ici... C'est toi!* (No, no! I'm not afraid, that I had answered him, because the first one who's gonna croak here... It's you!)

- *Non!... N'aie pas peur... Dis-moi!* (No! ... Do not be afraid, he had repeated... Tell me!)

And that's when I opened up to him.

Besides, he must have known about the whole affair, the motherfucker! And I went straight to the point, just as I always did when it mattered the most...

"*Je sais! Je sais!... Je suis au courant pour Mohamed et tout le reste... Ça fait plusieurs fois qu'on lui dit de te laisser tranquille. Notre guerre à nous, ce n'est pas une guerre de vengeance personnelle: c'est une guerre de terrorisme. On veut faire peur aux Européens pour qu'ils partent... Pas tous les tuer! Car après, il nous faudra bien rebâtir...* (I know! I know! ... I know about Mohamed and all the rest, said the Arab. We've told him many times to leave you alone. Our war is not a war of personal revenge: it is a war of terrorism. We want to scare the Europeans so they'll leave... Not kill them all! ... Because, after everything is over and done with, we'll have to rebuild...)

Yeah! Talk about fuckin' rebuilding! Rebuild with what, motherfucker?

The master had continued to speak... And his soothing words were gradually going to influence me, and, little by little, I began to relax and not want to kill him...

Well, not immediately!

"*Écoutez bien une chose... Si Mohamed continue à faire ça, moi aussi je vais essayer de tuer ses frères et ses soeurs... Et puis après j'vais liquider toute sa putain de famille au grand complet et terminer le travail avec ses cousins germains! Moi aussi je suis né dans le quartier arabe... Moi aussi j'ai grandi dans ce bled pourri... Comme lui! Pourquoi est-ce qu'il me pousserait à faire des choses pareilles?... Pourquoi?* (Listen to this one thing..." I had professed, "if Mohamed continues to do what he's doing, I, too, will try to kill his brothers and sisters... And then, after I will have liquidated the whole fuckin' family, I'll complete the work with his first cousins! ... I, too, was born in the Arab district... I, too, grew up in this rotten neighbourhood... Just like him! So, why would he push me to do such a thing? ... Why?)"

When I finished my plea, Abdel Tahar seemed to be touched by my words...

- *Comme ça, si je comprends bien ce que tu me dis, dans ton âme et conscience... Tu ne voudrais pas tuer tous ces gens-là?... Tes frères musulmans!* (So, if I understand what you are saying to me, in your heart and soul... You wouldn't want to kill any of these people? ... Your Muslim brothers!)

It was very similar to synthesizing a multivariate regression equation to find the unknowns... But since he was a brilliant mathematician, it seemed normal to me that he would.

- *Non! Non! Pas du tout!... Pourquoi ferais-je une chose pareille? C'est avec ces gens-là que j'ai grandi. Pourquoi devrais-je tous les tuer, maintenant? C'est Mohamed qui me pousse à faire ça... C'est lui qui me menace... Moi et ma famille!* (No! No! Not at all! ... Why would I do such a thing? I grew up with these people. Why should I kill them all, now? It's Mohamed who pushes me to do that... It's him who threatens me... Me and my family!)

My old teacher seemed to think about the whole affair for a moment. Then, he ordered:

- *Bon! Maintenant, je t'ai assez vu. Va-t'en!... Et si tu veux mon conseil, ne remonte plus jamais ici. Il y a beaucoup d'yeux qui t'ont vu et que toi tu ne vois pas... Et qui t'ont reconnu! Tu es très courageux d'être venu ici. Ça se récompense... Je vais arranger ton affaire avec Mohamed! Va! Va en paix! Salam alec cum.* (Good! ... Now, I've seen enough of you. Go away! ... And if you want my advice, never come down here again. There are many eyes that have seen you and that you do not see... And they recognized you! You are very brave to have come here to parlé. It's to be rewarded... I'll arrange your *feud* with Mohamed! Go! ... Go in peace! ... *Salam Aleikum.)*

The next moment, an Arab guide specialized in carpet labyrinths brought me back to the exit door. Arrived at the end of the maze, he greeted me as the Arabs usually do amongst themselves, and he touched his heart, his lips and his forehead saying: "*Salamalec!*"

- *Aleikum Salam!* (Peace be with you!)

From that day on, I never had to worry about Mohamed anymore... I learned later that he had been transferred to another *Katiba* (unit fighter group), very far from Bône.

9

The days had passed rapidly and the Algeria of the Pieds-Noirs had continued to sink in the doldrums. The Algerian cities were no longer safe for European colonists; the hunt for *Whites* was officially open... And three quarters of a million Pieds-Noirs were to leave their country from the end of May to mid-August of 1962.

After the Oran massacre of July 1962, a few days after the official recognition of the Independence of the *Djounouds* by general de Gaulle, it would be the drop that makes the cup overflow for many of us. And by mutual agreement, the majority of the Bônois families, who had stubbornly stayed in Algeria, had decided to flee before it was too late. We all had lost hope: several Pieds-Noirs had understood that, to leave their country alive was at least getting out of Algeria with something!

Uncle Nino, who lived on an isolated farm at about ten kilometers of the city, often said: "*Je n'ai pas peur de mourir en défendant ma terre, moi!* (I'm not afraid to die defending my land!)" He had finally been slaughtered in the early morning in front of his Arab employees, because he didn't want to abandon his domain to the Fellaghas.

Fuckin' Arab assholes! ... We wanted to kill them all before leaving. But it was impossible... There was too many of them!

In this troubled end of July 1962, while there was random shooting all around the city, my family had finally decided to embark on a steamer bound for Marseilles, and, even if we didn't like the climate of France, we no longer had a choice.

As for the patrols, it would be my last night of service for the UT, a final tour of the city to allow the greatest number of my compatriots to embark, and, after this last *baroud d'honneur* (lap of honour), I had to rejoin my family at dawn on the trans-Mediterranean.

This was the theory...

Some of my fellow citizens had been piling up for days in the port... It was a massive exodus with overflowing piers and overcrowded ships that never stopped parking passengers on decks so to get as many Pieds-Noirs as possible on board, because the other ships, those that the French authorities had to hurry to evacuate the population, were playing hard to get.

It was the fall of the Colonial Regime... The great retreat! The abandonment of the lands irrigated by our ancestors... Those who had revived this uncultivated desert that nobody wanted! ... Raised and milked the ewes to make the cheese... Planted the fruit trees, the vine and made full-bodied wines... Harvested olives and made the oil. Our Great general would keep all the black gold... The oil wells... The mineral oil... The gasoil... Greasing the palm of certain friends! Everything was not lost for big business in Ageria!

But for us, North Africans colonists, it was the flight to the motherland, a country we only had seen in pictures!

We had lost everything...

I walked silently in the streets of the Élysa district with my volunteers through the long tunnel that formed the plane trees; lined up straight and squeezed like sardines, they looked as if they were happy to see us parade one last time... I would have liked to be one, too, and remain rooted in this Arab land that had seen me born.

We ended up in the wharf section of the gas plant, at the other end of the harbor. I wandered aimlessly thinking of Ariane and my family, who, like thousands of Europeans of Algeria, were queuing up on the port, hoping to embark on a hypothetical Mediterranean crossing. The Bônois piled up on the docks, waiting in silence before leaving their country with the luggage of a lifetime in one hand and a heavy heart in the other... They were going to abandon their Algeria to the Muslims: they, alone, had seized the real message of our great general de Gaulle.

"*Je vous ai compris!* (I understood you!) That he had said in Algiers... But us, Pieds-Noirs of Bône, we didn't understand anything anymore!

My family brought back only a few suitcases of beige linen; they contained clothing and personal belongings of the first necessity, and on the quays they would surely darken to show our sorrow. Aunt Titine, who during her youth had briefly found herself *en odeur de sainteté* (with a reputation of sanctity) during a fruitless and brief stay with the nuns, had brought back only clothes and a pearly rosary with a small cross beatified by St. Augustine: the crucifix seemed to be hanging at the end of the chain, dying to detach itself from it, like French Algeria of Africa... A single suitcase that testified to a life spent in North Africa at the service of others.

My patrol had drowsed to the tip of the harbor pier. That port, it was the same that my father Giuseppe (Peppé) had rebuilt during the Second World War after the bombing of the Germans; the same he had rebuilt after the attacks of the Allies during the Liberation... The wharves stretched as far as the eye could see as I observed, in the distance, the Algerian mass waiting for the boarding. My heart was big as I was trying to find my family in this rough sea of people, hoping that they could, at least, embark.

I lit a cig, thoughtful, and glued it against my lower lip so it would stick on its own, because, with a machine gun in the hands, it wasn't the time to clutter one's paws with a cigarette. We continued patrolling and finally stopped just before the sea, as if the guardrail had repulsed us to keep us from ourselves, and after one last drag, I finally oriented myself. And so, in the middle of the night, we took the direction of the barracks at a good pace.

Naturally, I could have said to the captain of the UT: "*Ta mission, tu t'la fourres au cul, conard!* (Your mission, you can stick it up your ass, motherfucker!) And set sail with my family!

However, I would never have dared say such a truth to a superior because of my military training... But it was also because the officer was nearly two meters tall; that he weighed almost one hundred-forthy kilo; and that he mastered just about every fuckin' hand-to-hand combat technique imaginable. So...

If I was still patrolling that night, it was because the former legionaries had been asked to ensure the evacuation of ordinary citizens, so of Ariane, who had recently said "Yes!" and was oficially my wife, of my relatives, of my friends and other European families: these Pieds-Noirs who looked like a bunch of fuckin' tourists who returned to the old continent after endless holidays in the colonies!

Hippone, principal Roman city of Africa in antiquity; Bône for Europeans... But tomorrow it would be Annaba forever! On the other hand, the Arabs called our city Annaba, not Bône, and for them it will not change anything at all...

When I arrived at the garrison, my men and I entered the main door moving steadily: we wanted to dispose of our weapons and of our gear in a hurry. But when we arrived at the monitoring station, we immediately went down to a lower gear, since the duty corporal had decided to put away our instruments of peace, methodically, and check off his list... While we were just about to lose the fuckin' country! The carporal wanted to make sure that the cylinder heads of the automatic weapons had been emptied, that the serial numbers matched his inventory, that we didn't miss a strap, a charger or a cartridge: the labour of a monk! Even if it was the end of the world... My world.

"Hé! Ho! Ça fait! Magne-toi le cul, bordel! On a not'claque, nous! Et on voudrait aller rejoindre nos familles! (Hey! Ho! That's enough! ... Get off your ass, for fuck's sake! We're fuckin' tired! ... And we'd like to get the fuck out of here and join our families!) I had sent him.

But the carporal was still scribbling, completely deaf to my rudeness... *"Le règlement, c'est le règlement!* (The rules are the rules!) He said.

While waiting for the trooper to finish his Benedictine work, several people sat down against a wall to rest their exhausted feet by the night's patrol. Some smoked cigarettes; others took out bottles of Royal-Kebir (wine); one of our snipers had two liters of VS in his bag, bottles of Cognac he had confiscated at the Arab brothel and had already started...

"*C'est pour nous changer les idées et nous désaltérer un peu, Sergeant.* (It's to take one's mind off things and quench ourselves a little, Sergent.)" He had proposed.

The *litrons* - bottles of one litre - had barely been opened that a French army truck stopped at the front of the main entrance. Subsequently, a young beardless lieutenant came out with a distraught step - he was in his early twenties, like me -, soon to be followed by five sinistar faces.

"*Qu'est-ce qu'ils nous veulent, Sergent?* (What do they want of us, Sergeant?)" Had said Ricco, who, in addition of shooting down a wine bottle in no time, was also a good sniper.

The young officer's uniform was faded, sweaty, and I thought he was only missing a large yellow spot in the fork of his pants to complete the picture! A scar on his cheek was trying to reach the chin that was still fleeing... But? ... Where, exactly?

Towards France! I had supposed.

The French officer and his henchmen loaded all the weapons from the depot into the truck... As well as the valuables they could carry away without any difficulty. In a few minutes, the French army guys had loaded everything they wanted:

"*On ne doit rien laisser aux mains des rebelles... Ordre du commandant!* (We mustn't leave anything in the hands of the rebels... By order of the commander!)"

- *Et mes hommes?... Qui va les rapatrier, eux? Vous avez de la place pour nous dans le camion?* (And my men? ... Who will repatriate them? ... Have you got room for us in the truck?)

I was waiting for an answer... Any fuckin' answers! And I wondered if we should accompany these assholes of France, or not? But before being able to make a break for it, the truck had already disappeared: the French motherfukers had taken off... Without us!

The next moment, it began to stink of camel shit and of Towel Heads... On camels! And the insurgents of the FLN, like true Sand Niggers of the desert, materialized in a cloud of nauseating particles: the filthy *burnous* (long cloak of coarse wollen fabric with a hood) were already there: the Muslim cocksuckers were waiting their turn! The French soldiers had abandoned us... And there wasn't any fuckin' *"Vive la France"* intone that could have saved us from the Muslim vultures!

While I deliberated with my inner self, who used to rebel often, too, I caught a violent hit from behind the head... After, it was the turn of another bad smelling evil son of a bitch to hit me in the ribs! They were using old single-shot rifles of the First World War era, obsolete for shooting, but well balanced for croquet, cricket, or to fix tent pegs in the rocks of the *djebels.*

My head took the lead on the rest of my body and veered to the ground; my eyelids drooped and flinched for a moment; then my eyes rolled over as if to watch the assailants banging furiously from behind... And the rest of the body followed.

Gravity, I thought.

Afterwards, as if I were at the end of a long tunnel, I heard the muffled sound of torn stuffs that must have been shirts... Buttons were tingling on the terrazzo... Detonations sounded... Bodies slumped... And then... Nothing! It was the calm after the storm. Total! The silence of the deaf, but without the exasperating buzzing noise in the ears...

It was very similar to taking the big dirt nap, I thought, even though I didn't exactly know what dying entailed, because everything that I had learned during my three long years of service to the Foreign Legion was how to give it to others.

10

When I opened my eyes, there were four whitish walls that seemed to capsize on a sea of cement: four walls that dragged me into a dizzying farandole! I immediately recongnized where I was: one of the cells of the central police station of the sub-prefecture of Bône. And my ribs, reshaped by Arab boots, immediately called me to order. Motherfuckers! ... I was aching all-fuckin'-over; I hadn't died with my boots on in Little Bighorn with colonel Mustard, with the revolver, in the ballroom... But I, too, was ready to face the music!

I looked around and saw Ricco, one of the best sharp shooter in the garrison... His mouth was partially toothless, swollen and about to explode, with an almost closed eye that sketched a funny wink: he looked like these boxers a couple of hours after a twelve-round fight for the title!

"*Ric... co! Et? Les autres?* (Ric... co! And? ... The others?)"

I had articulated my best, despite the feeling of having a good dozen peppermint candies in my mouth, and, after having self-examined my dolorous ribcage, I waited in vain for my sniper's response... Who didn't give a shit about anything, now.

He didn't answer, escaping a long groan in his nauseating corner: the jail cell smelled of shit.

I tapped the pocket of my shirt, found my lighter, and lit a cigarette. I had sketched this gesture as a doped automaton lacking drugs... And a cloud of confusion had already enveloped me when the lock of the door cell began to moan.

Then, an Arab officer wearing a little bowler hat as black as death landed in the cell, immediately followed by two filthy *Ratagaz*.

I immediately laughed at seeing them enter... The two assholes of the desert... Real puppets! They held in their hands long curved daggers with coagulated blood on them... If they wanted to impress me, they had missed their fuckin' number, the bastards of *djebel!* ... Fellagha motherfuckers! ... It was a real fuckin' joke, this staging of clowns! ... And? ... Where did they get these two cocksuckers, anyway?

While I was laughing, I had not been able to stop myself even if it really hurt just to breath, the Fellagha in chief beat the fumes in which I comforted myself, and my face a little, too, and after two or three slaps in the face, I immediately returned to a better frame of mind.

I thought, for a moment, to try something and escape. With surprise on my side, maybe I had a chance to succeed? ... But in the pitiful state that I was, I could have perhaps, at best, steal the dagger of the one of the *Djounouds* and make him eat it for breakfast. But three goons! ... It was more than I could handle.

So, I looked at Ricco's side... But he declined my invitation with a discreet shake of the head: I wasn't fuckin' going anywhere, wasn't I?

I then relaxed my sore muscles. Well! ... If these gentlemen want to come forward and ruff me up... Let's get the show on the road, motherfuckers!

And I had no choice but to bite the bullet...

The black hat dude immediately began to interrogate me in Arabic. He questioned me with numerous pats with the back of the hand. I thought that he had learned, just like me, to communicate by sign with the deaf-mutes... But as I was already hurting everywhere, he couldn't have made me suffer much more than at this very moment, unless the cocksucker decited to cut my balls off and make me eat my dick in pita bread with lettuce, green onions and harissa!

Fuck me! ... There! ... I must admit that this wasn't a very good thought on my part.

The Fellagha told me that I had to convert to Islam, like all these Christian infidels who were born on Algerian soil... Child of Allah... The prophet Mo Ahmed had said... And yak, yak, yak! "You will not save your'self unless you submit, my brother", repeated the Arab officer with a heavy accent that seemed to come from Pakistan. Because there were a lot of fuckin' Paki motherfuckers who came to Algeria to support the war effort for the independence of their Muslim brothers... With trucks filled with AK-47!

- Yo, Bro! ... Islam'a bad, man... Vely, vely bad for you, my fliend!

I had tried to imitate his Paki accent!

Paf! Pif! Paf!

Okay! ... Okay! Maybe it wasn't my best effort!

The cocksucker was furious... And he banged me to a pulp. Under the force of the blows, I was thrown head first against a wall and ended up thinking that I, too, had a natural predisposition to swelling just like my friend Ricco.

- Is that all you got? ... Because you really hit like a fuckin' schoolgirl, motherfucker!

The Muslim interrogator looked at me, puzzled... And then he strarted laughing... A crazy laugh. After wiping out is tears, he advised me to think about it... Seriously. To sleep on the question, that is! He would come back at dawn to see if I had changed my mind about the conversion, otherwise... No need to draw me a picture: I was going to be executed.

"Hum!... Et c'est dans combien de temps, au juste, l'aube?" (Umm! ... And how long is it exactly before dawn?)" That I asked him.

I couldn't tell time because a bastard Muslim cocksucker had stolen my American watch when they caught me.

For any answer, I got another slap...

And my torturer came out of the cell with his two *djounouds* friends with curved blades. Fuckin' cocksuckin' Muslim sons of a bitch... They couldn't even make a strait blade, the assholes!

While we were languishing in our little cell, a prison gard was patrolling the corridor and clanging his key ring against the door, as he passed... They wanted to show us that they were still taking care of us, I thought. The guard, from time to time, was observing through the peephole the political prisoners that we were, and gradually, I managed to regain my senses...

Leaning against the wall, I pulled out another cig... The future is bleak... A few meters in a corridor... Then a flight of stairs... And the hangman's noose... Or the wooden block of the headsmans... Or the firing squad... The face covered with a hood... One wouldn't want to flinch and really ruined the execution...

Just gimme the fuckin' condemned man's cigarette and be done with it... Mothefuckers!

I took two or three successive puffs, lost in my thoughts, and once my lungs satisfied, I passed the cigarette to Ricco, who was still ruminating in his corner... And I understood that, this time, the shit really hit the fan.

11

I got up to take a sip of water, bathwater with the scent of army latrines that I had swallowed more to quiet down my anxiety than my thirst, and when I had finished, steps approached in the corridor... Fuck me man! ... Already? And I immediately prepared myself for another session of questions and answers with fists on the mouth... Islam 101 crash course!

The door's rusty hinges creaked... I raised my head just to see who was coming in, so I could prepare myself, mentally, for what was coming to me, but it wasn't my torturer who entered. I quickly recognized the dude who passed through the opening; in another life, we had gone to the same little rundown shit school and lived in the same rotten streets of the Arab quarter: his name was Mohamed, like the prophet...

They all were a bunch of fuckin' Mohameds!

I had already done something for him, in time, during a night patrol. He had been taken after curfew in the streets of the Élysa district, and it could have cost him dearly, his folly night out to join his wife-to-be, because there were Muslims who were eliminated for much less than that! But as we had been childhood friends, I had let him go without my troupe doing him any harm.

"*Mon frère!... Ils vont venir te chercher à l'aube... Tu es sur leur liste noire!* (My brother! ... The Arab whispered. They'll come and take you at dawn... You're on their blacklist!)"

Next, through the gaping opening, he looked behind him... He looked afraid.

"*Ils vont te tuer! Le Colonel de la Naya 1 a déjà été averti de ta capture... Il a déjà signé l'ordre pour ton exécution!* (They will kill you! The Colonel of Naya 1 has already been warned of your capture... He has already signed the order for your execution!)"

My exe-fucken'-cution? ... Fuck me harder, Mo!

- *Tu me laisses sortir, Mohamed?... Tu ne vas pas les laisser faire ça, non?* (You'll let me out, Mohamed? ... You're not going to let them do that to me, right?)

I had implored him! And despite my pride, I was not ashamed of it. Not anymore! Because I had felt that he wanted to help me.

"*J'ai déjà fait quelque chose pour toi, Mohamed... Tu ne l'as pas oublié, hein? On était des amis, autrefois! Tu pourrais me renvoyer l'ascenseur... Je ne suis pas ton ennemi, tu le sais bien.* (I have already done something for you, Mohamed... You have not forgotten it, huh? We once were friends! You could give something back... I'm not your enemy and you know it.)"

- *La guerre est finie... Et on l'a gagnée. On a notre pays à nous... Ça donnerait quoi de les laisser te tuer, maintenant?* (The war is over... And we have won it. We have our own country... What good would it do to let them kill you, now?)

- *Alors? Laisse-moi foutre le camp d'ici... Mohamed?* (So? ... Let me get the hell out of here... Mohamed?)

The Fellagha seemed to think about all of this, as if he weighed the pros and cons of his clemency towards me... for him and for his family! ... Fear of reprisals? ... Surely!

For my part, I was expecting to see my life scroll by fast if he ever told me no.

- *Voici ce que je vais faire, Jo... Je vais refermer la porte, sans tourner la clé dans la serrure. Attends encore une bonne heure pour qu'ils ne se doutent pas que c'est moi qui t'ai laissé sortir... Ensuite, tu vas tout droit et tu prends à gauche. Au bout du couloir, il y a une grille de fer, à l'arrière, et je la laisserai déverrouillée pour toi... Tu sortiras par-là! Personne ne monte la garde de ce côté... C'est tout ce que je peux faire pour toi, mon frère!... On ne se doit plus rien, maintenant... Inch Allah!* (Here's what I can do, Jo... I'll close the door without turning the key in the lock. Wait a good hour, so they don't suspect that I let you out... Then, you go straight and you take a left. At the end of the corridor there is an iron gate and I'll leave it unlocked for you... You'll get out that way! No one stands on guard to that side. That's all I can do for you, my brother! ... I do not owe you anything anymore... *Inch Allah!*)

- *Choukran jazilan... Merci, Mohamed!... Oui! On est quitte pour toujours... Inch Allah!* (Thank you, Mohamed! ... Yes! We're even... forever! ... God be with you!)

The revolutionary gard made me the sign that the Arabs do to greet each other. Then, he turned on his heels, without saying anything more, and he closed the heavy door behind him.

I heard the keys clash against the wall... Shit! ... Would Mohamed keep his word?

I waited a few more seconds, and then, without making a sound, I went to check the door. I was a little short of breath and eager, because if he had changed his mind... I was Kentucky fried!

I exerted a slight pressure on the metal... The steel didn't move a millimeter... Fuck me man!

I tried again and pushed harder: the door opened. Phew!

I closed it back with a heart full of hope, but immediately after, thinking of the watchman, I got a little concerned... Let's hope no one comes to see us before dawn, I had implored the gods!

I looked in the direction of my cellmate, but he seemed to be half dead in his corner, pondering. And I whispered to him:

"*T'as compris, Ricco? On va pouvoir s'échapper! Ricco! Mais secoue-toi, bon sang de merde!* (Did you understand, Ricco? We'll be able to escape! ... Ricco! Shake it, man... Damn you!)"

I took him by the shoulders to shake'n baked him a little... To try to make him listen to reason!

- *C'est foutu pour nous, Sergent... Foutu! Ils vont nous faire la peau dès qu'on va essayer de sortir... C'est tout vu! Ils vont se justifier auprès des autorités françaises en disant qu'on avait essayé de s'évader... Y a rien à faire, Jo. On est condamnés!* (We're fucked, Sergeant... Fucked! They'll do us as soon as we try to get out... There's nothing to talk about! ... They'll justify themselves to the French authorities by saying that we tried to escape... There's no two ways about it, Jo... We're really fucked!)

- *Ouais! Peut-être bien que oui... Mais mourir pour mourir, j'aime autant morfler en essayant de m'évader!* (Yeah! Maybe you're right... But, if I'm gonna die, anyway, I'd rather croak trying to escape!)

Ricco plunged his head in his knees as a sign of abandonment... Or maybe he was praying? I donno? ... I waited a moment longer; the seconds passed, slowly... Subsequently, I began to count in my head, because I had no watch and it was impossible for me to measure the time that went by: one steamboat, two steamboats, and three steamboats...

The more time passed, the more my heart bumped hard in my chest. And finally, exacerbated by an interminable wait, I got up and I bridged the distance that separated me from my friend... Maybe he was going to change his mind, this time?

"*Faut foutre le camp d'ici, bordel! Viens, Ricco! Et tout de suite!... C'est un ordre, soldat... Exécution!* (We must get out of here, for fuck's sake! Come on, Ricco! And right now! ... It is an order, soldier... Execution!)"

And I shook him like a fucken' olive tree as to make the fruit fall down to the ground.

- *Non! C'est foutu!... C'est foutu, Sergent. Bonne chance, Sergent... Buona fortuna!* (No! We're screwed! ... We're screwed, Sergeant, had cried Ricco. Good luck to you, Sergeant... *Buona fortuna!* [Good luck!])

- *Ouais! Toi aussi mon gars!... Toi aussi!* (Yeah! You too, my friend! ... You too!

And I left, alone...

I felt a little guilty to abandon Ricco, because I had not convinced him to, at least, try to get out of jail.

I wasn't such a great leader of men, after all...

I went to the door and listened... Nothing! No noise coming from the corridor. So, with a hopeful heart, I pushed on the armored door... Slowly, but with all my weight behind the steel plate, and by an opening just big enough for a man of my size, I escaped my jail cell on tiptoe.

I made a few meters in the narrow corridor, and then, stopping on a dime, my senses on alert, I paid attention to the sounds of the prison... Nothing! All I could hear, when I listened, was the sound of my heartbeat: it banged my eardrums like an engine about to explode. I got scared and started to quiver... Because for a second, I had thought that the noise from my *patato* would alert the prison guards!

But, as nothing seemed to have disturbed them, I went back to close the door of my cell so that everything seemed normal. Afterwards, a few meters away, I walked along the walls of the corridor leading to my freedom. I crossed three other cells on the way, and then I reached the rear gate; I was hoping that the screened door would not be locked, as Mohamed had promised me before. Otherwise... I was caught like a rat in a trap!

Glimmers blushed the horizon... Already, the first rays of this fateful morning of July were trying to lift the opaque lid that still weighed on the new Algeria of the Arabs, but I, like more than a million Pieds-Noirs, had lost mine. And there are things like the loss of one's country that a man can never get used to and... But there was no time to think about that!

I was there like an idiot wasting precious time; I scanned through the bars without daring to push on the fenced door, like the convict who discovers that, during all these years of incarceration, the door had never been locked and that he could have gone out when he wanted... I hesitated.

Outside, it was neither night nor day, but it was already very hot... Go! Enough time wasted, Jo... Go! ... Go for it, for Christ's sake!

And I went for it... I ran like the madman who still believes in his chances of survival and wants to take another bite at life. I dashed down and never looked back... Racing 'till I ran out of breath... I was looking for a way out of the city... I was wandering between two worlds that did not want of me anymore... Zigzagging and ondulating under the dark facades...

Hiding behind the palm trees... Avoiding Fellagha sentinels... These patrolers of a newly acquired freedom at the expense of mine! ... I felt their presence... They were there... Hidden... Lying in the darkness... Waiting... They wanted to kill me!

I galloped like a devil with his ass on fire and passed behind Caserne Yusuf, went down to the base of the Casbah hillock fearing to be gunned down at the corner of a crossroads, fatally hit by a bullet on the fly... And, almost relieved to have escaped the worst, I quickly reached the commercial train station of Bône without being spotted.

I hid under the wagons abandoned by the French; I was going to be lurking in the shadows of the cars, trying to see how I could escape it all... Wait for my chance.

Around the little railway office building, French berets were parked here and there like cattles waiting for some sort of strategic retreat, with sentinels guarding the quays. Patrols of reconnaissance passed by without seeing me, and all these army guys were waiting for other French soldiers, who had to come back from the interior of the country by train, before setting sail with the hope of making a final cross on French Algeria. They were now neutral and impassive on this soil hostile to the Pieds-Noirs, as stipulated in the conditions of surrender at the hands of the *victorious* FLN.

I was caught between two fires: on one side was the glorious army of General de Gaulle, who controlled the train station and had orders to fire on everything that moved; on the other were Fellaghas imbued with freedom patrolling the city and the surroundings of the port.

I didn't know how I was going to get out of that one, alive!

In the distance, an old liner was preparing to leave the pier, and it was at that moment that I began to think of my family: they must have been on the big ship. I knew that it wasn't the moment to worry one's head, that it wasn't the time to be discouraged and that every second of waiting could be fatal to me... But it was stronger than me!

I saw the big transatlantic that was about to abandon the wharf with what I had most precious in the world, and I thought of my proud Dad, that good old Peppé who had arrived at Bône a young teenager with only the richness of the contents of his pockets: a penknife that his father had left him for all inheritance; of Mémé, my adoptive mother, who had married my father a few years after *maman* died; of my sister Anna Maria, who was barely four years old and the fruit of my father's second union; of my brother Vincenzo and *Tia* (Aunt) Francesca, who had crossed the access footbridge with dad; and of Ariane who now was my wife and in charge of the little personal effects we'd accumulated together in the last weeks...

Then, escaping a last complaint, the siren of the ship seemed to give up it's soul, and at the same time the crew dropped the moorings.

The merchant seamen had a lot to do in the sea of passengers who were fussing on deck, overloaded, and as the liner was leaving the port, the short-winded ship attempted to clear the wharf with extreme difficuty... All the weight of the Pieds-Noirs nation on board must have slowed it down! The ocean liner was going along the coast at snail's pace and was trying to escape the high tide, which too, seemed to have chosen the Fellagha's camp and held the ship in the basin...

There's my chance, I thought!

I had spotted the position of the sentries at the station, established the route of the French patrols, and, bent in two, I crossed the yard with the assurance of a paratrooper during a final suicide mission. I crawled, when I had to, or stopped dead to make myself invisible to the new ennemy of the Pieds-Noirs: the Frenchman in beret! I wanted to join the crowded tub of passengers who was slowly going away to the open sea...

What a crazy fucken' idea! But the frills of foam carved by the propellers indicated the course to follow. So, I decided to try my luck. I didn't have much choice: what did I have to lose, trying?

I arrived at the pier, unnoticed. Then, I slipped along the rough wall, almost under the nose of the Fellagha vigils, which were busy smoking kif to pass time. Lost in their reverie, their finger on the trigger of their AK's, the Fells watched the cruise ship approach the jetty in slo-mo. The liner was closing in along side the breakwater before finally rush out to open sea.

Then, their call to prayer echoed throughout the city... I had never been so fuckin' happy to hear their Eden caller in all of my life, and the majority of the Fellaghas present at the warf turned in the direction of their beloved Mecca to pray... A bunch of fuckin' carpet crawlers!

While they were busy with their God, I took the opportunity to pass between men of faction spaced by about fifty meters, and subsequently, I dropped into the water; a dip of about two meters: plouchhh!

Alerted by the suspicious noises, a fish that had made a jump out of the water? ... A Fell roused the whole troop:

"Yallah! Yallah!" Shouted the Fellagha.

The next moment, most of the Fells abandoned the Morning Prayer to begin shooting in the sea with their Kalashnikov... To the great displeasure of Allah who, I suppose, was not going to be enchanted with the interrupted ritual. Just keep on praying, you fuckin' Muslim cocksukers... Will ya!

In the beginning was Water... And since I had long ago broken the sacred fluids in my mother's womb, when I came into being in North Africa, it almost made sense to get out of Algeria and escape death swimming... I had already done it once, motherfuckers! ... I sure could do it again.

And I swam as long as I could under water...

The quiet marine remained impassive in the face of the deadly battle that was taking place in its vast domain, but it allowed itself to be assailed by the victorious breaststrokes of the skilful swimmer that I had become over the years; and by the bullets of my Muslim brothers... The ones I had gone to school with in the Arab district!

My lungs were going to burst, when I came back up, in extremis... I had only taken one good breath before going under again... I moved through the wave like a gold medalist at the Olympic pool, while the Fellaghas kept firing away with their automatic weapons in the opaque immensity, temporarily protective like the waters of a mother for his son... And with all my strength, I stirred the salty water with the fear of not being able to swim fast enough... I wanted to reach the Transmediterranean... The ship was going to set sail towards the open sea and pass in front of me... Abandoning me in the Algerian waters forever... Continue its course to Marseilles without me!

On the banks, the AK's of the religious fanatics were rendered silent, the tiny moving target that I was being now out of reach of their bullets, except perhaps with the rifle of a sniper. Now, their only wishes was that I wouldn't reach the ship in time and drown... Or they would finish me off with paddles in a rowing boat.

I finally came within five meters of the huge steel frame; I had arrived just in time, out of breath: the letters Sidi Okba were encrusted on its rust. I had stopped my progression, slowed to a crawl... Then, I wondered how I was going to get on board, the hull of the ship being uniformly smooth and impossible to attack with bare hands. In addition, there were the propeller blades that could suck me in if I ever approached the stern of the sea monster too close and drag me by suction to a horrible death... I didn't want to be *chop sueyed!*

And that's when the miracle happened...

Almost at the waterline of the sea ship, a kitchen Negro opened a small wicket door and began to pour table scraps and other kitchen waste into the sea... Seeing the bloody residues all around, I told myself that, if there were no marine predators in the area, there was going to be a gathering very soon to deal with the feast... And with me! So, I had to hurry up... And while I was trying to get the attention of the guy working in the galley, I thought about what my uncle Vito always said, when barracudas were attacking the sponge fishermen of Catellammare del Golfo, in Sicily: "... *Non tentare mai di nuotare più veloce di una scuola di barracuda, perché era impossibile seminare questi abili cacciatori di mare... Dovrebbe piuttosto nuotare solo un po 'più veloce dei suoi compagni di immersioni!* (... That you should never try to swim faster than a school of barracudas, because it was impossible to elude these skilful sea hunters... One should rather try to swim just a little faster than his diving companions!)"

Except that I was alone in the sea!

When the African finally saw me, his eyes opened wide with amazement, and for a moment he hesitated, not knowing how to react. But as he must have had a good heart, he extended a helping hand to the exhausted swimmer who was imploring him, stretching his arm through the gaping hatch...

The doorway that led to salvation!

I filled the gap that separated me from the opening and I managed to get on board... I was saved!

"*Faut que tu 'estes caché dans la cale... Sinon le pat'uon va me faire des p'oblèmes* (You must 'emain hidden in the hold... Othe'wise the *pat'uon* (chief) wy make me p'oblems)", had explained the employee assigned to shit labour.

- *Me... Merci! Merci de... tout... que... cœur! Tu... Tu m'as sau... vé... sauvé la vie! Je... ja... jamais... je ne... l'oublierai!* (Thank you! Thank you for... everything... from the... heart! I had managed to say, between two breaths... You... you saved me... saved my life! I... will... never... I will never... forget it!)

The black dude immediately found me a hideout; it was a dark corner of the hold, not far from the galley. For all wealth, I had only my pants, stockings and a t-shirt with cigarettes and a gas lighter in the pocket!

The Cameroonian came back later to bring me food and drink: I thanked him sincerely. And I was sorry I had nothing to offer him as monetary compensation for his efforts... for saving my life! And I gave him the lighter; the silver lighter Ariane had bought me the day we got engaged, in Bône.

I, who had the reputation of being a racist, a heartless man and a serial killer because I had slaughtered more than a hundred Muslims and pretty much everything that had once walked, crawled or flown in God's creation, I now owed my life to two Africans: an Muslim with whom I had been to elementary school in the Arab district, and a kitchen Negro from Senegal!

When I was finally able to look through the circular porthole of my greasy recess, I could not distinguish the details of the street or the animation on the harbor where there were still many thousand Pieds-Noirs... Bône the elegant was slowly moving further away from view. Now, only its virginal whiteness and the ocher tones of its clay roof tiles were still visible...

Later, while the ship was steaming away at full speed, there would only be the distant lands from where the last Algerian coasts would blend with the landscape; and after that... Nothing! Only the azure of the sea that drowns everything as my heart was capsizing in the blue like a ship without a flag thrown into turmoil.

I was now a man without home or country...

Sadness brought tears to my eyes. My cheeks got wet. I, who swore never to cry again after the death of my mother, I sobbed; I was only a kid when I made that promise at the edge of her grave, just before the traditional earthen handle on her pine coffin... But now she would remain alone forever in her little plot at the cemetery, abandoned with relatives and friends who had fallen to the hands of the evil Muslim devil.

Not only was I giving up the country that had seen me born, I was also abandoning my deads forever...

12

The next morning, the ship arrived in the port of Marseilles. I had spent a whole night in the hold fighting bilge rats and bedbugs; I had neither passport nor identification papers on me, and it was impossible for me to mingle with other passengers or to go out by the bridge with them... I was fucked!

"*Mosieu!... Mosieu! Moi, pas connaît'e toi!* (Miste'! Miste'! I, not know you!)" Said the Negro.

He was going to turn his heels, because a fat grimy voice called him from the back of the kitchen: "*Où c'est qu'il est ce putain de Nègre?... Fainéant, va!* (Where the fuck is that asshole Niggar? ... Lazy bastard!)" Had shouted the knucklehead cook.

- *J'a'ive chef!... J'a'ive!* (Comin' Chef! ... Comin'!)

And I only had time to exchange a very brief handshake with the Black man, a short moment of life to show my eternal gratitude to this guy I didn't know... But who had saved my life!

While his eternal bondage still called him, I said:

"*Merci!... Du fond du cœur, merci!* (Thank you! ... From the bottom of my heart, thank you!)" And I waited in my filthy corner for the passengers to get off the ship...

I finally risked a clandestine exit and sneaked to the third-class passengers' deck, ready to knock out the first comer who would dare try to stop me... But there wasn't anybody home! On the quays, by the thousands, the Pieds-Noirs jostled each other on the pier. Many were looking for a relative, a friend, a husband, in the animation of end of colonial regime that reigned over the overflowing port of Marseilles. Other ocean steamers coming from Algiers, Mers-el-Kebir or Tenes were stowed there... A continual stream of passengers swept in random order the overwhelmed CRS (*Compagnies Républicaines de Sécurité* - French national police -), which tried to control the tens of thousands of Algerian refugees lashing out commands:

"*Restez dans le rang!* (Stay in line!)"

The government staffers were left with their head spinning so the Algerian sea was oppressive. An incredible rumor was coming up to me... Huge Pieds-Noirs waves were beating against the hull, and among this maddening crowd of people, there might have been my family! Somewhere? ... Drowned in that ocean of heads and shoulders that seemed to float like buoys in the ocean. And in vain I sought, in this disheveled sea, the little brunette with curly hair who had said "yes" to me for life... Ariane!

I crossed the bridge without further delay and I headed rapidly towards the stern. Then, I grabbed a big cable, which served as a mooring line to the floating monster, and I descended with the feet and hands wrapped around the big leash of hemp, like a tightrope sailor who goes down for a shore leave without permission to come ashore. I dropped on the neck of Quai de la Joliette, and, immediately on land, I stayed hidden in a dim corner until dusk... I waited my time in the dark, in the black which wrenches us out of hellfire and damnation, for "*il n'y a que dans l'ombre qu'un légionnaire y voit vraiment clair* (it's only in darkness that a legionary sees really clearly)", used to say my captain of the 1st REP, when we waited for the ennemy to come to us at night, embushed.

The sun had been falling for a long time, when I ventured onto the harbor. The quay was almost deserted, but there was a peculiar man who was strolling near the deserted steamers... He was a Tunisian who said he came from Bizerte.

"*Je viens de me sauver d'un bateau et je cherche ma famille... Pouvez-vous m'aider?* (I just escaped from a boat and I'm looking for my family... Can you help me?)" I had asked the onlooker, naively.

- *Comment ça, vous ne trouvez personne?* (How is that, you can't find anyone?) Had replied the Muslim.

He had taken a step back, as if I had transformed into a homeless man. But I have to say for his defense that I didn't have much on my back... And that I could have indeed been considered a tramp. I explained to him my story without going into all the sordid details, that I had escaped from a ship that had brought me here, and that I was looking for my family...

- *On va rester ensemble* (We'll stay together), had proposed the Arab.

He seemed to think that someone would come looking for me, that I had just lost my way like a real country yokel coming out of the boat on his first trip away from home.

He was walking step for step with me, and then he added:

"*Si t'as pas où aller, on verra! Reste avec moi, car je dois retrouver ma famille, moi aussi...* (If you don't have anywhere to go, we'll see about that later! ... Stay with me, because I also have to find my family, too...)"

But without papers, and with no money, I couldn't go anywhere; no reception service for immigrant, no possibility of leaving the port and pass by the check point... Unless I tried swimming!

I had been walking with the Muslim brother for a few minutes, only, when I saw from afar a guy who looked strangely like one of my brothers-in-law. I rubbed my eyes to make sure that it was not a vision and that I didn't imagine this in-law materialized right in front of me...

"*Rémy!... Par ici!* (Rémy! ... I'm here!) I shouted, glad to find someone I knew.

It was really Rémy! ... Ariane's brother... He was walking towards me, hopping and shouting his joy at finding me, and, since he was not a fool, he had thought that I would try to cross clandestinely. And as eighty percent of the boats leaving Algeria were to arrive here in Marseilles...

- *Viens! Dans mes bras, qu'on s'embrasse!* (Come! In my arms... let's kiss!)

After a very long hug and strong pats on the back, Rémy went back quickly to his appartment to get some ID papers my wife Ariane had surely brought back, because I had nothing on me and could'nt get out of the port, legally. I smoked the cigarettes he had given me to kill time, and then Rémy came back and took me to his place... I waved and old army identification *carnet* (Army ID booklet) at the checkpoint as the tired guard barely looked at the papers, nodding, when I went thru.

When she saw me enter with her brother, Ariane almost tore my head off... Peppé and Mémé wept with joy. Little Anna Maria, who didn't quite understand what was happening because of her young age, jumped on me. She had grabbed one of my legs and let herself be dragged around the appartment. My brother Vincent decided to play a freshly improvised saxophone piece in my honor... But the whole family fled to another room!

Tia Francesca was calling on us to pray with her the Rosary and to do penance, on the knees, as a *thank you* for her answered prayers. But I had preferred to let her peel rosaries alone and drink a good liter of pastis with the men, while the Auntie threatened the audience of excommunication. But by dint of being threatened with explusion, and on some occasions more than once, one ends up fearing nothing at all... Not even the wrath of the Church.

After a good night spent with my family, I went to the prefecture with an old birth certificate, my military booklet, and a second set of identity papers. The dates on the documents had expired, but Ariane had kept them, just in case.

It was better than nothing...

"*Cher Monsieur* (Dear Sir,)" the official had said, flipping through my documents except those that testified to my entry into the country, "*Comment êtes-vous arrivés ici?* (How did you get here?)"

I was tempted to say: *swimming!* But I stopped myself just in time. Besides, he would never have believed me...

"*Je suis arrivé sur le Sidi Okba* (I arrived on the Sidi Okba)," I said.

I did not want to make too many waves, because among these officials there were crooked ones in the lot. I was just hoping he didn't get in too deeply into my cover story...

- *Avec qui?* (With whom?) Asked the administrator, with a suspicious eye.

- *Avec qui, quoi, Monsieur?* (With whom, what, Sir?)

- *Bon sang! Mais avec qui êtes-vous arrivé à Marseille, voyons?* (Damn it! But with whom did you come to Marseilles? ... Don't you understand?)

- *Hé! Bien... Mais avec ma famille, pardieu!* (Well! ... But with my family, by God!)

- *Eeeet... Pourquoi n'étiez-vous pas là, hier?* (Annnd... Why weren't you here yesterday?)

- *Heu!... C'est parce qu'hier, je... Heu! Je n'ai pas pu être là... Voilà! J'attendais ma grand-mère! On l'avait perdu de vue, vous savez?... Avec tous ces gens qu'il y avait sur les quais... Elle est malade du coeur, vous comprenez!... Et comme c'est moi qui avais été chargé d'aller à sa recherche...* (Huh! ... It's because... yesterday, I... Huh! I could not be here... That's all! I was waiting for my grandmother! We had lost sight of her, you know? ... With all those people on the quay... She has a sickness of the heart, you understand! ... And since it was I who had been charged to go looking for her...

- *... Bon! Bon!* (... Good! Good!) Had snapped the official, chewing the tip of his pencil.

He didn't believe a single word of what he had heard... But since there were hundreds of Pieds-Noirs refugees clinging to his windows, he quickly stamped the various documents. Then, after handing me the papers, he sent me to the next department, incredulous...

"*Au suivant!* (Next!)"

13

When we, the Pieds-Noirs refugees, landed on the Quai de la Joliette, it was total indifference! We were Frenchmen completely foreign to our motherland, France, and the Marseillais never stopped showing their hostility towards us:

"*Pieds-Noirs, retournez chez vous!* (Pieds-Noirs... go back home!) Were they throwing at us, from everywhere.

It had even been written in giant letters in the city to better humiliate us. We were called "*putain de colonialistes!* (fuckin' colonialists!) *Racistes!* (Racists!) *Bandits!"*

But nobody had yet dared call me a killer...

"*Que les Pieds-Noirs aillent se réadapter ailleurs!* (Let the Pieds-Noirs rehabilate themselfes elsewhere!) They said to us, when we were looking for work in the city. But these same Marseillais had a short memory, since they had forgotten that they had acclaimed us, particularly those of the third Algerian Infantry Division, we, who delivered them from the Nazis in August 1944!

Nothing had been planned for our housing, in Marseilles or in the surrounding area, and our family had to pile up in disgusting dwellings. After that, it was in apartments in ruins. But other Pieds-Noirs, unluckier than we were, had to spend the night in hotel halls or even on sidewalks like vulgar tramps. These exiles dragged for the most part a suitcase and some knapsacks... It was all their fortune that they were dragging with them.

Before leaving Algeria, many of my Bônois compatriots had destroyed by fire the relics of several generations... To leave nothing in the hands of Fellaghas! After the assassination of Uncle Nino, just before leaving the country that had seen me born, I had been with friends to burn his house, his barn and his little cheese factory: the few Fellaghas who had taken possession of his domain had been cremated alive in memory of my *tio!*

My father and I had a lot of trouble finding work in and around Marseilles, despite our qualifications and especially Peppé's expertise: an urban infrastructure foreman who had already had several thousand workers at his charge. But as we were treated as slave traders and racists, we were not welcomed on any construction sites, and when I felt discouraged and seemed ready to sink into violence to assert my right to French culture, Peppé always said to me: "*Fiston, n'oublie pas ce que tu es... Ça évitera aux autres de te le rappeler tout le temps!* (Son, do not forget what you are... It will prevent others from reminding you all the time!)"

Yeah! Really good advice, Dad! ... Except that my problem was that, precisely, I didn't know who I was, anymore! ... I was neither an Algerian, nor a Frenchman, nor a Sicilian... I was something else: a countryless Pieds-Noirs with a passport from France!

And then one day, about two weeks after my arrival in Marseilles, an OAS activist contacted me... I never knew how the fuck he managed to find me, but he did in fact do it. I was at the Grand Hotel Mediterranean. I was very quiet with an anisette on the terrace, waiting for my brothers-in-law who were to join me and have a couple of drink, when a guy in a suit came to sit at my table. The dude said to me:

"*Salut! Sergent... Dis donc, ça fait une paye, mon vieux!... Je peux m'assoir un instant?* (Hi! Sergeant... It's been a while, old friend! ... Can I sit for a moment?)"

I didn't even have time to open my mouth that he had already sat in front of me. I had met Lieutenant Max on a few occasions while I was collaborating with the Deuxième Bureau (like England's MI5) in Tlemcen. The guy was working with French Intelligence and had heard of me through my captain of the 1st REP, then from a senior officer of the Air Force who worked under the command of Lieutenant Colonel Bastien-Thiry. Max then approached me in Bône, in 1962, for a special mission on behalf of the OAS: the slaying of a political Fellagha leader... He was looking, at the time, for an experienced sniper, a guy who wasn't afraid of anything, to bump off a high-ranking *Djounoud* in the fellagha hierarchy. The mark, an important Muslim, was rocking the boat and was pissing off almost everyone: a shot in the head of 300 meters in the city of Algiers and the problem had been resolved quickly!

- *Salut Max... Putain! Mais qu'est-ce que tu fous ici?* (Hi Max... What the fuck! ... What's you're doin' here, man?)

When we shook hands, I was still lost in my memories of previous missions... And I suspected the reason of his visit, because I had already worked for him in the past.

Max quickly explained to me that he was looking for a volunteer for a very special job in French territory, and since I had not found work, yet, he thought that it might interest me to do some *special labour* for him.

- *J'ai besoin d'un tireur expérimenté... Un gars à la hauteur, comme toi. Et de nos jours, un gars à la hauteur, c'est rare comme une pute qui travaille à son compte à Marseille!* (I need an experienced sharp shooter... A guy right up there, like you. And nowadays, a competent marksman is as rare as a self-employed whore in Marseilles!)

As I was actively looking for work, but not exactly in this highly specialized branch, I decided to listen to him. Who knows? ... What the fuck had I have to lose by listening?

- *Et c'est quoi, ce travail? Ça paye combien?... C'est où?* (And what's the job? How much does it pay? ... Where does it take place?)

- *Ho! Ho! Mais y a pas de presse, Sergent! Avant tout, est-ce qu'on peut toujours compter sur ta discrétion et ton implication pour la cause? ... Garçon! Deux autres Ricard par ici!* (Ho! Ho! But there is no hurry, Sergeant! Above all, can we still count on your discretion and your implication for the cause? ... Waiter! Two more Ricard, overhere!)

The attendant nodded, while I continued the casual chitchat.

- La cause?... Mais quelle cause? Mais y a plus de cause, bordel!... Depuis qu'on a perdu notre Algérie! (The cause? ... But what cause, for fuck's sake? But there's no more cause, for crying out loud! ... Since we lost our Algeria!)

- Ouais! Tu as raison. Tu as bien raison, Sergent... Et que dirais-tu de dégommer le grand responsable de cette débâcle? Veux-tu venger tes compatriotes pieds-noirs, oui ou non? (Yeah! You're right. You're maybe right, Sergeant... But what would you say about taking out the real person responsible of this debacle? ... Don't you want to avenge your Pieds-Noirs compatriots, yes or no?)

Max spoke of general de Gaulle... The Great General of all Gauls! The bastard who gave our country to the Djounouds!

The OAS had already tried to liquidate him in the past, and more than once, but without success. And on top of that, I would have taken care of him for free, that bastard generalissimo! But it was already too late to save our Algeria... We had already lost!

- C'est quoi ton plan, au juste? (What's your plan, exactly?)

Max bridged the distance that separated us, and told me:

- Je peux compter sur toi?... C'est une mission top secret! (Can I count on you? ... It's a top-secret mission!)

I nodded.

- Ouais! Ouais! Va-y... Déballe-moi ton opération. (Yeah! Yeah! Go ahead... You can tell me all about the operation.

- C'est un commando de 12 hommes avec fusils mitrailleurs, des explosifs et 4 véhicules... On prend le convoi sous un feu croisé, juste avant un rond-point menant à l'aéroport: Opération Charlotte Corday... Ça t'intéresse, Sergent? (It's a commando of 12 men with machine guns, explosives and 4 vehicles... We'll take the convoy in crossfire just before a roundabout leading to the airport: Operation Charlotte Corday... Are you interested in the job, Sergeant?)

I had never been very strong in history, but this name reminded me vaguely of something... With hints of the French revolution and all the rest. Ah! These fuckin' intellectual, cocksuckers the whole fuckin' bunch!, they always had the chic to classify their operation with evocative code names... But in the field, they all sucked big time, they weren't worth shit these motherfuckin' planners, and afterwards, when you got yourself in deep shit up to the wazoo, you could never count on any of them to get you out of trouble.

- *Et c'est pour quand, ce boulot?* (And when is it for, this job?)

- *C'est pour très bientôt, mon pote. Il ne me manque plus que quelques hommes de confiance pour compléter le peloton... Ça t'intéresse, Sergent?* (It will happen very soon, buddy. I only need a couple more men to complete the platoon... Interested, Sergeant?

- *Et ça paye combien... ta petite sauterie?* (And how much does it pay... your little dance?)

- *Pas si mal... 8,000 francs.* (Not so bad... 8,000 francs.)

- *Quoi?... 8,000 francs pour gommer le numéro Un de France!... Mais tu rigoles ou quoi, là?* (What? ... 8,000 francs to erase the Number One of France! ... But you've got to be joking, man?)

- *On n'est pas riches, tu sais... C'est tout ce que l'organisation peut t'offrir.* (We ain't rich, you know... That's all the organization can offer you.)

- *Et c'est qui?... Le commanditaire? On bosse pour qui?* (And? ... Who's the sponsor? ... Whom would I be working for?)

I always liked to know whom I worked for before taking a contract... So to stay alive once the job was done! And since I was now a newly married man, I certainly did not feel like taking part in a suicide mission and take the risk that my little Ariane would find herself a widow even before her first wedding anniversary.

- *Ça, c'est pas de tes putains d'affaires!... Tout ce que je puis te dire, pour te rassurer un peu, c'est que ça vient d'en haut... On a le soutien de politiques et de l'Armée... Le lieutenant Colonel Bastien-Thiry et des généraux sont du complot.* (That's not your fuckin' business! ... All I can say to you, to reassure you a little, it's that it comes from above... Way up. We have the support of policiens and of the Army... Lieutenant Colonel Bastien-Thiry and some generals are part of the conspiracy.)

- Putain! Le colonel B-T?... Avec lui vous êtes vernis, les gars! (Fuck me! Colonel B-T? ... With him, you'll all be in for a treat!)

Lieutenant-Colonel Bastien-Thiry was an organizer of the OAS who was known to be unstable and troubled with mental disorders. Shit! A fool good for the nut house was sending us to chew up the Great General of France... And it wasn't much doe if you liquidated a President of the Republic and had perhaps to spend the rest of your life watching behind your shoulder. In addition, I didn't like working with people I didn't know, or trusted, and with twelve men, it was likely to fuck up quickly... Their little motherfuckin' coup d'état!

Between two shots of anisette, I let Max know that I wasn't interested in this kind of work anymore and that I had a wife and wanted to move on...

- *Tu devras te passer de mes services, mon pote.* (You'll have to do without my services, buddy.)

Max seemed disappointed with my answer. Then, he added:

- *Pense-y bien, Sergent... Je suis à l'hôtel jusqu'à demain matin... Au cas où tu changerais d'idée.* (Think about it, Sergeant... I'm at the hotel until tomorrow morning... Just in case you change your mind.)

He left some doe on the table to pay for the drinks and then he left, quickly. I finished my pastis, while waiting for Ariane's brothers, and I never saw Lieutenant Max again.

A few weeks later, in the evening, I heard about his fucked-up operation! First, on the radio; and then the next morning in all the newspapers of France. Everyone spoke of it in Marseilles; *l'attentat du Petit-Clamart* (the attack of Petit-Clamart) of August 22, 1962:

"*Un attentat vient d'être dirigé contre le président de la République. Sa voiture a essuyé plusieurs rafales d'armes automatiques. Aucun des occupants n'a été atteint...* (An attack has just been attempted against the President of the Republic.

His car was hit by several bursts of automatic weapons. None of the occupants were injured...)"

The fuckin' idiots! Almost two hundred bullets fired with only fifteen or so projectiles that had hit the presidential car... And on top of all that, they had managed to miss their mark, the fools! I couldn't help but think that, by the end of August, 1962, I would have needed only one bullet to settle his account, this Great motherfuckin' General...

A few days after the failed attack of Petit-Clamart, while I was sitting in his hotel terrace, Antoine Guerini and Mémé, his brother, came to offer me a drink. Shit! I suddenly had become the most popular man in Marseilles, or what!!! ...

They, too, had heard about me and offered me a good paying job at the SNCF and on the docs of the seaport of Fos, work that involved stealing certain goods and smuggling cigarettes and heroin for his organization. And since I was of Sicilian descent, he had said that I was almost part of the family, so...

He, too, had heard of me through his contacts with French Intelligence Service, and had said that a good trigger like me would complement beautifully his Marseilles team... The French Connection!

The Guerinis then introduced me to a guy who called himself Lucien Sarti, a Corsican, like them, a man who would take me under his wing and teach me the basics of the trade, promised Mémé.

But to them, too, I had to say "no"... I didn't have the nerve to start trading in whores and heroin.

I had left the Guérini brothers in good terms; they had assured me that the doors of the Grand Hotel Méditerranée would always be open to me the day I decided to come work for them in the region...

14

After vegetating a few months in Marseilles, we were finally sent to the northwest of France, in Alençon, we who were accustomed to the Mediterranean climate of North Africa! And I froze my balls all winter in a shabby place turned into a dormitory for French refugees, with the guys on one side and the women on the other. We warmed ourselves with small camping stoves; Ariane was pregnant... I couldn't see any future for us in France.

In the end, we were offered the opportunity to immigrate to the Commonwealth country of our choice, and since we were francophones, we chose Quebec as our country of adoption...

Our transatlantic liner, the Normandy, arrived in the port of Quebec in March 1963. The captain had given a little party in honor of my younger sister's fifth birthday, Anna-Maria, and after seven days spent on a dismounted sea vomiting the day's before meals, it was for my family and for myself a real pleasure to see appear the old city of Quebec clinging to the edge of a precipice: the port of registry of our adoptive country.

When we descended onto the mainland, a strong explosion welcomed us into the city. From what the locals had said, a mailbox had just exploded. The letters had been sent to the skies with acknowledgment of receipt by spring gusts coming from Southwest Canada, a sure sign, according to the *Québécois,* that mild weather was to arrive for good in this rough corner of the country.

A fireworks amateur of the Front de Libération du Québec (FLQ) had managed to detonate dynamite sticks, we had learned in the newspaper on the next day.

Going down the footbridge, Peppé had looked at me dazedly, and he said to me:

"*J'pense qu'on a mal fait de venir ici... Ça saute comme chez nous, en Algérie. On est aussi bien de s'en retourner tout de suite avant que ça se remette à péter de partout!* (I think we were wrong to come here... It is exploding like at home in Algeria. We'd be better off to return right away before it starts to go off everywhere!)"

But it was already too late to back down...

We headed, almost backwards, to the Immigration Office of Canada: "Province of Quebec". A Mounty on a small reinforced concrete pedestal stood guard. He was dressed in a red uniform with a stupid German Scout hat on the head... There were others who watched us pass on their horse and made us a face: welfuckin'come to Canada, hey!

It was the start of our Canadian adventure!

- Hello my friends! *Bond Joooour!* Did you folks have a good trip? No? Bah! Do not worry about the explosion... It's only a small bunch of radical frenchies. We'll send the army soon, don't you worry! ... Your papers, please! ... *Papiii... ééé!*

Peppé had looked as if he had just received a blow on the noggin, as he slipped to me in the ear:

"*J'comprends pas un foutu mot de ce qu'il dit, ce con-là! J'pensais qu'ils parlaient le français, par ici? C'est pourtant ce qu'ils disaient au bureau d'Immigration du Canada, en France. Et puis ça saute comme à Bône, ici! On aurait peut-être mieux fait d'émigrer en Australie. Au moins, là-bas... il fait chaud!* (I don't understand a damn word of what he says, that asshole! I thought they spoke French, here? That's what they said at the Canadian Immigration office in France. And they blow up shit just like in Bône! ... It might have been better to immigrate to Australia. At least it's hot over there!)"

And I continued to make the translation for Peppé and for the family...

15

Without wasting any time, much to the displeasure of the folks of Quebec City, because we were francophones and Quebeckers wanted to keep us with them, the Canadian Immigration service sent us immediately to Montreal, to the West side of the Canadian metropolis. My brother Vince, who had been in the country for almost six months, worked as a machinist at Canadair and had found us an appartment on Barclay Street, near the corner of Victoria: a four and a half in the Côte-des-Neiges district... But when we arrived in the borough, it looked more like *Côte-des-Nègres.*

It was a good start in our new country, except that most of our neighbors only spoke a foreign language: Black people who were only fluent in English!

In addition to all that, my younger sister was going to have difficulties of adaptation in her pristine environment. Indeed, in addition to making everyone of her classmate laugh, because of her almost unpronounceable Italian surname, Anna Maria was often beaten when she came back from school; most often she was coming back with a torn blouse, a tress of hair plucked-out, a blood-stained face, or simply covered with bruises.

"Go home! ... *Retourne don' chez toi, maudite Italienne à marde!* (Go back home, you damn Italian little shit!" Was she told, in both official languages of the province of Quebec.

Born in Africa or not, the Blacks of Côte-des-Neiges did not really like her, and one afternoon, just after school, Peppé had to chase down a posse of little panthers with a shovel, a gang of adolescents trying to choke his daughter to death in a snow bank: they were picking on a school girl who was just in the first fuckin' grade! Giuseppe (Peppé) had arrived just in time to save her. Anna Maria, who was not more than five years old at the time, already had a blued face, when her father took her out of the snow... Fuckin' Negroes! After the Muslims of Algeria, it was now the turn of the Black Panthers of Côte-des-Neiges to try to kill us...

Peppé had complained to the police about his dauthter's daily abuse, but the Montreal cops said that they couldn't do anything to find the attackers "*parce que les Nègres de Côte-des-Neiges se ressemblent presque tous!* (Because the Neggars of Côte-des-Neiges all look alike!" Had explained one for the policeman. As the pigs weren't going to do anything for his daughter, Peppé had made it a point to go and pick her up at school... He had his penknife in a pocket... And beware to the first Neggar who was going to try something on his daughter!

And then one day, supposedly to allow us to better adapt to Montreal city life, we were forced to take English classes. A lady from the immigration department came to see us within a week of our arrival in Montreal, saying that in the metropolitan region "it was essential to know English if you wanted a good paying job".

But why force us to learn a foreign language if we were in a French-speaking country? ... Peppé did not understand it! Neigther did I! ... We thought we had emigrated to Quebec?

But we definitely were in Canada: a different country!

For I, who spoke English well enough to get by and entertain people with diverting conversation so I'd be understood, it had gone very well, and I had been able to raise the level of English I already had, especially oral. But for Peppé, who was in his fifties, it had been almost impossible to learn anything, although he already mastered Sicilian, French and Arabic. But English, never in his fuckin' life:

"*Ça rentrait pas pantoutte!* (It didn't get in at all!)" As the Quebec people said in their own coloured French dialect...

Peppé finally got a job for the city of Montreal without having to master English. He, who had been a foreman for more than twenty years, who had already managed construction sites of several millions francs, who had erected buildings of twenty stories high, and even bridges!, had to content himself with the underpaid work of the labourer; a non-specialized worker assigned to the thankless tasks of pick and shovel shit jobs: the equivalent of the *water boy* in American football... But at the time, we didn't understand anything about that sport, yet!

What an outrage for a man who knew how to do everything on a construction site and who could have teached the intricacies of structure work to almost anyone in Quebec! But Peppé had not been reluctant: he was happy to simply work in his field and earn some money for his family... At fifty, he would roll up his sleeves and start at the bottom of the ladder. But that was before he fell into a manhole that a co-worker had not covered, after doing the rounds, one night, to make sure that everything was okay... Peppé had broken his two legs and had lost his job on the next day.

Talk about bad fuckin luck!

For my part, I had not yet managed to find myself a stable job, even with my *maestria* of English, my third *second language* after French and Arabic, having worked for a while in commission sales, a difficult line of work that was not always lucrative, and I raged not to be able to earn a good living and provide the basic needs of life to support my family. Peppé was unemployed; Ariane was pregnant and was about to give birth: I didn't have a cent in my pocket and didn't know how I could find the necessary monies to pay for the delivery... Over $ 300! And the hospital demanded to be paid in cash before admitting Ariane in the maternity ward! ... Dollars that I still didn't have and that I would have to find, whatever the cost may be, because as it was so aptly put at Sainte-Jeanne-d'Arc Hospital: "No money, no candy!"

Motherfuckers! They would let Ariane give birth on the front steps of the health facility, if they were not paid cash-on-the-barrelhead... I was completely discouraged!

And then on day, Uncle Vito, my godfather, came to visit us in the Canadian metropolis just to see if his brother was recuperating from his fall and to make sure that we were well set up in Côte-des-Neiges.

Leaving his beloved *Nueva York* behind for the week, he said he had some business to settle on St. Lawrence Boulevard on behalf of his company, and that he had taken advantage of the trip to pay us a courtesy call. And it was then, seeing that I didn't have a job and that I needed money, urgently, because Ariane's belly was as big as a sperm whale about to burst open, that he told me that he may have a job for me; work within my capabilities, he had said... A good fuckin' paying job!

Next, he whispered in my ear:

"*Que cosa pensi di quindicimila dollari?*"

- *Ce que je pense de quinze mille dollars?* (What I think of fifteen thousand dollars?) I had repeated!

- *Dolari americani!*

In American dollars!

Fuck me man! That was a big hunk of money in October of 1963.

"*Et qui dois-je tuer pour me mériter une pareille somme?* (And who shall I kill to deserve such a sum?)"

I had joked, giggling a little, when I had replied to him.

But my Uncle Vito wasn't laughing at all, when he continued:

- I have something for you, my godson... Come have a drink and dinner with me... We'll talk more quietly in front of a good bottle of red wine.

Uncle Vito didn't want to discuss the matter in front of the family. And it's with little or no concern at all, 'cause the guy was my relative, for fuck's sake!, that I left with my *tio* (uncle)...

We crossed the city in his rental car, a gleaming automatic transmission Cadillac, going through the streets of the West side of Montreal: Victoria, Van Horne and Côte-des-Neiges, as we passed in front of the cemetery; then we crossed Mount Royal to finally get to the other side of the 200 and some meters little hill, which was actually a very old volcano, dormant, subsequently, we took St. Urbain Street to Sherbrooke, and then my uncle made a left on the all too famous Saint-Laurence Boulevard that divides the city in two: *The Main!*

And so we arrived at Chez Moïshes restaurant: a highly rated Jewish steakhouse of Montreal.

In the large dining room, there was a small bar and a huge espresso coffee machine, and a bunch of four-seater tables with leatherette benches that they called "booths", discreet little spots where customers could converse in peace with their sweetheart... those for whom a love-and-wine diet was far from enough.

Uncle Vito greeted the man behind the counter, who immediately gave him a series of "*Don Vito this, Don Vito that*", which made me wonder why so much respect and courtesy for a guy from the U.S. of A., and we subsequently walked through the dining room to find a quiet corner. Halfway through the restaurant, we stopped for a moment at the table of a dude who looked important, and Uncle Vito immediately introduced me to *Signore* Cotroni. The good fella, an impeccably dressed man, was finishing his meal with an eye-catching young beauty, the type of babe on high heels with two meters long legs that any guy, horny or not, would have loved doing on the spot, but I rather noticed the bodyguards siting at a near table: two hairy hulks built like a fuckin' nazi Panzer tank that checked me out, intensely.

I greeted Mr. Cotroni without knowing who the man was, exactly... And the famous Vic said to my *tio,* whispering:

"*E 'che lui è il nostro uomo?* (Is this our man?)"

- *Sì! Questo è il mio figlioccio, quella che ho già parlato.* (Yes! This is my godson, the one I already talked to you about.)

What the fuck? ... I was... their man?

And I was still in the dark, when I reached out a hand...

After seizing Don Cotroni's heavy claw, "*Hum!... Incantato di conoscerle!* (Umm! ... Delighted to meet you!)" The motherfucker had tried to break my hand in some fuckin' squeezing contest that I wasn't aware of, I followed my *tio* in the back of the dining room, massaging delicately from the fingertips to the wrist. And Uncle Vito quickly ordered T-bones, spaghetti with parsly and garlic, and a good bottle of red: a Chianti Ruffino in a bottle woven with straw.

It immediately took me back to Sicily... *La dolce vita!*

After a delicious meal, we had an espresso and I drank some Cognac, my *tio* knew my taste with regards to alcohol and had ordered a bottle, and then a guy came out of the blue. He joined us and made a point to drink with me: we were gonna empty the bottle of Fine Napoleon.

All that would surely cost my godfather an arm and a leg!

Uncle Vito quickly made the presentations; we shook hands heartily, and afterwards, we talked for a long while.

Lucien Rivard looked like a nice guy, a jovial dude: he was some king of a joker. And when I asked him what he was doing in real life, besides drinking Cognac like if it was water, he described himself as a French-Canadian underworld ringer who specialized in weapons smuggling, gambling and heroine, rather than "*vivre une petite vie tranquille à travailler dans une shop pour des pinottes!... Et c'est bien mieux qu'une job steady!* (living a quiet life working in a shop for peanuts! ... And it's much better than a steady job!)" He added.

Travailler pour des pinottes?... Une job steady? (Working for peanuts? ... A steady job?) In a shop? ... They really spoke a different French, these French-Canadians!

After telling me all this, he burst out laughing... a thunderous laugh.

Rivard, who said he had contacts in the *milieu* (underworld), and even overseas, didn't fit the mobster profile; he surely wasn't an enforcer, that's for sure! His weapon of choice seemed to be more on the side of discretion and intelligence rather than big arms! And just by looking at him, no one would have suspected that this ordinairy looking guy was actually working with organized crime *capos* (captains) from all over the world, and that Rivard was busting out tens of millions of dollars worth of business with the mafia.

"*Don Vito? ... Est-ce de lui dont tu me parlais, l'autre jour?* (Don Vito? Had Rivard queried, is he the guy you told me about the other day?)"

- *Si... Questo è nuestro uomo!* (Yes... This is our man!)

Once again, the famous "our man!"

What the fuck? ... What was it that made me so fuckin' famous? I didn't even have a job... I was fuckin' pennyless... Almost wandering in the street half naked, for fuck's sake!

And it was Rivard who finally told me about the *hit*...

- *Un hit?* (A hit?) I repeated, half in French, half in English!

I had repeated it out loud without really knowing what it was, exactly...

Rivard motioned me to lower the tone. And it was by talking with him that I understood that this was how they called this kind of work, here, "hit", or for me "*contrat* (contract)", work that consisted in killing people for money.

Rivard laughed, when he added: "*C'est le plus vieux métier du monde... Ha! Ha! Ha! Tout de suite après la prostitution!* (It's the oldest profession in the world... Ha! Ha! Ha! Immediately after prostitution!)"

Funny guy, this Lucien...

When the time came to tell me more, the friendly Rivard turned to my uncle to ask permission to continue, and my *tio* immediately reassured him, telling Lucien "*qu'il se portait garant de moi et qu'on pouvait avoir une totale confiance en ma discrétion!* (that he would act as a guarantor and that one could have total confidence in my discretion!)"

Oopsy doody do!

I didn't understand it at the time, but this was as if Uncle Vito had said that he would be responsible of my future conduct within the organization; if I fucked up in any way, he would take the rap for whatever went wrong!

My *tio* continued his blablabla... Adding that I was a former Foreign Legion paratrooper and that I already had several *hits* under my belt, including a shot from 300 meters in the center of Algiers.

- *Ton client sera beaucoup plus près... À moins de 250 pieds... Même pas besoin de savoir tirer pour faire le hit... Je serais peut-être capable de le faire moi-même avec un tire-pois!* (Your client will be much closer... At less than 250 feet, had cut off Rivard, to reassure me... Not even the need to know how to shoot to make the hit... I might even be able to do it myself with a peashooter!)

- *Alors, si c'est si facile que ça... pourquoi ne le fais-tu pas toi-même, Lucien?* (So, if it's that easy... why don't you do it yourself, Lucien? I replied, bragging a bit.

And I pretented to get up from my chair and go...

That almost cut Rivard's balls off. Uncle Vito had a good laugh just at looking at Lucien's panic reaction...

I imagined a silver plate with finely sliced roasted testicles on a bed of Basmati rice and a nice bottle of Chianti! ... Hiss! Hiss! Hissssssssssssss!

- *Heu!... C'est parce que... Heu!... J'sais pas tirer, moi...* (Uh! ... It's because... Uh! ... I donno how to shoot...)

- *Alors, mon p'tit Lucien, quand on ne sait pas tirer... on ferme sa grande putain de gueule!* (So, my dear little Lucien, people who don't know how to shoot... usually keep their big fuckin' mouth shut!)

My godfather gave me the look... Like if he was ordering me to take it down a notch and get back with the program! ... And I filled my glass with Cognac without adding anything more.

As I was of Sicilian origin, my *tio* told Rivard that he didn't have to worry about me... That I was almost *della familia* (of the family). And that talking to me was like "*parler à une tombe!* (to talk to a grave!)"

Une tombe! (A grave!)

Then, I wondered how one could talk to a grave? ... Or for that matter... *from* the motherfuckin' grave?

Even if I started to be in a good fuckin' mood, because of all the alcohol I was getting into, I didn't really appreciate the comparison of my godfather. And that's when I realized that my *tio,* besides being my godfather... was also a *Godfather!* That he was one of the captains of the Sicilian mafia of New York; that he wasn't here just to visit the family, the son of a bitch... he was there to recruit me.

Fuck me man!

Rivard continued to talk about everything and nothing for several minutes, small talk shit like the beautiful Cuban babes he had jumped in Havana, the almost perpetual good motherfuckin' weather of the Caribbean and of Florida, blablablablabla... Next, it was the cocksuckin' communist's turn, which had made him lose a small fortune, and then, finally, he talked about his nightclub in Sainte-Rose: a small city just North of Montreal, on Île Jésus.

Good! The guy had money... Lots of money!

I was just shitless in Quebec! "*Si vous aimez l'aventure!* (If adventure is what you're looking for!)" Had said the chick at the Canadian ambassy of France.

Afterwards, point-blank, Rivard asked me if I was interested in taking the contract... in doing *the hit!*

- *Et c'est pour quand ce... Hit?* (And when is it for... this hit?) That I asked.

- *Pour très bientôt... Probablement pour le début de novembre. On a deux ou trois dates possibles, mais je n'en sais pas plus pour l'instant. Tout ce que je peux te dire, c'est que le contrat vient de Marseille... Ce sont eux qui t'en diront plus; moi, je ne fais que recruter la bonne personne pour faire le travail... Une faveur pour l'ami d'un ami... Si tu vois ce que je veux dire.* (Very soon... Probably for the beginning of November. We have two or three possible dates, but I don't know anymore, for now. All I can tell you is that the contract comes from Marseilles... They're the ones who will tell you more; I'm only recruiting the right person for the job... A favor for the friend of a friend... If you know what I mean.)

He looked to be serious as he concluded his statement... But he ended his tirade with a slight wink.

- *Et ça se passe où... ce fameux contrat?* (And where will it take place... this famous contract?)

- *Ça n'est pas encore déterminé, ça non plus... Mais tout ce que je peux te dire, c'est que c'est un travail pour de vrais pros... Pour des professionnels de très haut calibre!* (That is not yet determined... But all that I can tell you is that it's a job for a real pro... For professionals of the highest caliber!)

However, I wasn't even a professional, but I didn't correct Lucien. I was just an average Joe who had learned how to kill a man at the *Légion Étrangère* (Foreign Legion). Nothing more. But a Joe with a lot of experience!

- *Et c'est qui... Notre client?* (And who is it... Our client?)

- *Aucune idée de qui ça peut être... Mais c'est sûrement un type important! Et même si je savais qui c'était, je n'aurais pas le droit de te le dévoiler. Va falloir que tu ailles à Marseille, si la job t'intéresse, et parler avec les Guérini... Moi, je ne suis que l'intermédiaire des Bonnano de New York qui, eux, collaborent étroitement avec les familles de Chicago et de la Louisiane. Par contre, les donneurs de contrat ce sont les Guérini et...* (No idea whom it can be... But it's surely an important guy! And even if I knew who he was, I wouldn't have the right to reveal it to you. You'll have to go to Marseilles, if the job interests you, and talk with the Guerinis... I'm only the intermediary of the Bonnanos of New York, who collaborate closely with the families of Chicago and Louisiana on this one. On the other hand, the contract givers are the Guérinis and...)

- *... Ouais! Ouais! Je connais les frères Guérini...* (... Yeah! Yeah! I know the Guérini brothers...)

- *... Non! Sans blague?... T'as déjà bouloté pour eux, Jo?* (... No! No kidding? ... Have you ever worked for them, Jo?)

- *Non! Jamais travaillé pour eux... Ils m'ont déjà proposé du boulot l'année dernière, mais j'ai dû refuser leur offre.* (No! Never worked for them... They offered me a job last year, but I had to refuse their offer.)

I didn't intend to elaborate on the subject and tell Rivard that I wanted to put this life behind me, forever.

- *Bon! Alors, va falloir que tu partes pour Marseille vers la fin d'octobre... Et tu ne seras pas de retour à Montréal avant... Hum!... Décembre. Ils t'expliqueront, à Marseille, et te feront connaître les tenants et les aboutissants. Jo?... Jo? T'es toujours avec nous?... Est-ce que ce genre de contrat pourrait t'intéresser?* (Good! ... So, you'll have to leave for Marseilles by the end of October... And you won't be back in Montreal before... Um! ... December. They will explain everything, in Marseilles, and make you understand the ins and outs of the contract... Jo? ... Jo? Are you with us? ... Could this kind of contract be of interest to you?

There was a long fuckin' silence... Heavy! Like carrying a ton of bricks on your shoulders... And I immediately thought of answering: "*Non! Fous-toi le au cul, Lucien, ton putain de contrat de merde!* (No! ... Stick it up your ass, Lucien, your fuckin' shit contract!"

A voice in my head was telling me to refuse... Not to go along with it... That it was pure madness! ... Unconscionable! ... A fuckin' nonsense! ... Next, I thought of Ariane who was about to give birth... Of my chronic lack of money... That I didn't have a steady job... Not even a fuckin' future!

And then, because I was a person in need, I turned on a dime like when you flip a coin in the air and you're just about to call "heads" and you change your mind at the last second... "Tails!"

- *C'est d'accord!... Je prends le contrat. Mais j'ai des factures à payer, moi... J'ai besoin de travailler, et tout de suite! Et si je prends ce putain de contrat, j'aurai besoin d'une avance. Disons... 5,000$, maintenant. Avec le reste payable une fois le contrat exécuté. Ça peut vous aller, comme arrangement?* (It's okay! ... I'll take the contract. But I have bills to pay... I need to work, and work right now! And if I take this fuckin' contract, I'll need an advance. Let's say... $ 5,000, now. With the rest payable once the contract is executed. Could this kind of arrangement work for you?)

- *Pas de problème pour moi si Don Vito est d'accord avec ce genre d'accommodement... Raisonnable! Ha! Ha! Ha! Car c'est lui qui va défrayer la note, et en cash. Alors...* (No problem if Don Vito agrees with this kind of accommodation... Reasonable! Ha! Ha! Ha! 'Cause he's the one who'll pay for the bill, and in cash. So...)

- ... *No vi è alcun problema* (I do not see any problem), said my godfather.

- *Bon! Excellent! Alors, si tout le monde est d'accord, prépare-toi à partir bientôt. Nous, on s'occupera de la logistique... T'as un passeport en règle, Jo?... Pour sortir de Montréal?* (Good! Excellent! So, if everyone agrees, get ready to leave soon. We'll take care of the logistics... Do you have a passport in order, Jo? ... To leave Montreal?

I nodded.

- *Parfait! Dans ce cas, c'est tiguidou. Tiguidou sa slide!* (Perfect! In this case, it's *tiguidou. Tiguidou sa slide!* - Okay! -)

After saying that, he rubbed his hands.

"Hostia! ... P'tit guidou?" I repeated. What the fuck?

As I must have been like the guy who didn't understand a fuckin' word of what he had said, Rivard immediately clarified his words by saying:

- *Alors, on a un deal?* (So, do we have a deal?)

- *Un deal?* (A deal?)

- *L'affaire est ketchup... C'est dans le sac, quoi!... C'est OK! ... Compris?* (It's over and done with... It's in the bag! ... It's Okay! ... You got it?

Rivard really spoke an intriguing French!

I concluded the pact by taking Rivard's outstretched hand: it was as if I had shaken hands with the devil himself... Like those generals who sign a truce after watching hundreds of thousand men got to their death... in vain.

After finishing the bottle of Cognac, Rivard invited us to La Plage Idéale, his Dance Club located in the small town of Sainte-Rose, but I had preferred to go back in my uncle's car. It was getting late and I didn't want to worry Ariane, unnecessarily. On the way home, I explained to my *tio* that, since I needed money, urgently, I was going to get out of my *retirement* and work for him, but that I was going to execute only one contract for his organization, and then, after the contract, he and his *familia* should forget about me... Forget about my existence forever! Which was something they could do at anytime after the hit just by having me killed by another hitman!

- *No problema ... Sarà solo per un contratto e no più. Hai la mia parola d'onore.* (No problem... it will only be for one contract and no more. You have my word of honor.)

But could I trust the words of a *Mafioso* from New York City? ... Even if the Mafia captain was, in addition to being a godfather... My godfather?

The next morning, Uncle Vito passed by the house just before heading back to the airport and his beloved *Bro-ké-lin.* He pulled out a huge roll of banknotes, tightly bound by an elastic band, and he handed me the reel, saying:

" *Qui è il deposito... Riceverà il resto dopo il viaggio di ritorno!* (Here's the deposit... You'll get the rest when you return from your trip!)

- *Et si jamais ça tournait mal et que je ne revenais pas... Qui s'occupera d'Ariane et de notre enfant à naître?* (And if it ever went sideways and I didn't come back... Who will take care of Ariane and our unborn child?)

- *Sarà come se fosse mia figlia e mio figlioletto!* (It will be just as if they were my daughter and my grandson!)

We had a long hug, with kisses on the cheeks and all the rest, the Sicilian way, and then my *tio* left without adding anything more...

I had finally found work. But what had I gotten myself into? A job that consisted of killing people for money!

I had done it for three long years in Algeria, although the pay had never been that great, and then in the streets of Bône... But killing people for the Legion had never been enough to live on.

However, I never divulged to anyone the true nature of the work that I had dug up... neither to Ariane nor to my father.

16

Finally, Ariane gave birth in mid-October at Sainte-Jeanne-d'Arc Hospital in Montreal, PQ, and I was able to pay for everything before her admission... in cash!

The delivery had not been too difficult for Ariane, a few hours of contractions and she had laid the little mermaid quickly, and the mother was doing extremely well after birth... Our daughter, too! I was happy. I had money in my pocket... And I was a dad, too!

When my sweetheart asked me where all that money came from, I told her that I had found a good paying job in an import-export company and that I now represented a group that imported olive oil in Canada, true Montreal; that the corporation was headquartered in Marseilles and that I should have to return to France very soon to complete a training of at least a month so I could learn whow to do big business on behalf of the company; that she shouldn't worry about anything: we wouldn't run out of money anytime soon.

I went to the Côte-des-Neiges City and District bank on Van Horne Street and opened a savings account on behalf of Ariane, and deposited $ 2,000. The rest of the money I had hidden in a stocking stuck in an old shoebox hidden in a bedroom closet with the wedding photos and other memories that Ariane had been able to bring back from Algeria.

Around the end of October, a few days before Halloween, Lucien Rivard posted a classified ad in the "Miscellaneous for Sale" section of the Montréal-Matin newspaper: Air ticket for Jo. Please contact Lulu at: (514) 636-6366.

I managed to pick-up the ticket at a café in Little Italy, on St. Laurence Boulevard: a Montreal-Paris-Marseilles return trip on Air France as well as a brown envelope containing $ 500 USD for my personal expenses. Between the bills of twenty was a little note written by hand that said: *Buona fortuna, Jo!* (Good luck, Jo!) And was signed: "V.C."

I assumed that V.C. was for Vic Cotroni and that Mr. Cotroni wanted to wish me "good luck!" for the job.

Napoleon, when it was time to choose a general, always said: "*Fort bien, mais a-t-il de la chance?* (Very well, but is he lucky?)" For he knew damn well that, on the battlefield, there were always unforeseen events, and that to win a war, a fight or a skirmish, you also had to have luck on your side...

I was hoping to have some, too, even if I had only been a sergeant... and Napoleon a general. But I consoled myself thinking that Adolf Hitler had only been a corporal! ... Thirty years and only a fuckin' corporal! ... What the fuck was wrong with that guy, anyway?

I left for France with the good words of the *Padrino* of Montreal, and yet, I had a heavy heart! I was about to leave Ariane and my daughter for a long month of absence... Without even knowing if, on day, I would see them again. It was the same feeling that I had experienced before, when our captain of the 1st REP had sent us, repeatedly, on suicide missions in the *djebels* of Algeria to force the Fellagha terrorists to emerge from their nest... And we didn't know if we were going to get out of it alive.

Perhaps I was being sent, one more time, straight to the scrap yard? ... I donno?

However, I couldn't go back on my word. Not now! I had to go ahead and earn the money my godfather had already advanced me for the hit. My fate was already sealed... It was for the gods to decide of my good fortune!

"Let the gods decide. For the gods had been silent all the while..."

17

When I arrived in Marseilles, I immediately took a taxi to the Grand Hôtel Méditerranée. Outside, the day was pleasant. It was the Mediterranean air that once again caressed my face... The climate where I had spent most of my life!

The Guérinis offered me their hospitality as when one opens the door to a long-time friend, and we immediately gave each other a warm hug. We talked about everything and nothing to break the ice, and then we took the stairs that led to the second floor of their domain. And it was in their little office that I would find out more about the famous hit...

Antoine Guérini immediately took out a bottle of pastis and some glasses, while I opened hostilities, first:

"*Et c'est quoi ce putain de contrat, au juste?* (And tell me... What's this fuckin' contract, exactly?) I had asked, eagerly waiting for a response.

Mémé (Barthélemy) Guérini handed me a glass of Ricard, which I filled with cool water, while Antoine Guérini, the other brother, unveiled the program, smiling:

- *T'inquiète, Jo! C'est du beau boulot. C'est un travail pour trois tireurs de qualité.* (Don't worry, Jo! It's an first-rate job. It's an assignment for three quality shooters.)

- *Trois?... Bordel! Mais vous ne rigolez pas, vous, à Marseille!* (Three? ... Fuck me man! You guys aren't kidding, in Marseilles!)

I rapidly thought of the assassination attempt of Petit-Clamart who had fucked up... Royally! And it immediately sent me a shudder down the back.

- *Trois tireurs d'élite...* (Three snipers...)

- *... Et en feux croisés, s'il vous plaît!* (... And in crossfire, if you please!) Had added Mémé.

- *Bon! Bon! Trois tireurs d'élite... C'est d'accord! Et c'est qui, votre client?... Le carton?* (Good! Good! Three snipers... It's okay! I had uttered, insolently. And who is the client? ... The mark?)

- *Un politicien... important!* (A politician... *important!*)

- *Un putain de politicien de mes fesses?... Encore!* (A fuckin' politician asshole? ... Again!)

- *Ouais! C'est un contrat **très** important!* (Yeah! ... It's a **very** important contract!) Had emphasized Mémé.

- *Et ça va se passer où, à Marseille, votre putain sauterie?* (And where will it take place, in Marseilles, your little motherfuckin' danse?)

Fuck me man! They wanted me to liquidate that bastard de Gaulle once again! And as I had gone to the south of France, I had thought that...

- *Non!... Ça n'est pas en France que ça va se passer, mon jeune ami...* (No! ... It's not in France that it will happen, my dear young friend...)

- *... C'est un contrat à l'étranger...* (... It's a contract abroad...)

- *... À l'étranger, vous dites? Où ça?... Une république de bananes?* (Abroad, you say? Where? ... A banana republic?)

I had thought of Africa and that they wanted to get rid of a politician, or vanish of the face of the earth a two-bit dictator... Algerian! I wished.

- *Non! Ça rime avec Afrique, mais c'est en Amérique...* (No! It rhymes with Africa, but it's in America...)

- *... En Amérique du Nord!* (... In North America!) Had cut off the other brother.

- *Putain! Un politicien d'Amérique du Nord? ... Mais, qui? ... Un ministre? ... Un congresman? ... Un sénateur?* (What the fuck? ... A politician of North America? But? ... Who? ... A minister? ... A congresman? ... A senator?)

- *Non! ... Encore plus haut que tout ça...* (No! ... Much higher than that...)

- *... Encore plus haut?* (... Much higher?)

I turned pale before Guérini had time to complete his answer. He, all smiles, had tried to prolong the effect, as when announcing an exploit out of this world of which one would be the author.

- ... *La plus haute des putains de légumes!* (... The highest motherfucker of them all!)

Oh! Shit. Fuck me two times! ... Once for tomorrow... Once just for today! Dah! Dah! Dah! Dah! Dah! ...

I saw my life flash by before my eyes... Their famous contract was to take out the President of the United States of America. Fuck! Fuck! And re-fuck me two more times! ... I was going to be part of a motherfuckin' suicide mission, once more, and go straight to hell!

"*Mais que diable allait-il foutre dans cette galère?* (But what the hell was he fuckin' doing in this galley?)" Would have surely said Molière, if he had walked in my shoes.

I tried to hide this moment of sheer terror, and after taking a sip of anisette to recover my senses, as if I wanted to pass the snake that I was forced to swallow, I was able to open my mouth and ask, all hesitant:

- *Et? ... Hum!... Où s'exécutera le contrat, au juste?* (And? ... Um! ... Where will the contract take place, precisely?)

- *Bonne question, Jo! Très bonne question!... Possiblement en Floride... Ou ce sera peut-être au Texas? Ça dépendra de...* (Good question, Jo! ... Very good question! ... Possibly in Florida... Or maybe will it occur in Texas? It will depend on...)

- ... *Ils viennent tout juste de manquer leur mec à Chicago, et le coup a foiré parce qu'un des gars s'est fait coincer par le FBI avec les armes... Un agent du renseignement américain aurait balancé l'un des tueurs, juste avant que nos amis de Chicago ne puissent finaliser leur coup, et ce n'est qu'après que la police a trouvé le nid des snipers.* (... They just missed their guy in Chicago, had added the other brother, and the coup went sideways because one of the guys got snatched by the FBI with the weapons... A US intelligence agent reportedly swayed one of the killers just before our Chicago friends could complete the hit, and it's only after that the police found the *snipers'* nest.)

Mémé had pronounced the word "sniper" with a heavy French accent... It sounded more like *"Se-ni-pè-re!"* than sniper.

It was hard not to stifle a laugh, despite the seriousness of my situation, but I was able to continue without smiling:

- *Mais c'est très risqué, ça, comme carton...* (But it's very risky, this turkey shoot...)

- *Oui! Très... C'est pourquoi vous serez trois gâchettes...* (Yes! Very... And that's why you'll be three triggers...)

- *... Trois tireurs expérimentés...* (Three experienced shooters...) Had said Mémé, trying to add more.

- *... Les meilleurs que l'on puisse trouver sur le marché! Des tireurs d'élite... Comme toi!* (... The best one can find on the market! Good snipers... Like you!)

After outbidding each other a moment, Antoine raised his glass as if he wanted to greet a gladiator who was going to be disemboweled in a Roman arena to appease the anger of the gods. Romans, too! But what had I ever fuckin' do to deserve such a fate? ... I was being fucked sideways by everyone... even by the gods who were trying desperately to two-time me.

Fuck me man! ... Talk about a shitty-fuckin'-deal!

I lifted my drink, relunctantly; Mémé raised his... And our glasses clashed. But in my head, even before having a tumbler of anisette, my neurons had already begun to collide; flying sparks where coming out of my head... I was fuckin' electrical!

- *Et?... On fait ça quand... ce putain de contrat?* (And? ... When will we dot it... this fuckin' contract?)

- *Vous prendrez l'avion dans deux jours pour Mexico.* (You will fly in two days to Mexico.)

Antoine had used the "*vous*" (*you* in French) that meant *more than one* - the plural form -, and not the "*vous*" that was used for politeness - which is singular -. So, I understood that I would leave with at least another "*tonton flingueurs*" (gunslingers): two pistoleros for Mexico.

Or more!

- *Et c'est qui, au juste, notre commanditaire? Parce que je dois vous avouer que, là... J'suis un peu confus, moi!* (And who is our sponsor, exactly? 'Cause I must confess that... I'm a little confused!)

I had thought of my godfather, associated with the Bonnano family; of Cotroni, from the Sicilian family of Montreal; of Rivard, who was into guns, gambling and heroin with his friends of Montreal and Louisiana; and now of the Guérinis from Marseilles! ... I didn't understand everything that was going on, and to execute a contract without knowing the ins and outs... It was never too good for the health of the ones who did the dirty work! And as I didn't intend to find myself in a garbage container with a bullet in the belly and another one in the head, I was going to try to find out as much as possible about the hit...

- *Comme tu fais presque parti de notre grande famille et que tu nous viens hautement recommandé par New York, je te raconte un peu... Ça nous vient de notre ami Santo Traficante, le bras droit de Carlos Marcello... Ce sont nos amis du syndicat de la Louisiane qui vont s'occuper de tout...* (As you're almost part of the family and that you come highly recommended by New York, I'll tell you a little more... The contract comes from our friend Santo Traficante, the right arm of Carlos Marcello... It's our Friends of the Louisiana syndicate who will take care of everything...)

- *... Mais ce contrat, ce n'est pas de son cru à lui... Traficante n'a jamais eu les roustons pour faire ça tout seul!* (... But this contract is not of his own volition... Traficante never had the stones to do someting like this alone!) Had belched out Mémé.

- *En effet!... En effet! C'est un contrat qui vient de plus haut, encore... De beaucoup plus haut!* (Indeed! ... Indeed! It's a contract that comes from higher, still... From much higher!)

- *Il a de puissants appuis, ce Marcello!* (He has powerful backings, this Marcello!)

- *Ça lui vient de politiques américains et des grands du monde de la finance, de l'armement et du pétrole. Ce sont eux qui veulent absolument se débarrasser de notre client... Une question de vengeance et d'argent, m'a dit Carlos, sans trop s'approfondir sur le sujet... Car beaucoup de familles ont perdu une petite fortune à Cuba, si tu vois ce que je veux dire...* (It comes from American politicians and big money from the world of finance, armaments and oil. They are the ones who absolutely want to get rid of our client... A question of revenge and money, Carlos told me, without expanding on the subject... Because many families have lost a small fortune in Cuba, if you know what I mean...)

Guérini meant that the mafia had lost millions when Castro took power in Cuba.

- *... Et c'est aussi une question de gonzesses!* (... And it's also about some chicks!) Had cut off the other, smiling.

- *... De gonzesses!* (Chicks?)

I had repeated it, very surprised. And I must admit that the Guérinis had totally lost me on that one.

- *Ouais! Apparemment notre carton a pilé sur les pieds d'à peu près tout le monde, aux États-Unis, et les gens du milieu sont arrivés à la conclusion que, avec le soutien des politiques et des services secrets, ça serait peut-être mieux pour tout le monde si quelqu'un s'occupait de la lui fermer une fois pour toutes... Sa sale gueule de con!* (Yeah! Apparently our mark has been stepping on the toes of just about everyone in the United States, and the crime syndicate has come to the conclusion that, with the support of the politicians and of the secret services, it might be better for everyone if someone took care of closing his big fuckin' mouth once and for all...)

- *... Et du même coup... Ha! Ha! Ha!... La fermeture éclair de son pantalon! Ha! Ha! Ha! Hum!... Parce qu'en plus de tout ça, il paraît que notre ami Carlos s'est fait piquer sa maîtresse par Kennedy...* (... And at the same time... Ha! Ha! Ha! ... The zipper of his pants! Ha! Ha! Ha! Um! ... Because, in addition to all this, it seems that our friend Carlos had lost his mistress to Kennedy...)

- ... *Mais les commanditaires tiennent absolument à ce que ça vienne d'en dehors... Pour brouiller les pistes...* (... But the sponsors really want this to come from outside, had added Antoine. To cover their tracks...)

- ... *Juste au cas où.* (... Just in case.) Had added Mémé.

Yeah! Just in case this impossible mission fucked up badly, had I deciphered... Like the failed invasion of Cuba!

The CIA and some influential members of the US crime syndicate had worked together in the past to overthrow Castro in Havana. But for the mafia, it was only for the recovery of their casinos and to save their own interest... Not democracy! Some sniper squads had been sent to eleminate Castro... But all the Coup d'Etat attempts went belly-up because of Kennedy's refusal to give to the CIA the resources to do the job; JFK was absolutely against strong-arm tactics in regards to the presidency of Fidel Castro: he wanted to see Cuban diplomacy triumph and didn't want to provoke a Third World War with Russia.

However, the American arms manufacturers - there was also a real gold mine to be exploited in Vietnam, but Kennedy was determined to pull out of the conflict - had not really liked this crazy idea of *not triggering a war* with the Russians. And now... I was going to be forced to press on the trigger on their behalf!

- *Et?... Comment on s'en sort, nous, après votre attentat suicide? Ce job, ça n'est pas du tout ce qui était prévu au programme... Mais pas du tout! J'suis pas suicidaire, moi!* (And? ... How' we gonna to get out of this after your suicide attack? This job is not at all what was planned for me... Not at all! ... I'm not fucken' suicidal, for Christ's sake!)

- *Holà! Du calme mon jeune ami... Du calme! Tu n'as pas à t'inquiéter pour ça. C'est du travail de pros... Je te l'ai déjà dit, tout à l'heure...* (Hey! Calm yourself, my young friend... Quiet down! You don't have to worry about anything. This is professionnal work at its highest level... I have already told you this before...)

- ... *Pour des professionnels!* (... For professionals!) Had put forth Mémé.

- Le Syndicat collabore avec la CIA depuis longtemps. Nous, on fait parfois de petits boulots pour eux, spécialement en Afrique et en Amérique du Sud... (The Syndicate has been working with the CIA for a long time. We sometimes do odd jobs for them, especially in Africa and South America...)

- ... Et même en France! (... and even in France!) Had cut in Mémé.

- ... Et lorsqu'ils ont besoin d'un tireur d'élite... (... And when they need a sniper...)

- ... Et qu'ils ne veulent pas se mouiller... (... And that they don't want to stick out their neck...)

- ... En effet. Merci, Barthélémy... Alors, pour rester net, la CIA nous refile le contrat, à nous. Tu comprends?... Ainsi, on collabore sur quelques dossiers à eux, quand ça fait notre affaire, et en échange ils nous laissent faire nos petits trafics en paix. (... Indeed. Thank you, Barthélémy... So, to stay clean, the CIA gives us the contract. Do you understand? ... This way, we collaborate on a few projects of theirs, when it ties in with our objectives, and in return they let us do our little traffic in peace.)

- C'est du gagnant-gagnant!... J'te t'assure, Jo! (It's a win-win for everybody! ... I assure you, Jo!)

- Mais il faut l'avouer... c'est la première fois qu'on nous propose de travailler sur un dossier d'une telle envergure... (But I must admit it... this is the first time we've been offered to work on such a vast project...

- ... Et en sol américain! (... And on American soil!) Had interrupted Mémé.

- Et c'est qui? ... Les autres professionnels? Ceux avec qui je dois bouloter? (And who are they? ... The other professionals? ... The ones with whom I must work with?

I had asked so I would know with whom I had the great pleasure of facing the gallows.

- Deux anciens du SAC. Tu vas partir pour le Mexique avec eux... (Two experienced SAC contractors - *Service d'Action Civique* [Civic Action Service] loyal to de Gaulle -. You'll be going to Mexico with them...)

- ... *Avec Lucien Sarti et son collègue et ami de toujours: "le Beau Serge". Tu connais Lucien, non?... Je te l'ai déjà présenté à au moins une occasion.* (... With Lucien Sarti and his colleague and best friend: "Beau Serge", said Mémé. You know Lucien, no? ... I've already presented him to you on at least one occasion.)

Mémé had given me another glass of Ricard to help me swallow everything.

- *Ouais, ouais! J'ai déjà rencontré Sarti à une ou deux occasions. L'autre... Je n'en ai qu'entendu parler. Je ne le connais que... Hum! ... De réputation.* (Yeah, yeah! I've already met Sarti on one or two occasions. The other... I only heard about him. I only know him... Um! ... By reputation.)

- *C'est l'un de nos hommes de confiance... Tu n'as pas à t'inquiéter pour le Beau Serge. Il est avec nous à 100%.* (This is one of our most trusted men... You do not have to worry about Beau Serge. He's a 100% with us.

Fuck me man! Working with these people would surely make some fuckin' sparks...

Lucien Sarti and Beau Serge were two mafia enforcers who had worked closely with General de Gaulle's *barbouzes* in Algeria, and they had the reputation of being dangerous lunatics; especially Sarti who, in addition to being completely fucked up in the head, was capable of almost anything!

Sarti had a reputation for taking risks... Big risks! He was the kind of guy with the finger on the trigger, always: even the Guérini brothers were fearful of him. They worked together and often gave him contracts, but they were afraid of him... Scared shitless! With the fear of being murdered by him for no reason!

That's why they never were alone with Sarti...

Beau Serge, in addition to having murdered just about everything that could be exterminated, had tortured or killed police officers in service in Algeria, not hesitating to execute high-ranking military personal who leaned towards the OAS... Something that was almost never acceptable in the *milieu!* These two men were bad fuckin' news... They had no code. And I never liked working with men who thaught that *to have no honor was insignificant!*

Usually, professionals did not kill policemen, judges, women and children... Never! It was an unwritten rule of conduct that was valued by all soldiers. The respect for life... To only take the life of another soldier when you had too! Every professional killer knew that... Except for Beau Serge and Lucien Sarti!

During the Algerian civil war, Sarti and Beau Serge had worked for the Gaullist camp, while I had been in the other, with the OAS. We had been enemies on Algerian soil and I would have liquidated them both without any hesitation if I had been ordered to. And now... We were going to work together on the same fuckin' contract!

- *Bon! Alors, Jo... C'est assez clair, maintenant?... Après une bonne nuit de sommeil, je te présenterai aux autres membres de l'équipe... C'est d'accord?* (Good! So, Jo... Clear enough, now? ... After a good night's sleep, I'll introduce you to the other members of the team... Okay?)

Um! ... So, the two other killers were here in Marseilles?

- *Oui! Limpide.* (Yes! Cristal.)

I started nodding off, very tired, because of the long trip and the jet lag, I suppose, and with all the alcohol I had drank with the Guérinis, I felt doubly tired...

I immediately took leave of my hosts at the first opportunity: I wasn't gonna let those motherfuckers drink me under the table and let them get the upper hand on me. As I was dead tired, I went straight to my room, like a zombie, and fell into my bed. I slept like a rock until the next morning... The alcohol! And it's the always affable Mémé who introduced me to my *teammates* at breakfast time.

Sitting together, we got to know each other a little while eating *croissants au beurre* and drinking our *café au lait*... Stuck in Sarti's belt, the pistol tight in the crotch and pointing downwards in the general direction of his scrotum, the butt of an automatic pistol was sticking out, clearly visible, and I joked, pointing at the caliber he had in his pants:

"*Lucien... Fais attention avec ton pétard, mec... Tu pourrais te faire latter une couille si jamais tu déchargeais ton instrument de combat... Prématurément!* (Lucien... Be careful with your firearm, dude... You could blow up your balls if you discharge, prematurely, your warfare tool!)"

The whole table burst out laughing.

Mémé was writhing in his chair, chuckling and laughing like crazy... Antoine could not take it anymore, almost pissing his pants, crying! Sarti had even spat a bit of *croissant,* almost choking... And I'm not sure he really appreciated Sicilian humor!

Afterwards, Beau Serge teased Sarti for a good fifteen minutes by saying things like:

"*Faut faire attention à tes roupettes, Lucien... Ça pourrait décharger tout seul, ton truc... Mais fait donc attention, couillon!* (Pay attention to your testicles, Lucien... They could discharge prematurely, your balls... Be careful with your nuts, bitch!)"

Then, he would burst out snorting.

Sarti asked him several times to stop riding him, but Beau Serge did not want to hear anything and continued over and over...

"*Attention! Tu vas te faire partir les couilles, Lucien...* (Careful! You're gonna blow your balls off, Lucien...)"

We all had a good laugh until Lucien came out swinging, really pissed off with his buddy... The gun in his hand!

Sarti had the look of a Holy madman of Tibet and no longer wanted to laugh, and then, out of spite, he stuck the cannon of his automatic pistol in the crotch of his colleague and best friend... Who was still writhing with laughter on his seat:

"*Si t'arrête pas tout de suite, mon coco, tu risques de te faire enculer par un gros calibre... Tu saisis?... Écarte un peu les fesses, pour voir un peu...* (If you don't stop it right now, my little goofbag friend, you risk getting fucked in the ass by my big caliber... Do you understand? ... Now, spread out your cheeks a little so I can see something...)"

We all looked at each other... Astounded! The hammer was cocked, the gun, ready to fire. Sarti had even removed the safety catch to make it look more authentic... Finger on the fuckin' trigger with all the trimmings!

All around the restaurant, it now was silence... Total! The clients eating breakfast were all time-frozen for a couple seconds like in the famous painting *au Moulin-Rouge* by Toulouse-Lautrec, but in Marseilles... And we all were afraid that his hand would start twitching a little and that Lucien would make Beau Serge another asshole, and, instinctively, I searched in my back, under my shirt... But I didn't have a firearm on me.

Fuck me man!

Ultimately, Sarti sheathed his 9 mil, bursting with a thunderous laugh; and we too, by ripple effect, I suppose, went on a rampage with him...

But Beau Serge's laughs had turned sour.

What a gang of mentally deranged souls! I was now part of a wild bunch who, in addition to being on the side of crazy, was manipilating handguns uncaringly.

At the Legion, there wasn't anything worst than having a soldier in your platoon you couldn't trust for shit with a gun... a guy at your 6... a brother-in-arms who covered your back and could have killed you as easily as your ennemy!

Now, I knew for sure that I would have to keep my two Corsican bozos in front of me at all times; they couldn't be trusted with anyone's life... Especially with mine!

And there it was... their fuckin' French Connection!

18

We flew to Mexico on the next day at around noon. Sarti and the Beau Serge had fake Italian papers; I had kept my French passport, since I wasn't on any "Ten most wanted fugitives" list.

After an uneventful journey, we went down the plane and strolled on the tarmac to Mexico airport. When I arrived at Customs, I said to the officer that I was in Mexico for a vacation. And the passage thru customs went well.

"*Esta aquí por la fiesta?* (Are you here to party?)" Had asked me the officer, as he examined my documents.

I wasn't sure that I understood the exact meening and what he had meant by "here to party"... But I nodded:

- *Si! ... Vacaciones.* (Yes! ... On vacation.)

I didn't want to elaborate with the Custom official and kept it short and sweet: Mexicans appeared to be very festive people.

Spanish was a little like Italian, and I didn't have too much trouble understanding the Mexicans during my stay. Moreover, my two colleagues spoke Castellano quite well... Enough to make conversation and build into a connection with girls! So, I thought we would have no communication problem in this country; but I would have *other* kind of problems with my partners in crime...

After getting our suitcases at the carousel, we went out, each on his side, not to draw too much attention to us. I didn't want to be regarded as a tourist whose art was death, a kind of French gringo who had come to America to paint his latest masterpiece with a spray gun.

Once in the open, we looked for our contact, and, for a long while, we waited for our guy to manifest himself in his own appropriate time. But there was no trace of the motherfucker tour guide anywhere!

So, we decided to wait in the shade, because the sun was still hot in Mexico at this time of year, and we grilled cigarettes without saying a word... I didn't want people to know that we spoke a foreign language and attract attention on us.

Finally, a guy wearing a cream suit and tie approached us.

- *Porqué estais aquí?* ... Why are you here?

-*¿ Qué?* ... What?

I had said it in Spanish, and then in English.

- Code name, please? ... What's the code name?

- Code name? Um! ... It's: "The Big Event," I said in my best English.

- *OK. Muy bien... Acompaña me, por favor.* (Okay. Very well... Please come with me.)

We followed the clear suit to the loading ramp, which also served as disembarkation point, and a big American sedan picked us up near the end of the ramp. The driver was quick to take our bags and store them in the trunk, and once in the car, which was slowly moving away from the Mexico City International Airport, our contact told us:

"My name is Diaz... How was your trip? ... Pleasant, I hope?"

When Diaz realized that my two crewmembers did not understand English very well, to say the least, he immediately spoke to us in Spanish. And since Sarti was Corsican from his mother's side, he spoke fluent Italian and good enough Castellano, and we didn't have any problem communicating with our contact... Ah, those Latin languages!

Diaz shook hands with all three of us, and then he gave us guns. It was some old Colt .45 of the American army, heavy motherfuckers that shooted 11.43 mm rounds... Miniature bazookas! I had had one at the Legion, but it was especially the side arm of choice of officers, in Algeria, and despite the impressive destructive energy of the weapon, past sixty meters, it was difficult to hit a target because of the weight and size of the bullet. But what a deafening bang at close range!

I much preferred the pistols that used 9mm Parabellum rounds, a caliber that was much more accurate and lighter... But I accepted my gift without complaning, saying to Diaz:

"*¡Gracias!* (Thank you!)"

Sarti immediately began to whine like a chick with a woah yeah between her legs... He wanted a fuckin' 9 mil Beretta and nothing else. He maintained that the Colt .45 he was given was an antiquity of the First fuckin' World War only good for cocksuckers... And Sarti was *not* a cocksucker.

He had made sure Diaz understood very well that he wouldn't suck cock... What a fuckin' asshole, that Sarti!

"*¿Me veo como un maldito hijo de puta, Diaz?* (Do I look like a fuckin' son of a bitch to you, Diaz?)" Had said Sarti. In essence, he didn't want the motherfuckin' gun he had received...

But Diaz didn't have anything else to give us, so Lucien, finally, ended his lamentations after a few minutes of whining...

One must never look a gift horse in the mouth!

We were taken to a high-end hideout and stayed in a beautifull colonial villa of Polanco, a small village in the Mexican megalopolis. Broad avenues gave a European character to the neighborhood with streets bearing names such as Lamartine, Musset and Alexandre Dumas... We were almost in fuckin' France, except for the air quality due to pollution. But it was also because the city of Mexico was resting at more than two thousand meters of altitude... on a fuckin' volcano!

As we had been ordered not to draw attention to ourselves, we only went out at night. Indeed, Diaz usually came to pick us up at dusk, but most of the time it was only to eat at a restaurant... We were forbidden to go into bars! And when we wanted to drink alcohol, wine or beer, it was only in our retreat that we were entitled to do so.

This dear Diaz, even though he claimed to have the Mexican police chief in his back pocket, was afraid that we'd make too many waves and be made by the *Federales:* the federal Mexican police. And Diaz was right to be suspicious, at least of the Corsicans, because Sarti and Beau Serge in a bar... They were like a fuckin' tsunami of hooch with a half twist of lime in a pike position!

On top of that, my two teammate killers were pissing me off almost all of the time; they were always complaining about something: they called Diaz so he would bring them whores; after that, it was more whores; different whores; more beautiful whores; taller whores; more dope; more alcohol; French food...

No French food here, motherfuckers!

And in addition to all that, they manipulated their pistol without making sure that the safety was on... And that really pissed me off!

They passed their pistols in the face of a Mexican whore or pointed their gun in my direction, completely drunk, and on top of that, they used drugs all the fuckin' time.

What the fuck? ... Was that what they called professionnal killers? Fly by the seat of their pants wannabe hitman?

And I didn't really like working with fuckin' addicts. To top it all, I was suspicious of their reputation for crazy, just as the Christians were of the notorius Barabbas in the Passion, because you could never trust a junky... And even less a drug addict son of a bitch on a high with a fully loaded handgun! And one evening, completely fed up with them, I seized Beau Serge by the collar and pressed my pistol in his gaping mouth, all the way to the back of the throat, saying:

"*Si tu pointes encore une fois ton pétard dans ma direction, je te bute... Enculé de ta race!* (If you point your gun in my direction again, I'll do you... You fuckin' piece of shit asshole!)"

His only answer to my threat was to throw up... He had pucked all over me, the cocksucker! And after the threat, frantic, I confiscated his Colt .45 and got a little upset with him; and I threw him against the walls a few times just to let off steam a little... Harvey's fuckin' wallbangers covered with Titus Flavius Agrippa vomitus!

But the motherfucker had trowned up on me several times, the bastard! ... There was vomit everywhere in the living room.

"Tu vas me nettoyer ça tout seul, fils de pute! (You're gonna clean your shit alone, you son of a bitch!"

Beau Serge continued for a while to bare his guts to the world, as Sarti was laughing like crazy, when he noticed his friend's puke all over my shirt and pants.

Beau Serge was having a tough time standing so he was intoxicated, and, after emptying his gun and throwing it, it too, at the other end of the living room, I went to change. And it was only then that I would calm down in the back yard with a fresh cervesa and a Mexican babe to cheer me up.

The next morning, Beau Serge could not remember what the fuck had happened the night before, so he couldn't blame me for throwing him on the walls and disarming him, but I already had it up to here with those two assholes even before arriving in Texas: they looked like two tourists who came to dance the *Voladores* in Mexico.

After spending a hell of a week in Mexico City, Diaz sent us a car with a driver: it was finally time to put an end to our *Mexican vacation* and cross the US border, 'cause I could not play babysitter one second more with the Corsican crazies.

Later, with more than fourteen hours of travel from Mexico to Matamauros - we had left at 6 p.m. the day before and drove all night -, we stopped just before the US border at around lunchtime. Sarti was very hungry, but we all decided to wait a bit more and eat in Brownsville, on American soil, just to see if the American fast food was worth it. We already had enough of the fuckin' nachos, tortillas and tacos, and, in addition to all that, with their shitty local spices they put in almost everything, the Mexican cooks had even found a way to make grilled chicken taste like shit!

When we arrived at the rendezvous point, a guy who called himself Roselli, he had been waiting for hours and was worried about not seeing us arrive on time, said he represented the interests of the Chicago *familia*. He had warmly welcomed us into his big dusty Ford, a car registered in Tennessee, and not in Texas.

Why, I thought?

Didn't have much time to think about it much as the American dude started: "*Hai fatto buon viaggio, ragazzi? ... Mi presento: Roselli. Sono io che lei accompagna a Houston, poi a Dallas.* (Have you had a good trip, guys? Let me do the presentations: My name is Roselli; I'll be the one taking you to Houston, and then to Dallas.)

Lucien was very happy to finally be able to speak Italian, so I didn't have to do simultaneous translation all the time.

"*Qual è tuo nome?* (What's your name?)" Roselli asked me.

- Jo.

- *Jo? ... Jo e che?* (Jo? ... Jo and what?)

- *Solo Jo!* (Only Jo!) ... No need to know more, Mr Roselli.

- Okay, Jo... Okay! If that's the way you want to play it. Fine with me! ... It's a real pleasure to see you all, guys.

Sarti and Beau Serge didn't reply...

There was an awkward moment... "*On nous souhaite la bienvenue, les gars* (We are being welcome, you guys)", avais-je dit aux deux Corses.

And then Roselli added, when he understood that my killer friends didn't comprehend much English: "*È un vero piacere vederti tutti*".

Lucien nodded: "*Piacere di conoscerle, Signor Roselli* (It's a pleasure to know you, Mr Roselli)".

And then Roselli turned to me, and said:

"Jo?... Since you're the only one who seems to speak English here, you'll have to take care of your friends and help us with communication."

Fuck me man! I was going to be the fuckin' official translator as soon as we reached the U. S. of fuckin' A.

- Yes, Mr Roselli... I'll do the best I can.

We transferred our luggage to the other American car. The guy who drove us to the American border recovered the Colts .45 Diaz had lent us and then quickly hid them under the spare tire of his car - we had taken the time to wipe them clean so that we wouldn't leave any fingerprints on them -.

After thanking our Mexican driver for taking us to Matamauros safe and sound, we quickly left with Roselli's Ford in the direction of Brownsville.

We traversed the city of *the killers of Maures* (*Mata* - to kill, *Mauros* - Maures: Matamoros), crossed a river, and on the other side of the bridge, we were already at the American border.

We cleared Customs quickly, friends of Roselli, I thought, and then we stopped at a Brownsville Diner for a bite to eat. We had burgers with greasy fries, Sarti had made a fuss because he wanted wine with his fuckin' burgers, but there was only Coca Cola, some orange shit and 7up!, and once everyone was satisfied, except Lucien Sarti, of course, we took the road to Houston... A six hours drive. Then another four hours before finally arriving in Dallas late in the night.

As soon as we got into the city of the Cowboys, we stopped in a nightclub named the Carousel Club, and that's when we met Mr. Jack Ruby for the first time: a pretty talkative guy who said he was a very good friend of the *familia!*

- Anything you want, guys... Anything!

He had repeated it several times, to make sure we all understood what he meant, and even if they didn't speak more than two fuckin' word of English, Sarti and Beau Serge immediately grabbed an erotic dance artist by the waist... They had understood very well the words of Mr. Ruby, it seemed, or was it the universal language of Dallas' nightclubs? ... The American dollar!

And immediately after our arrival, the staff of the Carousel Club treated us like oil moguls.

After drinking and playing a little with the babes, Sarti and Beau Serge had made sure to get noticed by all as they were not the type of men to share their chicks with anyone - they had made a scandal when they roughed up a horny Texan who had dared approache a night-owl bitch that they had kept in reserve for themselves -, Roselli had to pay the guy a few rounds to keep him quiet and shut him up, and it was then that I helped him drag Sarti and Beau Serge out of the club before they had time to make it into a diplomatic incident.

After our first encounter with the strip joint clubbers of Dallas, Roselli took us back to our hideaway: a small house a little away from the center of the city with a beautiful backyard.

But we wouldn't have the right to enjoy it because of my unstable Corsican friends...

Fuck me man!

- *Non si ottiene fuori di qui...* (You do not get out of here...) Ordered Roselli... And especially these two, Jo! They look a little fuckin' crasy to me...

- Yeah! Yeah! That I had said. Don't worry, Mister Roselli... I will keep an eye on them both.

- *Tornando ricerca che in due giorni* (We'll pick you up in two days)... *And donotte do so-me-thing he estupid!* He added, borrowing an Italian-American accent used in the Hollywood movies.

Roselli was a great connoisseur of American cinema; I learned it later by talking with him. And we all went to our respective rooms, rapidly; it had been almost two days since we really had slept in the comfort of a bed. I was tired... A dead man walking!

19

Roselli, a little *Capo* of the Chicago Outfit who had a thing for sexy B-movie starlets, I had had the confirmation when I spoke with his fellow *Mafiosi* friends, came back to see us like he had promised within two days of our arrival in Dallas. After asking us if our stay had been okay and if we needed anything special, I had told Sarti to shut it when he tried to open his hatch and complain about something, Roselli told us to prepare ourselves for a two-day getaway in Florida: he was going to send a car pick us up in the evening.

Sarti and the Beau Serge were pawing impatiently; we were going South of Miami: a night flight in New Orleans *padrino's* twin-engine plane... Special treatment for the Marseilles' crew!

Shortly before midnight, Mr. Ruby came to pick us up. He had his two *children* with him in the car, Sheba and Clipper, two Dachshunds grumbling and jumping in the air on the front seat of his four doors sedan. Ruby was very proud of his *kids:* he claimed they were his most precious possession in the world.

After a few minutes drive, we arrived at a small airport that was not too far from where we were staying. Just arrived on the tarmac of Red Bird Airport, a small airfield located south of downtown Dallas, Ruby immediately pulled into the direction of a twin-engine plane that was awaiting near a huge hangar: a sedan was parked next to the plane.

Roselli came out of the parked car and was quick to introduce his two trusted men, two Joes whose last names were Campisi and Civello, and another guy who called himself Lee.

Ruby told me that he knew Lee very well and that he was an ex-Marine training with a CIA-sponsored anti-Castro group who was supposed to overthrow Castro's regime. But Roselli's friends were only talking of regaining control of the casinos of the island... and of the Cuban beauties that were dying to meet wealty Americans hunks, like them.

It all seemed very convincing... except for the hunk part. But I was no beauty contest judge.

Lee explained that he needed to train a bit before his next mission, an action that was to take place towards the end of the year, according to Ruby, and that he was going to take advantage of the plane to shoot with us so he would stay sharp.

I moved away a little to talk with Roselli for a moment, and I didn't hesitate to let him know my mind:

- What's fuck, Mr Roselli? ... Is this some kind of fuckin' vacation at Miami Beach and everybody knows what we're doing here?

- No! No! Don't worry, Jo! Lee is with us for the long run... He knows nothing. Sweet fuck all! ... We've got him by the balls, actually!

At the time, I must confess that I had not understood Roselli's cruel humor. I only realized later what he had insinuated by his raillery.

Lee Oswald seemed to me to be a nice guy, rather reserved, about the same height as me, athletic in build: almost my age. But the guy didn't speak much. And I had the impression, seeing him operate, that he was only there to spy on us... To spy on me! ... And I didn't like it one bit.

Lee was the complete opposite of Jack Ruby, who was constantly jabbering like a magpie, a real used car salesman, that Jack Ruby, and seeing Lee act, the words Secret Service came naturally to mind. But I still did not understand what that guy was doing with us... And that made me a little nervous.

Roselli confided in us, but in Italian so that Lee wouldn't understand what he had to say to us, and ordered not to discuss our special mission with anyone, and especially in front of Lee: "*Non dice una parola circa la missione. Lee, lui, non sa niente... Capice?* (Don't say a word about the mission. Lee doesn't know anything... Is that understood?)

We all promised not to divulge anything, and I swore "we'd be silent dumb as an oyster!"

"*Muet comme une carpe!* (Dumb as a fish!)" Said Beau Serge.

- *No! Come una tomba...* (No, as silent as a grave...)

Roselli smiled...

That was Sarti humour all the fuckin' way.

And it was on the plane that we met David Ferrie, a guy who said he was the personal pilot of Carlos Marcello, the godfather of Louisiana and southern United States' mafia.

Ferrie was in his forties, had no eyebrows, and wore a kind of wig or ridiculous toupee on his head; but I only found out later that it was because of a strange hair system disease, alopecia, that he wore hairpieces and that he penciled in black at the top of the orbits to draw false hair on his arcades. After getting to know our pilot a bit, we fasened our seatbelts and then the plane took off smoothly, heading for Miami. Lee and Roselli were also part of the trip, but both Joes and Ruby stayed in Dallas. Jack Ruby had said that he couldn't come 'cause he had important things to do... And besides, he had his two children with him. So...

After takeoff, once at our cruising altitude, Roselli told Ferrie, our pilot:

"Okay, David. Let's go find these gentlemen some guns!"

- *Quoi? Qu'est-ce qu'il dit? ... Qu'est-ce qu'il dit?* (What? What is he saying? ... What is he saying?)

- *Ne t'énerve pas, Lucien... Monsieur Roselli dit simplement qu'on va nous trouver des armes, c'est tout...* (Don't get agitated, Lucien... Mr. Roselli just said that they would find us weapons, that's all...)

- *Hé! Ho! Mais j'suis calme, Jo!* (Hey! Ho! But I'm calm, Jo!)

I thought that Lucien did not like air travel very much... especially flying in small twin-engine planes!

- *Je pense que lucien a besoin d'un sac à vomi!* (I think Lucien needs a barf bag! Said Beau Serge, jokingly.

- T'as l'air nerveux, mon petit Lucien... Ça va comme tu veux? (You look nervous, my little Lucien... Is everything okay with you?)

- Ouais! Ça gaze! C'est que j'suis toujours un peu nerveux lorsqu'un pédé me tient par le manche à balais. (Yeah! Great! It's that I'm always a little nervous when a fag holds me by the broom handle stick.)

Beau Serge bursted out laughing...

Despite his unconventional appearance, I must admit, Mr. Ferrie seemed to me to be an excellent pilot; he even was a bush pilot, the type of aviator like *Saint-Exupéry* who could land an aircraft almost anywhere, even during a night flight, on a secular dirt road of a forsaken village...

But that didn't stop Sarti from having the jitters when we were crossing turbulent zones.

David Ferrie later told me that he had already been an airline pilot for a major airline, but it was in another life, and that he had been *fucked out of a job* because he had been falsely accused of "homosexual activities" outside working hours... He then had made a little complicit wink. And during the whole trip, Sarti and Beau Serge did not stop laughing and saying all sort of shit about our pilot:

"*Mais t'as vu la pédale aux commandes!... Qu'elle tantouze, ce mec!... Et en plus, il se fait épiler les sourcils comme une gonzesse, le connard!* (Have seen the fag at the controls! ... What a faggot, that queer, had laughed Beau Serge... And what's more, he has his eyebrows shaved like a fuckin' chick, the asshole!)"

- Ha! Ha! Ha! Quelle salope, ce clown! Il est mieux de ne pas trop s'approcher de moi... Sinon, je le bute. Et vite fait! (Ha! Ha! Ha! What a cocksucker, this clown! He'd better not get too close to me... Otherwise, I'll pop him like a zit. And quickly!)

- Attends au moins qu'on ait atterri... Ha! Ha! Ha! ... Avant de le flinguer! (Wait at least until we have landed... Ha! Ha! Ha! ... Before putting him out of his misery!)

- Quelle tante, ce Ferrie! (What a faery, this Ferrie!)

- What he said? Had murmured Ferrie who, him too, wanted to laugh a little with the Corsicans.

- Bah! Just some stupid Frenchie jokes... You wouldn't understand the humour. You know how the fuckin' Frenchies usually are...

I did not want to upset our pilot for nothing, and as no one else understood French apart from the two Corsicans and I, we did not really had time to make enemies on the flight. Ferrie probably suspected something, because of the wild laughter of my partners in crime and the intensity of the entire finger pointing at him, but he didn't say anything and he endured in silence... The motherfucker had to be used to it, I thought, with such an appearance.

I stayed in the co-pilot's seat for a long while. I had dreamed of being a pilot when I was a kid and even took a crash course on "how to land a plane in an emergency situation", a kind of learn to fly for Dummies course, when I was with the Foreign Legion, and I had received what they called a *Black permit* - an authorization to drive any army vehicule, including planes and helicopters, so they wouldn't fall into the hands of an enemy -.

I talked with David for a good part of the flight, and despite his divergent sexual practices - he organized homosexual parties with young men and teenagers for Texas businessmen and politicians, with Jack Ruby -, Ferrie seemed to be an okay guy. He was very smart, had knowledge and ideas on almost everything, and had a lot of humor. My kind of guy... except for the homo part!

And it was while conversing with Ferrie that I learned that he was working for the US Secret Service and for parallel organizations that wanted to overthrow Castro, like in *Operation Mongoose* - what madness! I thought -, and that his specialty was smuggling weapons under the guise of the FBI and the Border Police between Florida and Havana, in addition to carrying people and *powder* from South America when Don Marcello ordered him to. On occasion, he even performed missions on behalf of both sides, running drugs, CIA operatives,

Cubains contras and weapons at the same time... his only limitation being the weight of the cargo!

Finally, when I went to sit down with my two hitman *friends,* who had been dozing in their seats with Roselli for a good while, Lee immediately took the place I occupied, that of the co-pilot, and Oswald conversed with Ferrie for the rest of the flight. After twenty minutes, having seen them interact so armoniously, I had deduced that they must have been two long-time friends.

In the wee hours of the morning, we finally arrived in Miami. Ah! The smell of the sea... There's nothing like the smell of the sea for the ones who were born by the ocean!

No! ... There was only one exception to that assertion: the smell of napalm in the early morning... For those who were lucky enough to have experienced it!

I always felt that the odour of gazoline was as intoxicating as opium... And even today, when I smell gasoline vapors, it always reminds me of the poor bastards we had burned alive with jelly-like fuel falling from the sky, as our captain called for air support to make the enemy come out of a blazing village...

I would shoot them down, one by one, men, women and children in flames, to stop the agonizing screams that drilled my eardrums, even today, as the captain had ordered us "*que les démons musulmans brûlent en enfer* (to let the Muslim devils burn to hell)" as punishment for their evil deeds againts the Foreign Legion and the Pieds-Noirs population.

But the captain was wrong; no matter what the sin... Hell is other people!

And in less than a Florida second, the salty air immediately reminded me of the beautiful beaches of Algeria... and of the villages that we had burned to rat shit as retaliation for our fallen comrades when our army trucks were blown up by Fellaghas!

After a hearty American-style breakfast, *Canadian* bacon, *French* toasts with maple sirup from *Quebec* and American coffee from *Colombia,* our little commando specially hated the fuckin' drip coffee shit, Roselli drove us to some sort of makeship camp in the Florida Keys. Lost in the swamps of the Everglades, an archipelago that stretched out towards beautiful Cuba and seemed to be dying to join her, where thousands of snakes and crocodiles swarmed by the bazillions, men were training clandestinely for *la guéguerre* (squabble) against Cuba's Castro regime.

When we arrived at the scene, several Cuban exiles were practicing target shooting; others were doing the military assault course, which was adapted for jungle warfare, but we were only here to find ourselves weapons and adjust the scopes of our high-precision rifles.

Roselli led us aside and told us that, according to the official version, we had come here to practice shooting and that we were the three snipers who had to take care of the removal of Fidel Castro in the upcoming invasion of Cuba, in late December... *The Cuban Project... Operation 40... Operation Northwood ...* Choose your fuckin' operation, we were here to liquidate the Cuban dictator!

- What coup? Mister Roselli, I had asked, naively.

- *Non ti preoccupare, Jo, è solo per la vostra copertura...* (Do not worry, Jo, it's only for your cover...)

- *Donc, si j'ai bien compris... On fait semblant qu'on est ici pour descendre Castro?* (So, if I understand correctly... We're pretending to be here to gun down Castro?) Had said Sarti.

I nodded.

We were here in America to liquidate a president, but it was another one!

We arrived in a palm-leaf roof shack, and, on a large table, in the middle of the makeshift shelter, there was a whole assortment of pistols, revolvers, ammunition, and twenty or so rifles; many were high precision carbines.

Sarti saw a 9 mm Beretta that was lying in the middle of the table and immediately grabbed it; Beau Serge had set his sights on a Browning, another 9 mil; for my part, I selected a small Walter PP .380, a caliber almost equivalent to 9 mm, but in America they used .380 caliber instead of 9 mil for their semi automatic pistols, and as the gun was more compact than a regular size handgun, the weapon would be much easier to hide under the shirt.

"*Hé! Jo?... Sergent? Qu'est-ce que tu fous avec ce tire-pois de mes deux... Tu t'adonnes maintenant à la chasse aux papillons avec ton petit ami Ferrie?* (Hey! Jo? ... Sergeant? What are you doing with that peashooter for fags' apparatus? ... Are you now taking up butterfly hunting classes with your boyfriend Ferrie?)"

In addition to pissing me off most of the time, he was laughing at me, the motherfucker!

- *T'inquiète, Lucien, avec une balle de .380 entre les deux oeillets, le trou du cul s'étend par terre aussi vite qu'avec du 9... Tu veux que je te fasse une petite démonstration, juste pour voir?* (Don't you worry, Lucien, with a .380 slug between the eyes, the asshole lies down on the ground as quickly as with your 9 mil... Do you want me to do a little demonstration, just so you can see?)

Beau Serge immediately saw that I was not kidding, when he saw me waving my pistol in the air, but Lucien may have wanted to demonstrate his superiority as a shooter... Or a killer!

Maybe Lucien thought that this was the right time to show everybody who was the real boss, here: the undeniable star of the operation... Miss Marseilles in fuckin' person!

Sarti immediately raised his weapon: the pistol was pointed at me. And I didn't know if his gun was loaded or not, but I wasn't going to take the chance and get shot to find out. So, I put a clip in my Walter and loaded a bullet into the chamber by pulling the breach. The hammer was out... I only had to remove the safety catch and my handgun was ready to fire a round!

- *Hé! Ho! Mais on arrête les conneries, voyons... Lucien? Merde! Jo? ... Bon sang! Mais on est tous des amis, non?* (Hey! Ho! Stop that bullshit! Come on, guys... Lucien? What's that fuckin' shit? ... Damn it, Jo? We're all friends here, right?) Had squealed Beau Serge.

The Americans didn't comprehend what was being said, but they sure understood that, what was happening, wasn't part of the fuckin' Christian tradition. And as they were surely very religious, they came together to see what was going to happen during this very special ceremonial... They were going to attend a Mass that Sarti and I were going to celebrate with Holy fuckin' bullets!

Lucien came forward, his Beretta still pointed at me... He was not the kind of guy to back down, oh! No. He had the look of a mad dog from Alcatraz, empty of all emotion except perhaps rage: all that was missing to complete the picture was white foam oozing out of the corners of his mouth and a vet would have given Sarti the rabies-diagnosis.

I would have to play doctor Dolittle and take care of the problem myself and quickly put him out of his misery... Euthanasia, they called it!

- *Lucien... Mon petit Lucien... Si tu braques ton arme sur moi, t'es mieux de l'utiliser... Sinon, c'est moi qui vais te buter, mec. Légitime défense... Et je dormirai ce soir comme un môme!* (Lucien... My dear little Lucien... If you flash your gun at me, you better fuckin' use it... Otherwise, I'll be the one to pop you one in the balls, dude. Self-defense... And I'll sleep tonight like a fuckin' baby!)

Beau Serge immediately intervened to calm things down: he looked a bit panicked. But I think he was more afraid of taking one in the privates than to see me lying on the ground with a bullet in the nutsac.

- *Voyons, les gars... On est ici pour bouloter ensemble ... Allez! Merde! Serrez-vous la main... Et tout de suite! Sinon, moi je ne marche plus... Putain! Mais on ne peut pas travailler de cette manière, Jo!* (Come on, guys... We're here to work together, for fuck's sake! Shake hands and fuckin' hug each other... Now! Otherwise, I ain't gonna work with you guys no more... Fuck this shit! ... You know we can't work that way, Jo!)

- *C'est Lucien qui fait toujours chier... Dis-lui de baisser son arme le premier. Sinon... Je le flingue, et vite fait... Et toi avec lui si tu restes devant, enculé!* (It's Lucien who's the asshole... Tell him to lower his weapon, first. Otherwise... I'm gonna fuck him real good... And you with him if you stay in front of me, motherfucker!)

- Come on, guys... What the fuck is the matter with you all? We're all professionnals here. Had shouted Roselli.

And then he added, but in Italian: "*Così dovrebbe funzionare professionisti.* (So you must act like professionals.) And we don't have time to fuck around with your bullshit, Jo! ... Understood?"

Understood! ... Understood! ... Fuck me man! But it wasn't my fault... It was Sarti's! Fuck this shit!

- *Sì! Ha ragione, Signore Roselli... Scusame.* (Yes, you're right, Mr. Roselli... Excuse me.) We won't do it again... It's a promise.

Roselli then looked at Sarti... Who had sheathed his pistol, nodding: he had taken an air of submission. But nobody seemed to be convinced of his change of mood... Me first!

I put the safety on and hid my pistol under my open shirt, as I had always done it when I carried a gun on me, and I stuck my "peashooter" between my belt and my back. Then, to lower tension a few notches, I reached out a hand towards Sarti who, has always, hesitated before taking it...

Roselli smiled, saying:

"*Qui ci sono due galli veri, quelli!* (Here are two real cocks!) ... A real G.I. Joe, this Jo!"

And to the great relief of all, we shooked hand vigorously... Afterwards, Beau Serge hugged us both... At the same fuckin' time! We were only missing David Ferrie and we had a small orgy under the palm trees of Florida...

"A foursome!" Would have surely said Ferrie.

- *Si fa a scegliere un'arma... I al lavoro! Si vede sul campo de tiro* (Choose a weapon... And get to work! We'll see you guys on the shooting range.)

Roselli got out at a good pace. He was all smiles.

On a makeshift table, two sheets of plywood that had been put end to end on wooden easels, there was a bit of everything: a few USM1, an old FN 49, a few Mauser 7.62, a Musketeer II, a Mas 49, two Mannlicher, one Endfield, two Remington Fireball XP-100, a Walter 43... Finally, I opted for a model that had just been marketed in the United States: a brand new Savage model 10FP, a bolt action rifle with a retractable metal butt - it folded to the side to make the weapon more compact -. The gun was equipped with a 2.5 X 10 compact rifle scope and fired Winchester 7 mm caliber bullets (.270): *Winchester Cathedral you're bringing me down, you stood and you watched as, my baby left town...*

I had asked one of the controllers in my best English, a guy who called himself Morales, a Cuban who oversaw the training of one of the anti-Castro bands ready to invade Cuba: "Have you got some Winchester .270 shells with 165 grain bullets?"

Morales told me that he did, but that they usually were used for bear hunting in the mountains of Colorado and North Dakota and that...

- ... Yeah! This is just what I need... Bullets for big game!

Beau Serge has set his sights on the tiny Remington Fireball XP-100, a new compact weapon equipped with a scope: the mini rifle fired .222 shells with small bullets that weighed barely 60 grains. It was a mini gun the size of a very long revolver, but which could easily be hiden under the coat. On the other hand, the penetration and the range of this kind of weapon were rather restricted to about 90 meters, at the most. However, from close range and with a scope, it was very accurate, and as we were to be within 100 meters of our target, it was a wise choice if one wanted to pass incognito before and after firing a shot.

Moreover, Beau Serge had revealed to me that he had refused the Guérinis contract on at least one occasion, that it had happened in May, and that he had said "no!" because he was convinced that it was a suicide mission! Nonetheless, he had finally changed his mind when he found out that his friend Lucien was going to take the contract and that the *mechanics* would benefit from the help of the American Secret Service for the hit... And that he would be paid $ 50,000 in uncut heroin for his involvement in the project, if you please! ... It would be worth five times more on the street!

And I was only going to pocket $ 15,000 for my participation to the hit? ... I had the distinct impression that, with this contract, everyone was trying to fuck me up the ass, and that I was the poor fuckin' asshole of the French commando.

My *friend* Sarti had opted for a Mauser 7.62 mm with a 2.5 X 10 scope, a model that I loved, too, because the rifle was ultra precise: the Germans were not only renowned for their beautiful cars and their lovely blondes with blue eyes! I had stayed for a few months in Baden Baden, at the beginning of my training with the Foreign Legion's paratroopers, and had had the pleasure of going AWOL (*absent without official leave*) a few times, and to prison, because of my taste for Kraut beer and *wieners...* and for the *fräulein* of the bade.

We finally went to join Roselli on the shooting range and settled into the open stands. I took two small sandbags, leaned my weapon on it to stabilize it well, and put myself in the prone position. I took a 7 mm cartridge, inserted it into the chamber of my American rifle, and closed the bolt. I aimed at a target 100 yards away, about 90 meters, for us, and I took a shot... Baboummm! The bullet had barely touched the edge of the target, wide left.

Sarti burst out laughing... a mocking laugh.

"Um!" I uttered, as I adjusted the scope to bring the viewfinder to the right - three "click!" and it was quickly dealt with -, and my next shot hit the inside of the second circle...

But it was still a little to the left and down in regard to the center.

"Not bad!" Said Roselli.

- *Hé! Le jeune... Mais va falloir que tu manges tes Weetabix de bonne heure si tu veux me battre au tir, mon pote!* (Hey! Kiddo... Sarti added, you'd have to eat your Weetabix early in the morning if you want to beat me at shooting, buddy!

Weetabix? ... Sounded more like shit-a-brix to me!

I gave another click to the right, then another one to raise the aim, and then I put the next pill in the bull's-eye... Baboummm!

"Excellent shooting!" Said Morales... "*Increíble! Y solo con tres ballas. Muy bien, Jo! ... Muy jodidamente bien!* (Incredible! ... And with only three bullets! Very good, Jo! ... Very fuckin' good!)"

- *Gracias! Señor Morales.* (Thank you, Mr Morales.)

Lucien went to adjust his Mauser a little further, well away from the indiscreet eye of the recruits, and after shooting a good half dozen shots to adjust the scope of his German made rifle, he came back asking if someone wanted to participate at a small shooting competition...

He was looking at me. Intensely!

Sarti, who only saw with one eye, but it was the right one, had the reputation of being one of the best snipers in the world... Even the CIA had used his *services* in numerous occasions, in Africa and in South America, and, according to the popular rumor among professional killers, when Sarti came to an African country or a banana republic to do his evil deed, shortly after his passage, there was a change of regime.

- *On se fait un petit tournoi, Jo?* (Let's have a little tournament, Jo? Had proposed Sarti.

I thought he wanted to show to everyone that he was the best shooter in the regiment.

- *Une compétition?* (A competition?) I repeated... Just between the two of us?

- *Ouais! Une compétition entre G.I. Joe et moi!* (Yeah! A competition between G.I. Joe and myself!)

He had said it loudly and mocked me with the nickname that Roselli had given me, earlier, but no one here apart from the Beau Serge had understood the reason for his territorial gorilla scream.

Maybe the gorilla was a fuckin' shebah? ... In heat?

- *Ouais! Je ne dirais pas non, Lucien... Mais seulement entre nous, car ça ne sera pas réglo pour Beau Serge, parce que sa pétoire...* (Yeah! I wouldn't say no, Lucien... But only between us two, because it won't be fair for Beau Serge; his pea shooter...)

- *... Juste toi et moi, G.I. Joe... C'est pour le championnat!* (... Just you and I, G.I. Joe... It's for the championship!)

He was mocking me... again!

- *Bon! OK. Ça me va... Et ce sera quoi, au juste, la mise?* (Good! Okay. I'm fine with it... And what will the bet be?)

- *Une bonne bouteille de Cognac? ... Ça t'ira?* (A good bottle of Cognac? ... Will that be okay?)

The motherfucker knew my taste in alcohol.

- *C'est OK pour le Cognac... Mais on joue pour une bouteille de Fine Napoléon. Et rien de moins!* (It's OK for Cognac... But let's play for a bottle of Fine Napoleon. And nothing less!)

Lucien extended his hand.

- *C'est d'acc! ... Tape-là, mon pote!* (It's okay! ... Put it in there buddy!)

I seized the palm of the Corsican to conclude the deal: it was like grasping the forked hand of death.

Roselli wondered what was happening... And it was Lucien who explained to him that we were going to have a small shooting competition, just him and me... For the title of best shooter of the anticastrist battalion! ... And that Roselli should find us a good bottle of Cognac and give it to the winner of the tournament.

- *Si! Una buona bottiglia di Cognac per il vincitore* (Yes! A good bottle of Cognac to the winner), promised Roselli.

- *Grazie mille per la mia bottiglia, Senor Roselli!* (Thanks a million for my bottle, Mr. Roselli!)

I was able to fuck with someone's head, too, when I wanted.

When the word got out among the Cuban recruits and makeshift soldiers, almost everyone rushed behind the shooting range, with several men already betting on us.

But I wasn't the favored one to win the competition...

We started shooting at 200 yards distance, increasing the distance by 100 yards after each target. We had one bullet each to adjust our scope, and then another one for the competition itself. To piss Sarti off, when I shot at the second target, I aimed and fired from the left, even if I was right handed. Sarti, who only saw with one eye, could hardly do that... He was so fuckin' angry!

Maybe that would mess him up sufficiently and make him miss at least a shot.

We fired up to 800 yards, as there were no more distant targets to shoot at, both of us managing to hit the center on the second shot, which was the only shot that really mattered. But Sarti was getting tired of this little game, probably because I had hit all the targets right in the middle, too.

So, he asked Roselli:

- *Qual è il nome di questi grandi uccelli laggiù?* (What is the name of those big birds, over there?)

- *Cormorani, penso...* (Cormorants, I think...)

- *Quanto vicino sono?* (How far are they?)

- *1200 o 1400 iarde, almeno!* (1200 to 1400 yards, at least!)

- How much is it? ... I mean in meters? I had asked Roselli.

- Between 1100 to 1300 meters, I'd say... more or less.

There were great Florida Cormorants perched on poles planted near a mangrove swamp. From their perch, these seabirds plunged into the water to come back with a fish in the beak. In a standing position and without any support, Sarti targeted a bird and then... Baboummm! The bird fell down from his roost, wounded to death.

The other birds were frightened by the noise, and with at least a second off the sea raven that had fallen off from the pole, they flew to the coast when the detonation finally reached them, crying...

The Cuban recruits began to burst into spontaneous applause: some even demanded their winnings to the losers.

- *Il tuo turno, Sergente!* (Your turn, Sergeant!)

I would have liked to shoot, too, but all the palmipeds had flown away...

Sarti was all smiles, sure and certain to have won the shooting contest... and the good bottle of Cognac.

Shit!

About a minute later, while many congratulated Sarti for his prodigious shooting, another cormorant band came to rest at the same spot. So, without hurry, while the Cuban recruits claimed their due to those who had lost the bet, with my pocket knife, I made a small cross on the soft tip of a 7 mil bullet. Then, I inserted the cartridge into the chamber... Closed the bolt... Adjusted the scope of my Savage for about 1200 meters... Rated more or less the direction of the wind... Corrected the scope accordingly... Took the time to aim really well at my target... But just at the moment of firing, the birds began to fly away, frightened by the sound of a small motorboat that was passing near the quiet bay. While my cormorant began to take off, it must have been at fifty centimeters from its perch, I aimed a tiny bit higher then the head and just in front of the Cormoran path... And fired a shot... Babounmm!

Next, with a good second off, the time it took for the projectile to travel the distance, the .270 caliber bullet struck the palmiped in the thorax. And where the sea bird once was, there was only a heap of feathers and meat floating in the salty air of the Everglades... Crocodile food! I had hit my target in full flight!

"Fuckin' lucky shot!" Had said a Cuban recruit out loud.

- Incredible shooting, you guys! ... I wouldn't want to be in your line of sight... The both of you! Roselli had claimed, very impressed by our marksmanship.

He seemed proud to count us among his sniper squad, but Sarti still claimed the title of best rifleman in the regiment: he wanted to know which of us was really the best... The winner!

In short, Lucien wanted to continue shooting. But shooting at what?

Roselli told him that it was enough fuckin' shooting for today: "*Basta!* (Enough!)" And then he added: "Both of you are the winners of the competition!" And that he was going to find a good bottle of Cognac for the both of us.

Lucien nodded. Both of us were champions!

Before heading back to the car, I went to the firing range once more, just to see how our *friend* Oswald was doing with his firearm. Poor Lee had a Mannlicher-Carcano rifle in his hands, a real crappy shit rifle if there ever was one made, and the poor unlucky bastard had trouble just hitting the outside of the target at 200 yards.

Maybe he wasn't really gifted as a shooter and couldn't ajust the lens very well? ... Possibly. But I thought that, with a Mannlicher-Carcano in the hands, a guy did not put the odds on his side, especially with a Japanese scope of poor quality. And when I asked him "why he had chosen the Mannlicher rather than a Mauser or a Mas 49", he told me that it was Morales who had ordered that he trained especially with that weapon... Because he had been given one and that he kept at home for future use.

"If you want my advice, I told him, change your Mannlicher-Carcano for a Mauser, because you'll never be able to hit anything with that shit rifle of yours!"

And I left to join the others, because Roselli was waiving at me franticly to get me to come back... But I don't think that Lee took into consideration my friendly advice.

20

Roselli ordered us to pack up our gear and leave; we were going for another plane ride: direction New Orleans.

Lee didn't come with us on this trip. He stayed at the camp and was going to go back to Dallas by car with Morales; and it was already late in the afternoon when Ferrie raised engine speed to fly to Louisiana. Sarti was radiant; Beau Serge hummed like a child: "*Jo! On s'en va faire la fête... On s'en va faire la fête!... Dans les boîtes de nuit de la Nouvelle-Orléans!* (Jo! We're going to party... We're going to party! ... In the nightclubs of New Orleans!" But soon after, Beau Serge and Sarti got bitterly disappointed, when they found out that we only were going to New Orleans to meet with Don Marcello at his Town and Country Motel Restaurant, on Airline Highway... and not for a night on the tiles with the boys in Bourbon Street! And it was at around eleven p.m. that when we showed up at the Don's restaurant.

The Town and Country Motel Restaurant was an American bungalow-style building with huge a huge roof of asphalt shingles. The brick of the frame was of a color that pulled on a melancholic cyan yellow, as if the masons had taken the time to piss on each block before laying them. All rooms were arranged on one level. At the front of the Motel, there was a huge porch where people could take shelter when it was raining. The cars of the customers were parked in front of the small rental units, with in the back a beautiful swimming pool of about fifteen meters in length. However, as there was almost no water in it, I could never do lengths... "Too late in the season", had said the night manager!

Don Marcello was a smiling man, a good-natured and cheerful man who had started his career as a gangster during the Great Depression. After having married the daughter of one of the Louisiana mafia's capos at the end of the Second World War, he quickly climbed the ranks of the *milieu* to finally become the undisputed Bigshot of New Orleans. Don Marcello specialized in gambling, extortion, strip clubs, prostitution and drug trafficking, especially in the heroin drug business with his friends from Marseilles: *the French Connection.*

The Godfather of Louisiana was not a violent type of guy, unlike some other capos of his time who didn't hesitate to kill to arive to their objective. Carlos Marcello preferred to use his power and his money to buy senators, judges, police, and make alliances in the shadows, rather than attracting the spotlight on him by killing the competition. His territory ranged from Florida to Texas... But his influence was felt as far as Mexico, Las Vegas and even California.

Like many other organized crime families, the Don had lost a small fortune when Castro overthrew President Batista's regime, in Cuba. But the godfather of Louisiana had even bigger problems with the Kennedys... And especially with Robert Francis Kennedy, the new Attorney General of the United States who had tried to pin him down for years, and by all means, legal or otherwise. Don Marcello even said to me that he had been deported to Guatemala, illegally... On the express order of the Kennedys!

He had sworn to me on the Bible that it was Bobby Kennedy who had him kidnapped by secret agents, he and his lawyer, Mike Maroum, and that they had been dropped from a helicopter in the jungle not too far from the Honduras border, with the hope that they would both die of *natural causes...*

But Don Marcello and his accountant, after wandering in the wilderness for three days, had escaped alive... O! Miracle. The Don had only broken ribs and a twisted ankle, the result of an unfortunate fall in a ravine, and the New Orleans Godfather had finally returned to the USA, incognito, thanks to his faithful bush pilot, David Ferrie, who had brought him back from Central America in the Don's twin engine and dropped him in the Everglades, not far from Miami. As good an aviator he was,

Ferrie had managed to thwart American radars by flying at low altitude - at less than sixty feet - not to be detected, and since that day Don Marcello's only thoughts had been of taking revenge on the two Kennedy brothers. He didn't hesitate to say it, and even aloud: he wanted the fuckin' Kennedys assassinated!

The big boss of the Louisiana Bayou, nicknamed "little man" because of his small stature - he measured only 1.57 meters -, was born in Tunis. He was more or less the same age as my father, and was almost of the same height, too, and when I told him that, like him, I was born in North Africa to Sicilian parents and that my *genitori* (parents) were born in a small village south of Palermo, Sicily, Don Marcello immediately treated me as if I were one of the children of the family... And in less than five minutes he had already hit it off with me!

Roselli had booked rooms for the "Frenchies" we were - the Yanks used to call us that way - in the Don's Louisiana Motel, and as Sarti and Beau Serge were beat, but also very disappointed not to celebrate in the streets of Vieux Carré and go on a tour of the bars, I thought that the interdiction to go out had made them even more tired than the journey... And they quickly took one's leave and headed to their room.

For my part, as the connection seemed excellent between us, I had preferred to accept Don Marcello's invitation of and get to know him better in the small private office of the godfather of Louisiana; and in addition to all that, we had a good bottle of Cognac to savour!

Upon entering his office, just at eye level, there was a small poster stuck on one the back wall, that said:

Three Can Keep a Secret If Two Are Dead ...

Whew be do! On which planet did I fall on?

Don Marcello smiled, when he saw me jump, and after savoring my moment of panic, he motioned me to take a seat in front of him. Roselli took the chair next to mine. Subsequently, still standing, the *padrino* (godfather) tooked the air of a Greek tragedian with a suppository up his ass and pointed an index towards the small poster. Afterwards, several times, the finger pointed at me, he repeatedly folded the last phalanx of his index finger as if pressing the trigger of an imaginary gun to empty the charger on its target... Me!

"*Capice, Jo?* (Understood, Jo?)" That he had told me.

I nodded.

After the moment of terror, I was gagged with dismay.

Seeing my reaction, Don Marcello burst into laughter. Roselli followed him instantly.

Even though I knew he was joking, probably, the blood almost frozed into my veins... I had suddenly metamorphosed knee high to a grasshopper, as if I had entered a cathedral to meet a god in the flesh for the first time. But, I wasn't innocent... Far from it! I knew that in the *milieu,* people like my uncle Vito and Don Marcello never talked about what they were doing; that a *Mafioso* brought his memories with him into the other world; and that, finally, the best way for Don Marcello to make sure that I kept a secret was be to have me executed... after the contract!

Without knowing it, I had just set foot in the high-level decision-making office of the American *Cosa Nostra...* An insifigant motel lost in the depths of a Louisiana Bayou! And even though the greatest leader of American organized crime was only five feet and two inches tall, Don Marcello had managed to reduce me to the size of some Tom Thumb from far away in less than two tirades!

"*Dans les petits pots les meilleurs onguents!* (In small pots the best ointments!)" My aunt Titine often said to me.

I took a pause to collect myself, my voice was hoarse under the influence of emotion, and, finally, I managed to articulate some phonemes more or less intelligibly:

- *Sì... Um! ... Ho capito, Don Marcello... Ho capito...* (Yes... Umm! ... I understand, Don Marcello... I understand...)

Next, surely to create a more friendly climate, seeing the effect that had had his little staging on me, Don Marcello changed the subject and told me about the situation that prevailed in Algeria: "A fucking shame... " He had said, "... to leave a country in the hands of a band of fuckin' sand Niggars!"

He just couldn't believe it!

I wasn't outraged by the words of the Don, whose affinities seemed to lean more toward the Ku Klux Klan than Martin Luther King's supporters: we were in the Bayous of Louisiana... the Deep South of United States of America!

After talking a bit about my godfather, *tio* Vito, the Don finally discussed the contract. We were only half way through the bottle of VSOP, when Don Marcello started to wave in his chair, and it was then that he began to be more talkative than he had been at the beginning of the session... Perhaps it was the Cognac that had loosened his tongue? ... Or was it that he felt confident with his *adopted son from Algeria?* ... I donno? Subsequently, he started telling me some pretty incredible stuff: my ears were buzzing with amazement, like a bee in a rose garden.

"Jo! Listen to me... I want the little Irish son of a bitch killed... Do you understand me? I want him killed... And if I could, I would do it myself... Because the son of a bitch is a thorn in my side!"

- But? ... Don Marcello, the Catholic Church teaches us that God can forgive everything... Absolutely everything!

I had joked and, especially, I had not corrected the Don about the size of the famous *"Irish son of a bitch"*, who still measured nearly 1.82 meters: it was a pretty tall *"little"* son of a gun!

- Exactly, Jo! God can forgive... And your job, my little Jo, is to arrange the meeting with him... Let the motherfuckin' Irish son of a bitch meet his Maker!

- Sins do catch up with us in the end... That's what's happened to the Kennedys... Had preached Roselli.

He looked like a parish priest coming back from his tour of the New Orleans brothels with his hairy nutsack empty!

And it was after this volley of oratory that Don Marcello took the bottle and served us another balloon snifter of Fine Napoleon.

After refueling, he searched one of the drawers in his office desk and pulled out a pack of long cigars. He offered me a *puros,* but I declined his offer and shook my head, content with cigarettes. He then cut his Havana with a small guillotine, lit it on, pulled several drags to make sure that the burning of the tobacco leaves was going well, and when the small room was completely invaded by a thick cloud of conspiracy, he added:

- Jo! Puf! Pchhhh! ... You've got to cut the head off the dog to stop the tail from wagging... Puf! Pchhhh! ... It's that simple!

- But? ... Don Marcello? ... He's the president! ... The president of the United States of America! How am I going to get out of this alive? ... All the police force is gonna to be looking for us after such a hit.

- Not to worry, Jo... Not to worry... Everything has been arranged, said Roselli.

- Everything? ... Really? And how the fuck are we gonna get out of the city after the hit? ... What's the plan?

Then, looking pensive, I added:

"Merde! Mais j'suis pas suicidaire... Bordel de merde!"

- What's that you say, Jo?

I didn't realize that I had exclaimed in French. So, I said, but in English:

- I said: I'm not fuckin' suicidal, for fuck's sake! ... Jesus Christ! Who do I have to fuck to get off that boat!

Roselli gave me a funny look, when he heard the word "fuck". And after seeing the face he had made, I hoped that my comment had not created any misunderstanding about my sexual allegiance...

- Jo! My little Jo! ... Don't you worry about anything! Ferrie will fly you guys out of Dallas in a jiffy. It's all been planned... Afterwards, we'll keep you here until things cool down a bit... And later on, when everybody will be looking the other way, we'll fly you out to New York, and then to France... *Chiaro?*

Yeah! Clear... Except that I wasn't going to France! And I didn't dare correct the Don... Perhaps it was better that he thought I was going back with *the other two:* the Corsicans.

- Cristal! ... So, if I understand it well, it's David Ferrie who's gonna help us escape... by plane... after the hit. Is that the plan?

I didn't dare say "*votre plan de Nègre!* (a plan which made no sense)", although I was sure he would have loved the colourfull expression. Besides, I wasn't sure that I could have made the exact translation, even though I would have wanted to pitch it to Don Marcello... "Your Niggar's plan (plan de nègre)" not making much sense to anyone except to the Cajuns of Louisiana Bayous.

- Yes! Ferrie... That homo son of a bitch is gonna get you guys out of Dallas... You know, Jo, I cannot stand homos...

Oh! Boy... Here we go again!

- ... Never did like them, Jo... But the guy helped me once, big time! So, he now is on the payroll. And like it or not, Jo, he's just a homo and not a Niggar... And he and his little friends...

- ... Okay! ... Got it! Don Marcello... Got the picture!

Good! A real triple K guy, this Marcello! He didn't like Negroes or homos... Duly noted. But as long as his homo could fly a plane to get us out of Dallas... I didn't give a flying fuck about anyone's sexual orientation, or the colour of one's skin!

The Don was in a state of total intoxication, when he continued his mafia boy sales pitch, and, unintentionally, I had become a sort of involuntary confidant to the man... But I was suspicious, because with a godfather like Don Marcello, one could quickly go from *a kind of confidant to an endangered species* in less than a Louisiana second.

- ... Wait a minute! Let me finish, Jo! The plan is to get rid of the top man... THE TOP MAN! ... Do you understand what the fuck I'm saying to you?

Fuck me man! ... He was completely drunk!

So, out of respect for the man, I nodded... I understood exactly what Don Marcello meant!

- But to pull it off, we had to get some nut for it, Jo... Some fuckin' crasy guy! ... And we just got the right man for the job... Said Roselli.

- ... Who? ... Sarti? ... Serge? ...

I was afraid that he would pronounce my name and that it would no longer be on eggs that I would have to walk, but on hot embers...

"... Me?" I added, my face like a fuckin' question mark.

- No! Not you, Jo! ... Some crasy nut job that thinks he's working for the good guys...

- Who?

- ... That queer guy named Lee!

- Jesus Christ! ... Another motherfuckin' queer?

Fuck me man! ... What had I got myself mixed up with this time: a motherfuckin' homosexual plot?

- You know, Jo? ... Lee! ... Ferrie's boyfriend! Added Roselli to help clarify things.

- Lee? ... You mean... Lee fuckin' Oswald? ... That Lee?

- Yes!

- The guy who couldn't shoot shit if his life depended on it!

- Yes!

- You're not joking! ... Seriously? ... That Lee?

- Yes! The one and the same... Lee Oswald!

- Jo! Jo... Don Marcello is not saying that Lee Oswald is going to **actually shoot** the President... Corrected Roselli.

Fuck me man! I was lost... And I have to admit that I had not grasped the complexity of their plan: it wasn't a fly by the seat of your pants mafia operation at all!

- ... No! The plan is to make it look like a Castro sympathizer killed the son of a bitch. Lee Oswald is not gonna kill the President... Lee is the patsy! Clarified Don Marcello.

- Even better if the patsy has been trained by Naval Intelligence and is currently working for the Secret Service...

- ... He's on their payroll, for Christ's sake!

- The Justice Department won't be able to touch anyone after the hit, since it's one of their own that will be accused of killing the President. That's the gift from the heads of the CIA, my little Jo! ... We'll supply a team of hitmen; the Texas politicians will send their own; and the Secret Service will supervise the whole operation... Killing the president was never the problem, Jo; we could have done it a long time ago... It's not getting caught afterwards that is! This is why we needed a patsy and the help of the guys upstairs to cover it up. Do you understand, now?

- And on top of that, Jo, the patsy is also a communist sympathizer... It's a double wamo! The're going to pin this on a deranged nut who tried to defect to Russia, and then to Cuba! Public opinion will be on our side and every American media will be outrage by Oswald action.

- Yeah! The media! ... They're all in the CIA's back pocket! They'll say whatever the CIA tells them to... Cronkite, Koppel, Jennings, Rather and the rest!

Roselli explained that the Secret Service had asked Oswald to infiltrate an anti-Castro nationals cell who was planning the assassination of Fidel Castro and the invasion of Cuba; that Lee was actually a double agent who worked for Clay Shaw, aka Clay Bertrand - another fuckin' homosexual! -, an influential businessman in addition to being a CIA operative, and with Guy Banister, a former high-ranking police officer from New Orleans and ex-FBI agent: a private investigator who was spawning in anti-communist circles with the CIA and the *mafiosi* of the Southern United States. All these people were controlling Oswald, one way or another, who thought he was in the service of the Nation. They really were a bunch of fuckin' bastards... Never trust a motherfuckin' CIA operative. Or the FBI!

For my part, I never trusted anyone, anyway... These cocksuckin' mafia boys and their secret service assholes friends didn't know whom they were fucking with!

- Listen, Jo... As I understood it at the meeting with Hoover's friends in that Texas cocksucker's oilman mansion, the power structure of the establishment would not be displeased by the possibility of our dear President departing for a better world...

- ... And Jo... believe it or not... you're just the guy who's gonna pull it off for us!

- Me? ... Alone?

- No! ... You and your Frenchy friends, of course... And some other guys, too. It's a team effort, you know.

- But there's one condition... Added Roselli.

- One condition? ... What is it? ... What's the condition?

- The top man said that he didn't want anything to happen to the little lady!

- The little lady? But? ... What little lady?

I really didn't understand what he was talking about.

- Don Marcello was referring to the first lady of the United States of America: *the* little lady!

Do not touch the First Lady... The little lady... *"She's a lady... Oh, whoa, whoa, she's a lady!"*

Fuck me man! ... So, if the *little lady* in question was next to the president, as the protocol dictated in such circumstances, we would have to hit the target from the front or from behind, but certainly not from the side... It was going to complicate matters, because a bullet could reach the target, go thru it, and then continue its course to hit another. *"Collateral damage!"* Use to say our captain of the 1st REP (*Régiment Étranger de Parachutistes*: paratroopers). In order to do the job correctly, I would only have one option: use expansive bullets...

We used to say "dum-dum", in the Foreign Legion.

- Have you understood your mission, my little Jo? ... A good sniper like you must be able to do that easily... Right?

- Yes! Don Marcello... *Sarà come lo desidera.* (... It will be done as you wish.)

- Good! Excellent! ... Let's have another drink and celebrate "The Big Event!"

- The Big Event? But? ... Why that name, Don Marcello?

- 'Cause that's the code name those cocksuckers use at the CIA for this very, very special mission, explained Roselli.

- But here we prefer the term: "Fireworks".

- Fireworks? ... You mean like on the 4th of July?

- Precisely, Jo! Just ask Jack Ruby... He'll tell ya.

- Yeah! Ruby... Another queer, this one! But he's a useful queer. A good queer! Him and his faggy friends from the Dallas police force let me know everything that's going on in the city!

Don Marcello's outfit seemed to be one of the only criminal organizations in the world that discriminated positively with the hiring of homosexual workers. Personally, I had nothing against faggots; I only felt a little awkward when a motherfuckin' fag asked me if I wanted to suck this dick or to take it in the ass for twenty bucks... But besides that, I had no real problem working with homos. But unfortunatly for me, I really didn't have time to explore the idea of a homosexual hit team any further...

- Got it, Jo?

Roselli had got me out of my reverie.

- Um! ... Ya! Got it. Um! ... Would you happen to have by any chance the final itinerary of the presidential limousine?

- The final itinerary? ... Yeah! We have it... But what's really final about it, Jo, is that the son of a bitch is not gonna come out of Dallas alive! They've just modified the route so that the convoy passes precisely where we want it to...

- ... The CIA got Oswald a job in Dallas a couple of weeks ago... Just in the right building. Added Roselli.

- Tomorrow, we'll take you back to Dallas, and then we'll send our man to show you the site so you can choose your spot for the hit.

- *Chiaro. Ho capito! ... Grazie por la buona bottiglia di Cognac, Don Marcello.* (Cristal! I understand! ... Thank you for the exquisite bottle of Cognac, Don Marcello.)

- *Volio un buon lavoro, figlio mio... Capice?* (I want good work done, my son... Understood?) And you kill me dead that good for nothing Irish son of a bitch will ya?

- Crystal, Don Marcello... It will be done according to your whishes...

The godfather stood up: our interview was officially over.

After walking me to the door, I extended a hand, but Don Marcello had preferred to give me a long hug... He reeked of alcohol and cigar, the bastard! Afterwards, he pointed a casual finger towards the wall... In the general direction of the small sign!

Fuck me man! Not again...

- Jo, my little Jo! ... Do not forget!

- *Ho capito, Don Marcello... Non si deve preoccupare.* (I understand, Don Marcello... You don't have to worry about it.)

But I must admit that I was pretty worried, because I had no confidence in the word of this Don Marcello...

When Roselli walked me to the exit, he quickly realized that I was somewhat troubled by our little heart-to-heart. So, to comfort me a little, I suppose, he said to me:

- Don't worry, Jo. Everything is going to be allright for you. You're just like family to us. I know your uncle Don Vito very well. We did some great work together in New York and...

- ... So? ... You know my uncle Vito... Really?

- We're very good friends; actually...

- ... But...

- ... Listen to me, Jo! And let me finish... Tomorrow you'll wake up rested and you'll tell yourself that you don't give a shit about the client you're gonna hit... President or not! Because I know what kind of a guy you are, Jo, and that all your life you've been able to do the dirty work and keep secrets... Want it or not, Jo, all your adult life you've been a professional killer... It's not your fault: that's how it is! And believe me when I say to you that we have total confidence in your capabilities... And when the job is done, you'll feel good knowing that you're going back to your family... Safe and sound! ... Do you understand what I am trying to tell you, Jo?

- Yes, Mister Roselli... Thank you for everything.

And I took the direction of my double bed motel room.

Great! They all trusted in my abilities to kill people... Whoopie fuckin' doo!

And I went to bed straightaway...

21

Two days later, when Ruby rang our door in Dallas, we were all happy to finally go outside for a ride. Jack Ruby was here to take us to town and show us the official presidential limousine's route. He had on him two Kodak Instamatic 100s, small cameras that took 35mm color shots; the film was mounted in small easy-to-load plastic cassettes: six twenty-four exposures rolls. But the lens was shitty, to say the least...

When we decided to start taking pictures during the circuit, Ruby told us: "No! Not here... Wait till we get to the spot". We must have looked like a band of Japanese tourists ready to shoot downtown Dallas, entirely!

Jack took Main Street, turned right on Houston, and at the corner of the Dallas County Records Building, he slowed down and made a left on Elm Street. We had time admire the Dallas School Book Depository, and, a little further, he stopped on the right side of the street in an area where we weren't allowed to park, just in front of a small green hill that he had called: "The Grassy Knoll". And that's when he turned to us, saying: "This is where you get him!"

He then continued his speech, explaining:

"The presidential car is gonna slow down here and make a complete stop for you guys right here..." He had pointed out the exact spot, a location that was just in front of the little hill, in between a traffic sign and a staircase leading to a parking lot behind the mount: "... and from that point on to the overpass, he's all yours... That's your kill zone, guys!"

He had said "your" kill zone and not "the" kill zone... I had deduced that there would be other snipers to help us make the hit, but posted elsewhere... In their own kill zone!

Sarti liked the tall building on the corner of Helm and Houston Street, the Texas School Book Depository - it was called the TSBD, in Dallas - and claimed that from that building one could have a perfect frontal shot while the president's limo would still be on Houston Street and would, unquestionably, slow down to make the left turn on Elm Street. Lucien thought that it was the perfect spot and that it was the easiest shot to make on a moving target, and that's where he wanted to position himself... Nothing less!

But Jack Rudy responded vigorously by saying that we absolutely had to position ourselves in Dealey Plaza, on top of the Grassy Knoll... And nowhere else!

So, I didn't go any further with my translation of Ruby's words, and I told Sarti:

- *Tu ne peux pas tirer de là, Lucien... Les ordres sont de faire feu d'ici: le Grassy Knoll... Ça ne donne rien de discuter avec lui... On tire de la butte!* (You cannot shoot from there, Lucien... The orders are to fire from there: the Grassy Knoll... It won't change anything arguing with him... We'll do our guy from the hill!)

- *On le bute de la butte?* (We'll kill from the hill?) Said Lucien.

- What he said? ... What he said? Asked Jack Ruby.

- Bah! Nothing important, Mister Ruby... Everything is under control. Don't you worry about it...

- Swell, Jo! ... Fine! ... So, why the fuck is he complaining all the time like a fuckin' Primadonna?

- Umm! ... This guy is always complaining about something. You know how he is! ... But I have a question for you, Mister Ruby: are you at least sure of the itinerary of the presidential limousine?

- You betcha, Jo! ... Comin' strait up from the top man!

- How high up is that, Mister Ruby? ... I'd like to know so...

- ... All the fuckin' way up, Jo! Don't you worry about it and stop asking so many fuckin' questions! ... What the fuck is wrong with you Frenchies, anyway?

He was laughing at me, the cocksucker!

- But, Mister Ruby, it's my job to worry about that kind of detail... Don't you think so? I'm the one who's gonna get buttfucked if it derails... Not you!

If I didn't worry about this kind of trivial thing, who else was going to take care of it in my place? ... Sarti?

"So? ... We have no choice in the matter; this is where we'll have to operate: the Grassy Knoll.

- You betcha, Jo! This is your spot... And that's that!

While I was doing simultaneous translation for Sarti and Beau Serge, who kept telling me "*mais qu'est-ce qu'il raconte encore, ce putain de pédé?* (But what is he saying again, this fuckin' fag?)" Because they both were useless in English, Ruby continued his explanation by saying that "the big boss had the itinerary modified at the last moment" and that the secret service guys hadn't appreciated not having been consulted ahead of time. They had claimed that they never would have time to check if the route was safe for the president.

- You see the planning, Jo? ... You see the fuckin' planning?

Ruby had even smiled as he voiced the word *planning,* as if he had orchestrated the coup on his own! ... Or was it big pride? I donno?

Beau Serge was very nervous, not a happy camper at all, and kept complaining all the time about the location:

"*Mais Lucien, tu ne te rends pas compte?... Ça n'a pas de sens de travailler dans de telles conditions... On est ouverts de tous les côtés, ici! Jamais je n'aurais dû accepter de te suivre!* (But Lucien, don't you realize it? ... It doesn't make any sense to work in such conditions... We're open on all sides, here! ... I should have never agreed to follow you!)"

He took a few steps in a futile attempt to get away, but Sarti held him back.

- *Mais non, mais non! Du calme, Serge... C'est ouvert, ouais! Mais ça nous facilitera la fuite après avoir exécuté le contrat. Je t'assure, Serge!... Qu'en penses-tu, toi, Jo?* (No! No! Quiet, Serge... It's open, yeah! But it will make for an easier get away after the hit. I assure you, Serge! ... What do you think of it, Jo?)

I nodded. Sarti was right. While talking, Lucien and I had started to take pictures of Dealey Plaza, and especially of the small hillock and the huge pergola on the other side of the picket fence. There was behind the grassy hill a huge dirt parking lot with a small fenced area at the top of the hill, well sheltered under the trees and directly overlooking Elm Street. A plan had started to burst out of my brain: a front shooter hidden behind the wooden fence; another frontal shot down the viaduct spanning the boulevard; and a shot at plus or minus 125 degrees from the pergola... So, I reasoned with the Corsicans:

- *Je pense qu'ici, finalement, c'est un bon endroit... Dans la panique générale qui va suivre la pétarade, on aura au moins trente secondes, peut-être même une bonne minute avant que la police ne réagisse. Amplement de temps pour sortir par le parking et disparaître dans la nature, de l'autre côté du TSBD.* (I think that here, finally, it's a good place... In the general panic that will follow the shooting, we'll have at least thirty seconds, maybe even a good minute, before the police responds to the shots fired. Ample time to get out by the parking lot and disappear into the Wild West on the other side of the TSBD.)

- *Ça va nous prendre des silencieux... Et je veux aussi un uniforme de policier...* (It'll take us silencers, said Sarti... And I want a police uniform, too...)

- *Quoi?... Un uniforme de poulet? Mais t'es fou, Lucien: tu ne parles même pas l'anglais! Et si jamais on t'interpelle après le carton, tu fais quoi? Hein?... J'vais te le dire, moi... Tu es cuit, et nous avec! Alors, non! Pas d'uniforme de flic pour toi, Lucien.* (What's that you say? ... A pig's uniform? Said Beau Serge. But are you fuckin' crazy in the head, Lucien? You don't even speak English! ... And if they grab you after the hit... What will you do? ... Hey? ... I'll tell you what will occur... You're gonna get fucked up the ass, and us with you! ... So, no! ... No fuckin' cop's uniform for you, Lucien.)

- Bon! Bon! Juste une idée comme ça... Fais-en pas tout un plat, bordel! Mais ça va me prendre un accoutrement. (Good! Okay! Just an idea... Don't make a fuss of it, for fuck's sake! ... But I'm gonna need some accessories... Something!)

- ... On verra pour l'habillement. T'occupes... On va motiver Ruby à nous ouvrir tout grand sa garde-robe! (We'll see for the clothing later, I answered. I'll take care of it. I'll motivate Ruby to open his wardrobe for us... Wide open!)

- Et si Ruby ne veut pas coopérer?... Qu'est-ce qu'on fait? (And if Ruby does not want to cooperate? ... What will we do?)

- Hé bien!... Tu peux toujours lui sucer la bite pour m'aider à le convaincre, Lucien! (Well! ... You can always suck his johnson and help me convince him, Lucien!)

- Putain! Jamais... Je n'ai jamais sucé de queue et ce n'est pas aujourd'hui que je vais commencer! (No fuckin' way... Never sucked cock and I'm not gonna start today!

- Tu devras en prendre une pour l'équipe, Lucien! (You'll have to take one for the team, Lucien!) Had said Beau Serge.

He was laughing at the thought of Lucien going down on his knees to suck dick...

- Allez vous faire foutre!... Tous les deux! (Go fuck yourselves! ... The both of you!)

- Ha! Ha! Ha! ... On t'a bien eu, enfoiré! (Ha! Ha! Ha! ... Got ya good, cocksucker!)

Sarti gave us the finger... But now it was Jack Ruby's turn to question me about what the *Frenchies* had said; the Corsicans, too, had a lot to say about Ruby... I was lost in translation... Couldn't do it fast enough to please everyone... I was caught between a rock and a hard place! Ruby thought that my colleagues didn't have the stones to go with it anymore, and that they wanted to get the fuck out of Dodge; he seemed rather anxious, as if the smooth running of the operation could have an incidence on him: "What's wrong, now? ... What the fuck is going on? ... They have to do the hit, Jo! Tell them they have to! It's too late to back down, now... Otherwise, we'll all be in a major shitload of problems, man!"

- Why worry so much, Mister Ruby? They're just talking about the hit. We've signed up for it... We'll do the job!

I signaled to the frenchies that everything was fine with a thumbs-up, and then I asked the strip club owner:

- At what time is *the Big Event* supposed to happen?

- It's gonna take place around noon. Twelve thirty at the most... Just before the president's speech at the Trade Mart Center! ... Why do you want to know everything, Jo? ... Why are you guys complaining all the fuckin' time? ... Like a band of little girls with their panties in a bunch, for fuck's sake!

Ruby was starting to annoy me, because I felt that he didn't tell me everything: he was rationing out information to us in tidbits... In addition to making fun of us! This contract was extremely perilous for anyone who wanted to save his skin after firing at the president; and I cared more about mine than his...

"*Savoir, c'est pouvoir, mon fils!* (Knowledge is power, my son!")" Daddy often told me. So, if I wanted to get out of this Texan shithole alive, I would have to know everything about this contract... Every-fuckin'-thing! Even if I had to use strong-arm tactics with our good old friend Mister Ruby!

So, I quickly seized Ruby by the lapel for a one-on-one:

- When I do a contract, Mister Ruby, I just need to know three things: What? When? How? ... And where?

- What?

- Okay... Four things! Got it, Mr Ruby? Clear enough for you, Mr Ruby? ... Need more explanations, Mr Ruby?

And every time I said *Mister Ruby,* I shook him up...

Sarti had a good laugh; Beau Serge did not give a shit about the whole thing. Ruby was already beginning to lose his legendary stature, when he stuttered:

- Ro... roger that, Jo!

Jack Ruby had a hoarse voice, and I think that he understood the message I wanted to pass on to him: *we were'nt here on a fuckin' vacation!*

So, I maintained my grip, shaking him from time to time:

- Don't you fuck with me, Mister Ruby! ... Understood?

- No! No! ... No fucking around, Jo... It's a Promise!
- Will there be other shooters, Mr Ruby?

I already knew the answer to the question, but I wanted to see if Mister Jack Ruby was going to play fair with us.

- Um! ... Yeah! In the big building at the corner of Elm Street and Houston: The Texas School Book Depository.
- Will they use rifles with sound suppressors?
- No! ... 'Cause that's where the shots are supposed to come from! The patsy is expected to have taken all the shots from the TSBD. That's the plan... So, everybody in Dealey Plaza is gonna be looking that way.
- Perfect! That will make a nice distraction for our getaway.
- ... *Ça va nous prendre des silencieux, Jo... Demande à ta tantouze de nous en procurer, et rapido.* (... We'll need silencers for the job, Jo, had interjected Sarti... Ask your faggy friend to get us some, and presto.)

Lucien had more or less understood the content of the conversation. I nodded, and continued with Mister Ruby:

- We'll need silencers for our rifles... Can you arrange this for us, Mister Ruby? ... Or do I need to contact Don Marcello, personally?

When Ruby heard the name of Don Marcello come out of my mouth, he had a slight flinch. But he couldn't go far... I still had my hands firmly on his collar!

- Ya! No problem, Jo! ... No need to call Don Marcello. I'll be glad to take care of it for you.
- We'll also need to go shooting with the guys... And make sure that the mufflers work well, and I would appreciate if...
- ... Yeah! ... Consider it done, Jo!
- ... In a remote place... Very fuckin' remote place! ... Can you take care of this for me, Mister Ruby?
- I know just the place, Jo! Gimme has a couple of days and I will make sure that...
- ... Good! Thanks for the help, Mister Ruby.

And I released his jacket, smoothed the lapel so that the jacket returned to its original fold, and then I said to Sarti:

- Lucien, faisons le tour de la place pour voir comment on peut faire le travail tout en minimisant les risques pour nous... Explorons les alentours et après on décidera où se trouvent les meilleurs perchoirs pour exécuter notre mission... Et on arrête de rechigner tout le temps devant monsieur Ruby! C'est clair? (Lucien, let's go around the place to see how we can do the work while minimizing the risks for us... Let's explore the surroundings, and only after we'll decide where are the best perches for our mission... And stop fuckin' complaining all the time in front of Mr. Ruby! ... Is that clear?)

- Ouais! C'est d'acc... Allons prendre des photos et faisons du repérage. Jo, dis donc à ton ami pédé d'aller faire un tour de bagnole... Qu'il revienne nous chercher devant la butte dans... Combien, Serge? ... Une heure? ... Ça t'ira? (Yeah! Okay... Let's take pictures and spot the best places for the job. Jo, tell your fagot friend to go for a ride... Let him come back and pick us up in front of the Knoll in... How much time do you need, Serge? ... An hour? ... Will that be enough?

- Une heure et demi... Minimum! Mais je te le dis encore, Lucien... Je ne le sens pas très bien, ce putain de contrat! (An hour and a half... At minimum! ... But I tell you again, Lucien... I don't feel good about this fuckin' contract!

After the grievances of Beau Serge, I told Jack Ruby:

- Mister Ruby, we'll need about an hour and a half to check the place out and take pictures... Can you drop us off here and come back a little later to pick us up?

- Betcha, Jo! I'll give you guys a couple hours to survey Dealey Plaza and take pictures. No Problem!

Then, a little uncomfortable, he took me aside, pulling me gently by the sleeve, and then he slipped in my ear:

- Jo? ... I would appreciate if you did not do it again.

- What's that, Mister Ruby?

Ruby pointed at the collar of his jacket, adding:

- That! ... Grabbing me by the collar in front of everyone and shaking me like a fuckin' dead leaf!

- Yeah! Yeah! Got it, Mister Ruby. Got it! But in the future, so that you know, don't fuck with us... 'Cause you're dealing with professional killers, here... Don't you ever forget that!

- I just wanted to be treated with respect, Jo. That's all!

- Well, then you should respect this, Mister Ruby... 'Cause this is your fuckin' lucky day...

- ... Oh yeah? ... And why is that, Jo? ... I have a revolver too, just so you know...

Ruby tapped the right pocket of his jacket to show me he wasn't kidding.

I smoothed his collar, smiling with all my teeth:

- ... It's your lucky day 'cause I'm the nicest one of the three, Mister Ruby... And the only one who wouldn't want to kill you just for the fun of it! You got that, Mister Ruby? Clear enough?

- Okay, Jo! Okay! You're the nicest one of the three Stooges... Ho oh! ... Why didn't I think of that one before? ... Ho oh! Yeah! Got it, now. Ho oh! ... Got it!

I ignored Mister Ruby's derogatory remark and did not explain to him that I would not even need a gun to kill him, and decided to let go of his sarcasm because I didn't want him to feel more humiliated than he was already, at the moment.

- *Faudra aussi faire développer les films... Demande-lui de s'en charger, Jo!* (We'll also need to have the films developed... Ask him to take care of it, Jo!) Ordered Sarti.

I looked at him sideways, and then I said to Lucien:

- *Hey! Calma... Calmati!* (Hey! Calm down... Calm down!)

- What he said? ... What he said? Asked Ruby.

- *Qu'est-ce qu'il dit encore, ce pédé?* (What is he saying again, this fag?) Had said Lucien.

- *Il dit qu'il te faut lui sucer la bite, Lucien, si tu souhaites faire développer la pellicule plus rapidement!* (He says you have to suck his cock, Lucien, if you want the films developed faster!)

- *Quoi?* (What?)

Sarti looked at me funny, not sure if I was clowning.

- What did he said?

I turned to Ruby, and then I asked him:

192

- Mister Ruby? ... Would you know of a place where we can have these films developed in a hurry?

- Betcha! ... Consider it done, Jo. I know just the place. You'll have your pictures tonight. Guaranteed! ... Scouts honor!

Fuck me man! ... On his scout honor! I thought that there was nothing more to fear.

- Yeah! Thanks, Mister Ruby! ... See you right here in a bit.

- You got it, Jo ... See you guys later.

Lucien continued shelling Dealey Plaza with his camera; I had the other Instamatic in hand, and with Beau Serge, we went to explore the Grassy Knoll in full force. We followed the parking and reached Houston Street, behind the TSBD... It seemed to be the best place for a discreet exit after the hit.

Sarti agreed with me about the evacuation plan, but he said he wanted to shoot from the top of the viaduct:

"*C'est le meilleur endroit pour un tir de face.* (It's the best location for a frontal shot.)"

- *Mais si jamais il y avait foule, Lucien... Jamais tu ne pourras tirer de là!* (But if there ever was a crowd, Lucien... You'll never be able to shoot from there!)

- *On verra bien... Mais c'est l'endroit idéal pour lui en mettre une en plein dans la tronche. C'est élevé, alors la balle pourra voyager sans obstruction et passer au-dessus du pare-brise.* (We'll see... But it's the perfect angle to put one into his head. It's high, so the bullet will travel unobstructed and will easily clear the windshield.)

Beau Serge was pensive as he was making a face, when we came down the Grassy Knoll to join Ruby: he definitely regretted his involvement in the assassination plot. But it was too late to back down, now.

Jack was parked at the bottom of the stairs with the engine running; he was waiting for us with his two hairy kids on the front seat, flipping through a newspaper.

22

It was already late in the evening when Jack Ruby came to join us in the safehouse; he had four envelopes on him, as well as a scale map of Dealey Plaza: Sarti and the Beau Serge immediately rushed at Ruby like mad dogs and Englishmen. When I finally joined them, they had already spread the color shots on the small dining room table.

We took a good look at the photos. Then, as to make it more official, I started writing x's to mark everyone's position on the Dealey Plaza map...

Sarti still loved the "Triple Underpass" site, the Stemmons Freeway viaduct where three major motorways ran below, including Elm Street, just off the Grassy Knoll. There was a concrete retaining wall at the bottom of the bridge, which would make it easy for a sniper to fire from and go unnoticed. So, Lucien officially opted for the Stemmons viaduct; and I made an x to mark the exact place where the shooter was going to be.

Beau Serge was anxious... He said it would be better to position one's self in the building at the corner of Elm and Houston street: the Texas School Book Depository. And that...

"Not again, Jo! Just forget about that fuckin' building, will ya? ... The boss wants you there!" And Jack pointed a resolute index on the little mound in Dealey Plaza.

Then, out of spite, Beau Serge chose to stand behind the fence of wooden stakes at the top of the little grassy hill; a more discreet place from which one could discharge a weapon without attracting attention. At the top of the Grassy Knoll was an interesting place, a sort of huge half-moon cement pergola, one end of which was about a hundred feet or more from the street, just in front of the exact spot where the presidential motorcade was supposed to stop. There was a small vestibule with four rectangular openings, like some kind of reinforced concrete window frame, from which a sniper could easily fire without attracting the attention of passers-by. The back of the cement arch was sitting right on the parking lot, and from there one could go around the Texas School Book Depository and then get out on Houston Street... Get lost in the crowd!

Not only would the Grassy Knoll site allow for close-range shooting, but in addition to all this, we would have the opportunity to escape without getting noticed once the job was done; the only downside for me being the sign posted to the left of my perch that partially obstructed my view. In such working conditions, and with the vision partially obstructed by the traffic sign, I would see appear, then disappear, and then reappear again the presidential limousine... I would only have a fraction of a second to adjust, aim and shoot before being completely aside... and risk striking the First Lady.

Despite the slight obstruction problem I had, the grassy hill seemed to be the ideal place for a successful mission: Sarti perched on the rise, at the bottom of the viaduct; Beau Serge hidden behind the fence of stakes; and I in the agora... *Kiss my aura ... Dora! Hummm! Feels like real angora, this pergola... Ya want some mora?*

I opened my mouth, but refrained myself at the last moment and said nothing. Jack Ruby looked at me kind of funny... The president had just won the Grassy Knoll Trifecta!

***

The next day at around noon a man rang the door. We were all a little nervous before I decided to open, because we didn't know who could be knocking at the door. Ruby had advised us that someone would pick us up during the day to go shooting at the range, but...

I opened the entrance with one hand in the back, the butt of my pistol in the palm, and I said to the dude at the door:

- Yeah! ... What's that you want, man?

- Hi, guys! ... My name is Frank. I'm the one who's supposed to pick you up. So, let's get cracking and go target shooting!

Sarti, too, had a gun in his hand, but when Frank unpacked his gear, an assortment of silencers he had taken out of an army fabric bag, the Corsican calmed down rapidly... And that's when we got to know Frank a little more.

The dude had said his name was Fiorini: Frank Fiorini. He was in his late thirties, early forties at the most, with black hair glued with gel neatly combed from behind. The guy was quite sturdy, well muscled, with a stern look, and said he supervised some of the teams: he claimed that it was the big boss himself who had sent him.

It confirmed once again that we wouldn't be the only sniper team, but not who was the famous big boss!

- OK guys! We don't have time to fuck around. So, if you please, let's go... Now would be a good time, Jo!

We wrapped our weapons in small blankets to make a discreet exit from our refuge, and we quickly loaded everything into the trunk of the car. Once everyone aboard, Frank left for Garland, just north of Highland Park. We drove to the north for a while, and then Fiorini made a right turn to the east. After a moment, we found ourselves on a deserted country road, a path that seemed to lead nowhere fast, and we wandered in a cloud of dust for a few miles. At the end of the dirt road, we arrived in a small clearing at the entrance of a peaceful wooded area, and it was in this lost corner of Texas that we tried the suppressors.

- Ok guys! ... We're here!

Fiorini pulled out of the trunk a big box filled with watermelons. I took the crate on one side, Frank had the other, and we slowly walked towards the woods together. After laying the box at the foot of a dead tree trunk, there was a big arm lying on its side, I started to take out the melons of the crate, one by one, and then I spread them on the big shoot at a distance of not more than twenty centimeters from each other. While I was emptying the bin, Fiorini decided to search in his jacket... And, for a moment, I thought he was going to pull a gun and do me in the woods... Shit! I had recoiled in horror; the blood almost sub-zero in my veins; and with my heartbeat rising, as I shouted:

- Wow! ... What's that you're doing, man?

But afterwards, I thought it was ridiculous to be scared for nothing, because, if they had planned to kill me, they would surely wait until I had completed the mission before doing so.

Frank finally took out a huge felt pencil from his inside pocket... And I did, gradually, calm myself.

- We must make it just a little more realistic... Don't you think so, Jo?

- I guess so!

And while I finished spreading the melons, Fiorini drew eyes, mouths and noses to make the faces more authentic.

I finally laughed, when I admired his work...

- Not bad, hey Jo?

- Yeah! ... Not bad at all, Mister Fiorini!

But Frank's scribbling, in addition to making it more realistic, was especially useful to aim at a specific point and better evaluate the accuracy of our shots.

As we turned back to the car, I began to count my steps: sixty, in all. And after taking the sixtieth stride, when I stopped, I drew a coarse furrow, raking the soft earth with the heel of my shoe: "*Soixante mètres, les gars... D'ici!* (Sixty meters, guys... From here!)" And I went to get my Winchester .270.

Sarti and Beau Serge were already equipped with their rifles: they were waiting while smoking cigarettes. Fiorini finally opened his surprise bag, and like a Texan Santa Claus who would do his run well in advance, he distributed our Christmas gifts... But it felt more like Thanksgiving to me.

- That's for the Mauser, said Fiorini, passing the dull metal tube to Sarti... That one is for the mini gun... And this one is for you, Jo.

- Thank you, Mister Fiorini.

- You can call me Frank...

- Okay, Frank. I will... Thanks!

- You know Jo, I'am a very good friend of Roselli...

- Oh yeah?

- All you Frenchies have come highly recommended. Morales has been impressed by your shooting skills. They were especially mesmerized with your migratory bird hunting abilities in Miami! ... It will be a real pleasure working with you guys.

- Thanks for the complement... I'll try not to disappoint you!

- Jo! ... If you shoot as good as they say you shoot... Good God! ... What a day it's gonna be for the Nation!

Fuck me man! ... I looked at him for a moment, without really knowing what I could answer to that one!

Later, I asked:

- Will you be shooting with us, Frank?

- You mean? ... Shooting at the prez on the Grassy Knoll?

- Yeah! ... Will you be part of our hit team?

- No! Unfortunately, no! ... Not that I don't want to shoot. I'll just insure security for you guys and make sure you get out easy and clean. Apparently, someone high up in the chain of command doesn't want anything bad to occur to you, Jo.

- Umm! ... It's good to know that I still have friends in high places.

- Yeah! ... We'll talk about everything later on the way back to Dallas. For now, let's do some fuckin' shooting guys!

My silencer was at least twenty-five centimeters long, and in addition to that, it had to be screwed on the barrel of the rifle with a butterfly screw... With such a length at the end of the weapon, it would be difficult to hide my Savage .270 after firing: I would have to take the time to remove the muffler and lose precious seconds before I could leave my spot.

As I was about to shoot at an angle of about one hundred and twenty-five degrees, one hundred and eighty being absolutely from the front and ninety from the side, and that we were ordered not to wound the First Lady, I was going to have to go for a fragmentation bullet and make sure that the missile wouldn't come out of the president's head and then hit her!

But we didn't have any... So, I pulled out my pocketknife and made two deep cross-shaped cuts on the soft tip of the 165-

gram bullets, as I did at the Foreign Legion when I needed to eliminate recalcitrant Muslims terrorists: the ones that I absolutely couldn't miss with a single bullet! It was absolutely illegal to do this in the Army, but... Desperate times called for desperate measures, as the saying goes. Thus streaked, the projectile would fragment in at least four pieces after encountering something hard... Like the bones of a presidential skull!

From an upright position, I aimed at a melon... And fired: tac! ... The silencer dampened the sound of the detonation, but there was still enough noise to attract attention. The bullet made a small hole through the front of the fruit, and then the back of the fruit exploded into pieces... *Shloouuch!*

Frank went to inspect the damage that the fragmentation projectile had caused... He then came back saying that there was a hole as big as the fist in behind the crown! I ejected the cartridge of my bolt-action rifle, put in another dum-dum 7 mil in the chamber, ajusted the rifle's scope, but hardly, because the shot had gone only a few millimeters away from the nose, a bit off and to the left of the center, and then I hit the nostril of another melon: tac! And the back of another watermelon bursted open with a juicy sound: *Shloouuch!* A red jet flared at the back of the fruit... Everything behind the melon had turned reddish!

- Good fuckin' shooting! Congratulated me Fiorini.

Despite the silencer, the detonations had still produced a certain noise, a kind of muffled but powerful sound coming out of the barrel of the rifle, as well as a supersonic "zooom!" produced by the supersonic velocity of the projectile. However, I had judged that the sound level was still acceptable and that I could pass almost incognito after firing. Otherwise, I would have to remove half of the powder charge from the cartridges to further reduce the sound of the detonation. But in doing so, I would lose a lot of speed and punching power... Consequently, I decided not to have the cartridges modified to make sure I would kill with one bullet, because I was sure that I would only have time to discharge no more than a single shot.

Sarti and Beau Serge had their fun shooting melons, Lucien having also crossed his bullets on the tip to have the rear part of cucurbitaceae erupt...

When we finally got back to the car, Frank told me that the "*Big Event*" would be soon. Very soon... Too fuckin' soon!

- What? ... The day after tomorrow, you say? And you're telling me this less then 48 hours before the hit? ... We're not ready, Frank. We've got to go over the plan and fine-tune it a little... Maybe make some changes... I donno, Frank? A little...

- ... Why don't you stop arguing? ... All the fuckin' time! ... Let us grown ups come up with the plan... A good plan... A plan that does'nt involve mass suicide for all of you! ... Is that fuckin' clear, Jo?

- *Quoi? Qu'est-ce qu'il dit?... Qu'est-ce qu'il dit?* (What? What is he saying? ... What is he saying?) Repeated Sarti.

- *Hum!... Frank vient de m'annoncer que... Hum!... Le "Grand Événement" c'est pour après-demain!* (Umm! ... Frank just told me that... Umm! ... The "*Big Event*"... It's for the day after tomorrow!)

- *Bon... Parfait! Aussi bien en finir tout de suite avec ce putain de contrat de merde!* (Good... Perfect! We might as well be finished already with this shit contract an be done with it!) Sighed Beau Serge.

- *Ils nous gardent cloîtrés comme des putains de curés! ... Et en plus de tout ça, la bouffe américaine est infecte!* (They keep us cloistered like fuckin' priests! ... And on top of all that, American food is shit!)

- *Et leur café filtre l'est encore plus: de la merde liquide! Ils veulent nous assassiner... Je te le jure, Jo! Ils vont finir par nous tuer avec leur putain de bouffe!* (And their filtered coffee is even nastier! ... Liquid shit! And on top of it all, they want to murder us with their fuckin' fast food! ... I swear it, Jo! ... They want to kill us all!) Added the Beau Serge.

Yeah! Maybe they will after the hit, I thought. But I refrained from telling them my own thinking on that one.

- Bon! Vous n'avez pas fini de vous plaindre?... Bordel de merde! Vous m'avez l'air de deux poufiasses en manque! (Good! You're finished complaining, no? ... Fuckin' pussies! ... You look like two whores in need of dope!)

- Justement, Jo... Quand Ruby va-t-il nous en envoyer d'autres?... Où sont les gonzesses qu'on nous avait promises? (Exactly, Jo... When is Ruby gonna send us others? ... Where are the chicks we've been promised?)

Fuck me man! It's as if they thought only about one thing in life... To drink, to copulate with whores and party!

Okay! ... Three things!

- On n'est pas ici en vacances, bordel! On est ici pour le boulot!... C'est compris? (We're not here on fuckin' vacation! ... We're here to do a job! ... Got that?)

- Justement, Jo! En parlant de boulot, peux-tu demander à Frank de repasser par le Grassy Knoll? (Exactly, Jo! ... Speaking of work, can you ask Frank to pass by the Grassy Knoll?) Sarti had asked.

- Putain! Et pourquoi ça? (Shit! ... And why the fuck for?)

- J'aimerais qu'on aille revoir le site une dernière fois et mirer la rue du haut de mon perchoir avec ma carabine... Histoire de m'assurer que j'ai un bon angle de tir, c'est tout. (I wish we went to see the site one last time and look at the street from the top of my perch with my scope... Just to make sure I have a good shooting angle, that's all.)

- Super bonne idée... Une espèce de répète en direct de la butte! (Super clever idea, added Beau Serge... Some kind of live repetition from the Knoll!)

When I presented the demands of my Corsican friends, Frank Fiorini was not at all in favor of doing it. But Sarti had made a big enough fuss in the car to convince him to go...

- Fuckin' Primadonna! Had belched Fiorini... They're all the fuckin' same!

We passed by Houston Street. Frank quickly parked the car in the TSBD car park, which was the same parking lot as the Grassy Knoll dirt car park, but a little further: he was going to backup and hide in the shadow of the trees, just at the edge of the wooden fence. Lucien and Beau Serge picked up their rifle and took the time to fix the silencers. Then, as snipers on a special mission, they went to shoot down the street through the lens of their rifle. They positioned themselves here and there, changing site several times behind the wooden fence to find the ideal position or the perfect shooting angle...

If they had been discreet, there would surely have been no problem, except that discretion had never been part of their habits, and like matamores, they had had their fun pointing at passers-by who were walking on the sidewalk, pretending to shoot at them with onomatopoeia: Booouuum! Badabooouuum!

I had stayed in the car with Frank, who always maintained that it was a very bad idea to have come here with the two crazies because he was afraid they would be spotted and that it could messed up the boss's plan. And we just had time to smoke a cigarette before it all went to shit: the two Corsicans had done their usual baloney!

Or they were denounced by frantic pedestrians going up Dealey Plaza to Houston Street, or it was Dallas patrollers doing their rounds who had seen them... Anyway, what was supposed to happen happened, and in the minutes that followed, respecting Murphy's Law, a police car stopped at the bottom of the hill, on Elm Street, and with their gun in hand, two cops came out rapidly of their patrol car to investigate the plaintiff's say... Inspect the premises.

- Hey? You! ... You! ... Over there! ... What you doin' up there? ... Come on down with your hands up!

Frank immediately blew a long whistle to bring back Lucien and the Beau Serge, the two Corsican dogs of war, and as soon as the two freaks had closed the door behind them, Fiorini put the car in first gear and left the parking lot with the pedal to the metal.

We managed to get out of the parking lot, safely, and Frank thought he had preserved our team from the worst.

"I think we're OK, guys!" He said, finally.

But another police car came up from behind and immediately chased us, as soon as we drove down Houston Street - the other patrol car had possibly called for reinforcements on the police radio band -, and, fortunately for us, Frank was a skilled driver and knew the city perfectly well, otherwise... Winnie-the-fuckin'-pooh is going to jail!

Fiorini managed to lose the pigs, driving like crazy, sneaking between cars when he could, even spinning against traffic when possible, and, oh miracle on Elm street! He finally managed to dodge the cops through side streets and alleyways.

Whew! ... It was a close call. Sarti, slumped in the backseat, laughed out loud like an escapee from Hell and slapped on the backs of the seats like a hyperactive kid who forgot to take his Ritalin, laughing loudly. This guy... He was completely fuckin' crazy!

Once out of danger, Fiorini turned to me, very displeased, as if it were my fault, and slid to me:

- Man! ... What a bad fuckin' idea that was! ... What the fuck is wrong with that guy? ... Is he really fuckin' mentally insane?

- Yeah! Sorry, Frank... I should have known better. With Sarti, anything is possible!

Afterwards, Lucien took out his 9 mil and waved it in the car, vociferating like, precisely, a demented soul:

- *Allez, Jo. On s'fait un poulet! Une police judiciaire américaine: un professionnel, comme nous! ... Qu'est-ce que t'en dis, mon petit Jo? J'ai le doigt qui me démange...* (Come on, Jo. Let's do us a pig! An American cop: a professional, like us! ... What do you say to that, my little Jo? I've got the itchy finger...)

- What was that? ... What the fuck does he want, now?

- Oh! Nothing much, Frank... Sarti just said that he wanted to do an American cop. A pro, just like him!

- Is he really fuckin' crasy in the head, or is it just me?

- It may be just you, Frank! Or you're just like me... Surrounded by fuckin' idiots with guns!

- Well, even more dangerous! ... You better get a handle on your fucked-up friends, Jo... I tell you this so...

- ... They're not my fuckin' friends, as you say. They're just fucked-up in the head... And I'm stuck with them, too!

- Then, you better take care of your crazy dogs. Now! ... And make sure they walk the fuckin' line with their ass tight! Otherwise... I'll have no other choice but to take care of the problem for you, my little Jo.

My little Jo? ... But I wasn't that fuckin' short, for Christ's sake!

- My problem, you say? ... Yeah! Shure, Frank. **My** crazy dogs... Owoooo!

And I bursted out laughing, if only to cheer up the rotten atmosphere in the car... But to take this kind of contract and work with armed people who, in addition, were mentally unstable, you had to be a little crazy yourself. However, I didn't have much choice anymore... I had to go through with it no matter what the future had in store for me.

Frank loosened his teeth a bit. But during the drive to the safe house, he looked a little worried about the whole thing, and when he parked in front of our place, he looked like a captain about to call an all hands on deck on the fuckin' Titanic:

- Jo... I'm counting on you. Make sure your fucked-up Frenchy friends do not do anything stupid before the hit. I don't want any fuckups. You got me? ... Jo? ... Understood? Otherwise, I'll just have to do them both myself... And solve their fuckin' problem once and for all. We can't work like this... Make sure you tell them... Please! So they understand the situation we're in.

Yeah! Yeah! Jo, do this. Jo, do that... Jesus Christ! But I wasn't a babysitter, for fuck's sake! And besides all that, I was the youngest of the three. What the fuck man?

- Don't you worry, Frank, I'll keep an eye on them both. And especially on Lucien... For everyone's sake!

23

***

Once the contract had been executed, back in the safe house, we drank a lot of alcohol, because taking a swig from a good bottle always helped me forget the sadness of the days... And the corpses that piled up in the attic. Still, I had no remorse for what I had done, because killing men, I had learned to do it at the Foreign Legion long ago, and with time taking a life had become easier and kind of a second nature for me. But as I had swore to Ariane that I would put this life aside forever, I had made that promise just before getting married, the contract on the head of a president would perhaps give me the financial means to rebuild a stable life in Quebec... I hoped.

The day after the *Big Event,* Sarti and Beau Serge, once again, wanted to celebrate with the girls at the Carrousel Club. But because of the assassination of President Kennedy, most of the Clubs and the bars of Dallas were closed. And when Jack Ruby came to see us at lunchtime, we were all still under the influence of alcohol, he repeated to Sarti and Beau Serge: No! No! No! ... Absolutely no Carrousel Club for anyone!"

- Is that a definitive no? I dared ask, smiling.

- Jo! ... You guys are not leaving this place until things quiet down a bit. It's a fuckin' free for all in Dallas at the moment! You Frenchies are going nowhere fast... and that's that!

- ... My friends wanted to play with your babes. They wanted some dope. You know these guys? ... What the hell do I tell them to keep them quiet, Mister Ruby?

- You tell them what you want, Jo, but they've got to keep a low profile and behave! ... Be-fuckin'-have! Is that clear? There will be no girls, no drugs, no nothing! You tell them. I have enough problems as it is... I don't need two fuckin' more!

Sarti was making a face. Deception, I thought.

- What kind of problems are you talking about, Mister Ruby? ... I thought the job was done? Can I do something to...

- ... Yeah! Sure you can, Jo. Certain! ... Make sure these two bozos don't make any fuckin' waves!

While he was talking to me, he had made a gesture and had pointed towards the Corsicans... *The other two!*

- Umm! ... I saw it on TV. They caught your buddy, Lee. Do you know what will happen to him, now?

- He's fucked! ... From day one, he was fucked. All the way fucked! And now, I'm fucked too! ... It's a fuckin' nightmare, Jo!

- Huh! How do you figure that, Mister Ruby? I don't understand what are you're trying to say to me?

- The guys upstairs are not satisfied with the job. The Dallas police was not supposed to capture Lee alive... 'Cause Lee may talk! And they're afraid he will! ... By the way, thanks for the help regarding Tippit. I heard that you...

- ... I did'nt do much... The cocksucker was already dead when Frank ordered me to kill him for the second time.

- Yeah! ... But thanks anyway.

- Do you know why Tippit had to be wacked like this?

- That's all on Frank... Frank's improvisation! That's his kind of bullshit. He's the worst fuckin' cold-blooded killer if I've ever seen one. Beware, Jo! He's Secret Service scum... Thru and thru! A very dangerous man! He could kill his own mother without a blink and then go to church and pray for her eternal soul!

- Don't worry, Mister Ruby, I don't have an eternal soul... and I sure don't trust anyone. I believe that everyone is out to get me... Even my Frenchy friends! So, I'm always looking behing my shoulder, ready to defend myself at the first sign of trouble... And I'll pop the first motherfucker who tries anything on me!

- That's good, Jo. Don't you trust any of these guys...

- ... And I don't trust you either, if you want to know.

- That's fine too, Jo. And you shouldn't!

I sure as hell didn't trust any of these motherfuckers!

- And you, Mister Ruby... Do you trust any of them?

- If I trust them? Fuck you very much, Jo! That's just about the extent of my trust! But do I have any fuckin' choice, now?

- So? ... What's you gonna do about Lee?

- I'll have to do him myself... Do Lee before he testifies in court... Before he goes on record in front of a juge. It's that simple! ... Otherwise, I'm a dead man too!

- A dead man? ... I don't understand, Mr Ruby? ... How can it be your fuckin' problem?

- Lee was my responsibility. And since Tippit didn't do his fuckin' job... And the idiots at the theatre arrested him instead of putting him down when he went to meet with his CIA controller... You know, Lee was supposed to escape by the back door of the theatre! ... They gave him all the fuckin' time in the world to get outta Dodge. Instead, he chose to let them arrest him and see where it goes... And now, because of some fuckin' police hero who wanted his photo on the front page of the Dallas Morning News, I'll have no choice but to do Lee myself.

A dozen police cars had been dispached because someone supposably entered the theatre without paying for his ticket... A dozen fuckin' cars! While every available cop in Dallas was suppose to be looking for JFK's and Tippit's assassin!?!

- And? ... Just like that? You're gonna take care of Lee?

- Yeah! Just like that, Jo. I got a call from Chicago, you know... And they said that I had to drive to the police station and take care of business, personnally! Otherwise... Umm! They told me what would happen if I didn't make the problem disappear...

- And? ... What will happen if you don't do it?

- Kill everyone I love and break my legs in seventy fuckin' places!

- Fuck me man! ... What a bad predicament!

- And then, on top of everything, the cocksuker laughed at me over the phone and said: "will it be behind the wheel or in a fuckin' wheelchair, Jack?"

- Motherfuckers! ... What a shitty deal that is if there was ever one! ... So? What's you gonna do, Mister Ruby?

Jack got lost in his own thoughts, and then he said:

- I donno, Jo? ... I donno? ... Go North to Oklahoma City and then head West on the 40 until I run out of froad...

- ... Or gaz! That looks like a plan. But? ... Seriously? How do you plan to kill a guy in the custody of the police? ... In jail?

- I don't know, Jo. I don't know! ... You let me worry about that one. I'll find a way; there's always a way. That's not your problem... You did your part of the contract and I'll do what I have to do, and that's that. You can't unfuck what's been fucked!

- Man! I wouldn't wanna be in your shoes even for a minute.

Ruby looked at his watch...

- Change of subject, Jo... So, you guys are leaving tomorrow, I hear. I may not see you before your departure, since I've got to take care of the problem you know of... And I just wanted to say thank you for a job well done... Thanks a million!

- It was a pleasure working with you, Mister Ruby.

And with that, he gave me his hand, a sincere grip, and then he added:

- From what I've seen, Jo, you're a pretty good guy... A very good guy! ... Way too fuckin' good for this kind of life. A little piece of advice from an old fella, if I may... Jo, you're young and you have your whole life ahead of you; it's not too late to think of a career change. Next time they ask you to do something stupid like the killing of a President, you do what I should have done from day one... You just say no and then you run! ... You run your ass off! ... You run like a bat strait out of hell! ... And you leave it all behind and you and you never go back! Otherwise, you'll work all your fuckin' life for them, and then one day you'll wake up in bed and realize that you just were Satan's little fuckin' helper! ... Do you understand what I am trying to say to you, Jo? ... Do you?

- Yes! ... I do! Thanks for the advice. It was a real pleasure knowing you, Mister Ruby. I hope everything turns out okay for you, too.

Jack greeted the Corsicans, quickly, and then he left: it was the last time I would see Jack Ruby in the flesh...

The next morning, at three o'clock, it was Frank Fiorini who picked us up and took our little commando to Red Bird Airport.

We made the trip in silence; Sarti and Beau Serge were heavy-eyed and slept all the way to the airport. Once on the tarmac, Fiorini woke them up, abruptly. He looked a little worried: "Wake up, guys. We're here. Come on... Let's go! ... You wouldn't want a miss your plane." I guess he didn't want to be stuck with the Corsicans even for all the gold in the world.

Frank helped us out with the suitcases, and afterwards we had a good hug. But Fiorini looked like a guy in a hurry to leave and didn't linger too long in a show of affection. He said he had bigger fish to fry... I thought he had to be working on Lee Oswald's case, too.

- It was a pleasure working with an elite shooter like you, Jo... Our paths will surely cross once again. You take care and say hello to Don Marcello for me... Have a safe trip, guys!

David Ferrie welcomed us on the plane: he had waited for us all night drinking coffee from a Thermos bottle.

- Nice fuckin' shooting, you guys... Un-fuckin'-believable!

- Thanks, Mister Ferrie... We did what we had to do to complete our mission and no more.

I didn't want to add anything, because I didn't deserve to rest on any laurels with a shot from a distance of less than 70 meters with a scope... Anyone could have done it in my place.

- Jo? ... Got some fresh news about Lee? I overheard that...

- ... Yeah! Got some news for you. I could give you the good news or the bad news... Which is it gonna be?

- Gimme the good news, Jo! ... One should always start with the good news and get the bad news out of the way...

- Okay! ... Then the good news is that there's nothing anyone can do for Lee any longer.

- Shit! That's your good news? And? ... The bad news?

- I heard he's fucked! ... All the way fucked! ... And so is your friend Jack Ruby.

- What?

- Apparently, they both got a shitty deal with this crazy government contract...

- What do you mean, Jo? ... I don't understand?

- Ruby was orerdered by his Chicago pals to take care of Lee in the police station, or else... Jack got to go in there to shut him up... Permanently!

- Jack is gonna do Lee? ... In jail?

- Yeah! ... Looks like it! ... So, you better forget about them both, because Lee is a dead man walking and Ruby is on a suicide mission to shut him up for good.

- Is there anything that can be done for Lee?

- Yeah! ... You can burn a candle for the poor bastard in New Orleans. For now, let's go! ... Let's get the fuck out of this miserable town. I hate all these fuckin' Dallas cowboys!

David Ferrie had a tear in his eye when he took control of the plane, and as soon as we were installed on our seats, he put the throttle on full. And so we flew from the small Dallas airport before the sun came up; Ferrie had told me that he hadn't even recorded a flight plan... We were going to fly at less than 1,500 feet and go under the radar control towers of Texas and Louisiana!

It was still morning when we arrived in New Orleans. Later, Don Marcello's chauffeur drove us back to the Town and Country Motel: my two Corsican friends were not very happy to return. And the next day, on TV, we saw Jack Ruby gun down his friend Lee Oswald in the garage of a Dallas police station... Live on T.V. You can watch them die! Pictures that had upset me deeply... Seeing it on TV had shaken me, probably because I knew all the actors in the plot!

"Bah!... C'est juste un pédé qui descend un autre pédé! (Bah! ... It's only a fag who guns down another fag!)"

Sarti had made it clear, laughing: it was a fag's problem.

Maybe Lucien was right? ... Because they both were fags! But, I new better. And I never understood why Ruby had done it this way... The desperate way! Afterwards, I thaught that he might have been promised that he would be released soon after his hit on Oswald, alleging something like temporary insanity or any other defense in the same vein, because Lyndon Baines Johnson had the long arm and heavy hand of the federal government at his disposal and had already used his influence to have his friend Mac Wallace acquitted of a charge of first degree murder, in Texas. So... Nothing was impossible in the land of cowboys! But things were not gonna go that well for Jack Ruby.

Poor Oswald, who was actually a smart guy and a patriot, would go down in history as the illustrious "lone gunman" of the famous Warren Commission. He would then be portrayed in the history books as the assassin of President Kennedy, even though he didn't really know how to shoot and that no sniper in the world could have, with a Mannlicher-Carcano rifle also called "the humanitary gun", because it was so inaccurate that one rarely touched the target, been able to do the shooting he was accused of in the Texas School Book Depository: three shots in less than seven seconds with two of which hit the target. And on top of all that, the Warren Commission was going to conclude that the first shot, the easiest one of the three, had missed the target! ... It just didn't make any sense. Lee Harvey Oswald, as newspapers around the world would call him, even if he only used Lee Oswald in everyday's life, would go down in history...

But what a history! Because from J Edgar Hoover to Robert Kennedy, from the CIA leaders to the big Texas financiers, from arms dealers to the mob, all knew that it wasn't Oswald who had killed the President of the United States of America. Poor Lee had never even fired a single shot from the TSBD... The paraffin tests to detect traces of nitrate on the face of Lee had proved inconclusive!

***

We spent a long week sequestered in the Town and Country Motel, but Don Marcello never came to see us, not even once, question of degree of separation, I understood, and one morning, Roselli came to tell us the good news... We were going by plane to Albany, New York, and then to Montreal by car through I-89. Afterwards, we'd cross the border at night in Frelighsburg... The border post being open only during the day!

And so, Uncle Vito picked us up in Albany, New York. We then drove to Montreal during the night, and in the early morning, my godfather dropped the two Corsicans at Dorval International Airport.

"*Ça serait mieux pour tout le monde si on ne se revoyait plus jamais, mon petit Jo!* (It would be better for everyone if we never saw each other again, my little Jo!)" Had suggested Sarti, laughing.

- *T'inquiète, Lucien... Si on se revoit encore une fois, j'te fous mon gros pétard dans l'cul et je décharge le tout prématurément... Comme toi et le Beau Serge le faites, habituellement!* (Don't you worry, Lucien... If I see you again, I'm gonna stick my big firecracker up your ass and I will unload it all, prematurely... As you and the Beau Serge usually do it!

And as I was saying it, I grabbed my balls and shook hard.

Sarti and Beau Serge sketched out a tired smile.

- *Jo, mon petit Jo!... Tu me dois toujours une bouteille de cognac pour le concours de tir!* (Jo, my little Jo! ... You still owe me a bottle of Cognac for the shooting contest!) Sarti pointed out to me.

- *Non!... C'est plutôt toi qui m'en dois une... Et une bonne!* (No! ... It's rather you who owe me one... And a good one!)

- *Qu'est-il arrivé à l'autre bouteille?* (What happened to the other bottle?) Had said Sarti.

- *Je l'ai bue avec Roselli et Don Marcello pendant que vous dormiez...* (I drank it with Roselli and Don Marcello while your were sleeping...)

- *... Ho! Mais ça n'est pas juste, tout ça!... Tu me dois une bouteille, vieux!* (... Ho! But that's not fair at all! ... You now owe me a bottle, buddy!)

- *Bon! Bon! OK, les enfants! C'est moi qui régalerai la prochaine fois!... Au plaisir, Jo!* (Good! Okay! ... Okay, children! It will be my treat next time! ... Looking forward to seeing you again, Jo!) Had uttered Beau Serge.

And we all gave each other a long hug...

Next, the two Corsicans went towards the Air France counter to get their ticket: a one-way fare to Marseilles via Paris.

After seeing them disappear behind the gate, Don Vito quickly took me home, because I had declined his offer to break fast with him at Moishe Steakhouse, even if the idea of eating a good T-bone with Fried eggs for breakfast would not have really displeased me. But since I had no intention of meeting Mr. Cotroni again, or to be recruited by his criminal organization...

Arriving on Barclay Street, my *Padrino* had parked a bit further than my block, Don Vito handed me the ten thousand dollars he owed me; the second installment of the payment for the hit. I thanked him, sincerely; we kissed each other on the cheeks and hugged for some time; then I told him, just before leaving him: "*Jamais plus! Si capisce, Don Vito?* (Never again! ... Have you understood, Don Vito?)

- *Sì! Capisco, Jo... Io non ti chiederò mai di uccidere per mi. Hai la mia parola d'onore... Se mento sto andando all'inferno!* (Yes! Unterstood, Jo... I will never ask you to kill for me again. You have my word of honor... If I lie, I'll go to hell!)

Yeah, hell! ... I was going straight for it, too. But only if there really was one. And since we all knew, in France, that "l'enfer, c'est les autres (hell is other people)", all I had to do is worry about my *Cosa Nostra* (our cause) friends... The other people... The kind of people that could easily have me killed!

I got out of Vito's car and went to meet with my little family... I was especially eager to see my daughter again, whom I had held in my arms for only a few hours, barely!

When I spoke to her and pressed her against me for a hug, she seemed to recognize my voice, immediately... And she gave me the biggest smile a father could ever get! She seemed happy to see her daddy again. It was as if she had told me:

"*Bienvenue au Québec, Jo!* (Welcome to Quebec, Jo!)"

Epilogue

Although he was offered several times thereafter, Jo never worked as a sniper for anyone and led a very quiet family and professional life for the rest of his existence. His godfather, Don Vito, came to visit him on several occasions to test the waters in the years that followed, but Jo always refused to work for the *familia*.

As his Uncle was the only one who knew his true identity and that he had brought his secret with him to the grave in the late eighties, no one ever knew who this sharp shooter of the Foreign Legion really was: a sniper simply known as "Jo".

I really enjoyed the company of this Jo and I always had known him as a man of his word, a good father, a kind and loyal person. And when Jo told me the story of his life and what he had done while serving with the Foreign Legion in Algeria, and later on his involvement in the Kennedy plot, just six months before his death, I was absolutely stunned to hear his revelations... and I must confess that I didn't really believe him!

But Jo was not the king of guy talking without saying anything and not saying anything for the sake of talking...

All I can attest to is that there was no remorse or even pride in his voice, when he told me about his involvement in President Kennedy's slaying in Dealey Plaza, Dallas. He had said he only did it for the survival of his family and that's all! I was then doing research on the life of former paratroopers who had participated in the Algerian civil war with the objective of writing a novel, a work of fiction, of fiction! When, after having sharing me the tumultuous story of his life in North Africa, he told me that incredible story about the Kennedy assassination plot.

After telling me his rather farfetched version of an historical event that had traumatized the whole of humanity, Jo had demanded, expressly, that I did not reveal his true identity to the world... *Nel caso in cui?* (Just in case?) For all his life he had feared for the safety of his family.

Jo had always been somewhat mistrustful in his dealings with people, trying not to draw too much attention to him, and I must confess that, even today, I have a lot of trouble reconciling his story with that of the man I had known for more than thirty years... A man who seemed to have disseminated love and death with the same passion!

Later, looking back at Jo's memorable early life, I concluded that human beings were complex beasts; that a man, apparently so good in his later life, was capable of the best as well as the worst, of being a creator and a killer... And often both sides of the same coin!

So, do not look for meaning in Jo's incredible story, because there is none... Jo was an ordinary man who had to do extraordinary things in order to survive. No more.

A B

Historical notes

1963 - November 22: **John Fitzgerald Kennedy**, 35th President of the United States, is murdered in Dallas, Texas.

1963 - November 22: Police officer **JD Tippit** is shot dead in the Oak Cliff neighborhood of Dallas, Texas... Lee Oswald will be accused of killing him, but they have never been able to prove it... or find the real perpetrators.

1963 - November 24: Jack Ruby executes **Lee Oswald** during his transfer to County Jail in the garage of a police station in Dallas, Texas. In the corridor, as he was going down to the basement, Lee Oswald claims his innocence to the journalists: "I'm a patsy!" Rushed to hospital, he will not get out of alive...

1964 - September 27: **The Warren Commission** delivers its conclusions. It determines that Lee Harvey Oswald's worked alone in the assassination of President Kennedy, as did Ruby in the assassination of Lee H Oswald. The Commission's report, a voluminous 888-page *tale,* concludes that Lee Harvey Oswald was the only sniper on the 6th floor of the Texas School Book Depository... and the murderer of JFK. It was the famous "lone gunman" scheme and the later legendary "magic bullet" theory; a missile that would have crossed the body of JFK and obliqued thereafter to reach John Connally (back, chest, wrist and thigh!), the valiant Governor of Texas who was sitting right in front John F Kennedy in a jump seat. "My God, **they** are going to kill us all!" Governor Connally shouted, after being hit several times in the presidential limousine.

There were more than 400 witnesses present in Dealy Plaza on the day of the assassination of John F Kennedy: 216 will be questioned by the FBI on the origin of the shooting; 52 will say that they heard one or more shots coming from the Grassy Knoll; 48 will say they heard one or more shots coming from the Texas School Book Depository; 5 will say that they heard one or more shots from the Texas School Book Depository and the Grassy Knoll; 4 will say that the shots seemed to come from somewhere else; 37 will be unable to respond; and the remaining 70... they will never be questioned about it! The Warren commission will also reject 40 testimonials for so-called "erroneous memories". As luck would have it, they were amongst the 40 witnesses who had said that they heard shots coming from the Grassy Knoll, statements that contradicted the theory of the lone assassin!

1965 - **Jack Ruby** (Jacob Leon Rubenstein) dies of cancer in prison before testifying in front of a committee of the United States Congress and unload all that he knew of the plot in exchange for a reduction of sentence... On his deathbed he would claim that the CIA had inoculated him with cancer.

1967 - February 22: **David Ferrie** is found dead of "accidental death" in his apartment! (A blow to the neck allegedly inflicted by accidental fall, had said the police!) Just prior to his testimony in a Louisiana Court before Attorney Jim Garrisson, who suspected him of involvement in a conspiracy to murder John F Kennedy. David Ferrie allegedly worked clandestinely on a virus with Dr. Mary Sherman, Lee Oswald alledged mistress, a virus that, once injected into the victim, would have transmitted cancer to the subject! Ferrie and Sherman allegedly tried to develop this weapon for the CIA in order to eliminate Fidel Castro.

1967 - June 23: **Antoine Guérini** is executed while refuelling his Mercedes in the Saint-Julien district, in Marseilles. He was the godfather of the French Connection.

1968 - June 5: **Robert F. Kennedy** is shot dead after a reception to celebrate the end of the campaign for the Democratic primaries in the United States Presidency. He was the favorite in the polls and should have been elected President of the United States of America... In place of Richard Nixon.

What have you done this time, Dick?

1971 - January 7: **Malcolm Wallace** is found dead in his car where he would have *lost control* of his automobile on Highway 271, in Texas. He would have been LBJ "personal" killer and would have allegedly murdered more than 5 individuals for him.

1972 - April 27: **Lucien Sarti**, Corsican bandit and notorious drug dealer, is killed in Mexico City: he had several hits to his credit during his very successful career as a hitman on behalf of the *Barbouzes,* the mafia... and of the CIA.

1972 - May 2: **J Edgar Hoover,** first director of the FBI, dies of a heart attack. He will later be suspected of abuse of trust, political blackmail, abuse of power, to have been corrupted by the mafia... And of being a homosexual! Several Kennedy specialists believe that he was involved in the plot and that his role was to ensure that the official version of the single gunner was the only version retained by the Warren Commission... And the world!

1973 - January 22: **Lyndon Baines Johnson** dies of a heart attack on his Texas ranch. When reporters asked Jack Ruby, when he returned to jail after testifying at the Warren Commission, "But who killed the President?" Jack Ruby had replied: "Look on the side of those who have benefited the most from his death!"

1976 - August 9: **John Roselli**, nicknamed "Handsome Johnny", is found in a metal drum floating in Dumfounding Bay near Miami, Florida. Roselli had been strangled and his legs had been severed (to get him into the container).

1982 - March 1st: **Mémé (Barthélemy) Guérini**, after spending 10 years in prison, dies of cancer in a private clinic in Montpellier. He was, with his brother, the leader of the famous French Connection.

1988 - August ??: **Don Vito**, suffering of lung cancer, dies peacefully at the age of 63 in his Miami home in Florida.

1993 - March 3: **Don Carlos Marcello**, head of the Louisiana Mafia, dies at home after a stay in prison.

1993 - December 5: **Frank Fiorini, aka Frank Sturgis**, dies of cancer at Miami Veterans Hospital, Florida. Involved in the Watergate affair with E. Howard Hunt, he was a spy and mercenary on contract with the CIA and the Mafia. He reportedly took part in several *special* missions around the world, both for the CIA and for organized crime.

2002 - June 22: **Madeleine Duncan Brown**, LBJ's mistress, said that Johnson was behind the murder of Kennedy and of several other men. In her memoir, *Texas In The Morning* (1997), she wrote about a social event in honor of J Edgar Hoover at a Texas oil Millionaire's mansion (Clint Murchison) held on November 21, 1963... The night before the assassination of JFK!

Shortly after the closed meeting, Lyndon B Johnson, anxious and blushing, reappeared and whispered in her ear: "After tomorrow, those goddamn Kennedys will never embarrass me again - that's NOT a threat - that's a promise."

2007 - January 23: Edouardo, Alias **E. Howard Hunt**, dies of pneumonia in Miami, Florida. A CIA officer for more than 20 years and Nixon's "plumber" in the Watergate affair, Hunt confesses on his deathbed that he was involved in the assassination of John F Kennedy and involves several other people in the plot, including **Lyndon Baines Johnson** (Vice-President), **Cord Meyer** (CIA), **David Atlee Philips** (CIA), **Frank Sturgis** (Operators for the CIA and mercenary for the Mafia), **David Morales** (Hitman for the CIA), **Antonio Veciana** (Cuban exiled founder of Alpha-66 [funded by the CIA]), **William Harvey** (CIA), and a Corsican killer named **Lucien Sarti** (French Connection). It was not the confession of a man who wanted to repent, but rather that of a man proud of what he had done for the Nation. Did Hunt continue to lie on his deathbed? Did he hide the involvement of people he had remained loyal to, people still alive? ... Certainly. Nonetheless, we all know that anything that comes from a CIA agent can only be taken with a grain of salt.

2011 - November: **Jo** dies from pulmonary embolism at the age of 71 in a hospital in Montreal. He leaves his wife, his two daughters and three grandchildren in mourning.

To this day - **Beau Serge,** whose real name is Christian David, a notorious bandit linked to the French Connection, is still incarcerated in prison for the murder of a policeman. He swears that had refused to participate in the assassination of JFK...